J. F. RIVKIN
WEB OF WIND

ACE BOOKS, NEW YORK

This book is an Ace original
edition, and has never
been previously published.

WEB OF WIND

An Ace Book / published by arrangement with
the author

PRINTING HISTORY
Ace edition / December 1987

ISBN: 0-441-87883-0

GOING, GOING . . . GONE?

"Surely only criminals can be sold—or captives of war?"

A gleam of deviltry lit Corson's blue eyes. Seizing Nyctasia by the collar, she called out lustily, "Who'll buy a beautiful foreign princess, stolen from the courts of the coast? Take note of her pale skin and delicate features . . ."

"You'll regret this!" Nyctasia bit her, hard, and Corson hastily released her.

"You venomous little snake!" Corson exclaimed, waving her wounded hand about. "You're poisonous as a viper! My hand'll turn black! I'll die . . ." She was laughing too hard to go on.

Nyctasia regarded her coldly. "Corson, you go too far."

Corson interrupted her tirade. "Nyc, look! That fellow —don't you remember him?"

"Where?" Nyctasia asked anxiously. Which of her enemies would pursue her so far?

Praise for *Silverglass*

"It's fun to see a tall, handsome, hard-fighting, hard-drinking, barbarian hero—who is female."

—Piers Anthony

"Open-roading romance!"

—Fritz Leiber

"Rousing adventure by, for, and about women."

—Jessica Amanda Salmonson

Ace Books by J. F. Rivkin

SILVERGLASS
WEB OF WIND

1

CORSON BRENN TORISK looked irritably at her companion. Nyctasia was toying with her dinner in gloomy silence, lost in thought, and Corson had had enough of her brooding.

"Are you going to eat that or aren't you?"

"I haven't much appetite, I'm afraid," Nyctasia said listlessly.

Corson shrugged and scraped the rabbit pie from Nyctasia's plate onto her own. "Since we got to Osela you've done nothing but mope about," she complained. "You've hardly left the inn. We came here to see the fair!"

"And after I've seen it, what then? On the way here I had at least a destination. Now we're here, I've lost even that."

Corson had long been accustomed to the life of a wandering mercenary, but the Lady Nyctasia ar'n Edonaris had never known what it was to be homeless. She had passed all her life in the city-state of Rhostshyl, and she could not resign herself to exile.

Corson sighed. She was losing all patience with Nyctasia's melancholy. "I thought you planned to go south to the Valley-lands, to visit the Edonaris who own vineyards at Vale."

"Even if they should prove to be of my blood, I'll only be a stranger to them. I've no place or purpose among them. Why should they welcome me?"

"It's true you're useless," Corson agreed, "but do you have to be boring as well? You know I'm dangerous when I'm bored."

"Nothing keeps you with me, Corson. I no longer need a bodyguard—I've no enemies this far from Rhostshyl."

Corson smiled her dangerous smile. "Well then, it's time I gave you those lessons in swordfighting you wanted. If you mean to travel without an escort you'd best be able to defend yourself. There's more than thieves and cutthroats in these parts—you'd make a pretty prize for a pack of slavers."

"You needn't worry about me. I can fend for myself."

"Come along," Corson ordered. She mopped up the last of the gravy with a piece of bread and gulped it down. "We may as well begin at once, since time's so heavy on your hands." Ignoring Nyctasia's protests, she all but dragged her out to the courtyard of the inn.

"Stand ready!" Corson commanded. "That's a sword, not a pen—hold fast to it! Watch this—" She made a move, and Nyctasia's sword landed several feet away, out of her reach.

"Impressive," admitted Nyctasia, "but I think you broke my wrist."

"No I didn't. If I'd wanted to break your wrist I'd have done it differently. And I will, the next time I see you with such a lax grip. Pick it up."

Nyctasia obeyed, and instinctively took up a fencing stance, which Corson regarded with scorn. "Forget those fool fencing rules. There aren't any rules in a fight." She came at Nyctasia swiftly.

Nyctasia parried successfully at first, but Corson seemed to be everywhere, and within minutes Nyctasia was ready to surrender.

Corson brought the flat of her blade down hard on Nyctasia's shoulder. "That's cut off your arm."

By the end of the lesson Nyctasia was bruised and aching all over, and bleeding from numerous pricks and scratches. Corson was an effective teacher. Her pupils had to learn quickly, purely in self-defense.

"You might make a fair fighter for someone your size," Corson said with a grin. "You've a good eye, and you're light on your feet. But you need plenty of practice. Tomorrow we'll work on the attack."

"No we won't," said a faint voice from the depths of a tub of steaming water. "I'm not leaving this tub for a week, and when I

do I have every intention of poisoning your ale. I should have let you die back in Lhestreq, you great overgrown ox."

Corson laughed. "In a real fight you can't choose the size of your enemy."

"No one's as big as you are!"

"At least I gave you something to think of besides your woes."

Nyctasia looked at her sharply. "Corson, sometimes I suspect you might be clever—for a simpleminded barbarian."

"I must have learned my crafty ways from you then. You weave schemes like a spider spins webs. A poisonous spider."

"Not anymore," Nyctasia said gravely. She only wanted to forget the measures she'd taken in the past to outwit her enemies. That life was behind her now. "Such webs are only snares for one's own spirit."

Corson yawned. "Your philosophy's too lofty for a simpleminded barbarian like me. You can stay here and rack your wits with riddles—I'm for the fair."

"Oh, very well," said Nyctasia. "Wait for me."

Osela was famous for its harvest fair, the largest of its kind in the Midlands. Farmers came from far and wide, bringing their crops and livestock to market. Merchants and traders hawked their wares, gossip was exchanged, performers vied for the crowd's attention, and thieves and beggars were kept busy. The city guard had all they could do to keep the peace, and summary justice was the order of the day.

In spite of herself, Nyctasia was fascinated by the chaos of revelry that overflowed the market square and spilled into the streets. The markets of the coastal towns she'd seen seemed tame in comparison. If she lingered too long to watch the dancing bear, she missed the performance of the swordswallower. All about her, storytellers chanted, mummers danced, and fortunetellers offered to reveal the secrets of destiny for a fee.

As usual, Corson was drawn irresistibly to the rows of merchants' stalls. She was greedy as a magpie for glittering trinkets, and she would not be satisfied till she'd squandered money on something impractical and garish. She tried on gloves embroidered with silk and stitched with tiny pearls, but their price was too dear even for a spendthrift like Corson. Flinging them down carelessly, she strolled off to find something that was more within her means.

But Nyctasia went her own way. The swordplay with Corson

and the excitement of the fair had shaken her from her despondency, and she had quite recovered her appetite. It was the hawkers of fruits, sweetmeats, buns and savories who tempted her.

"Pork pies, threepence! Hot pork pies!"

"Fine, ripe pears! Sweet pears!"

"Roast potatoes! Who'll buy?"

It all looked inviting to Nyctasia, and she wanted to sample everything. A smell of frying meat and spices lured her toward a crowded stall where a young boy was spooning a mixture of meat and vegetables onto thin pieces of dough. A heavyset woman deftly rolled the pasties and set them to sizzle in a greasy pan. A girl was selling them, two for a penny, as fast as the pair could make them. Nyctasia gave her a copper, and received her meat-cakes wrapped in a waxy green leaf. She devoured one of them in a single bite. With the other halfway to her mouth, she suddenly gasped and started to choke.

"I've been poisoned! My throat's afire!" she said hoarsely, as Corson came up to her, chewing one of the spicy delicacies.

"Poisoned! What—who—?" Then Corson saw the uneaten pasty that Nyctasia was still clutching. She started to laugh, and thumped Nyctasia cheerfully on the back. "Haven't you ever eaten zhetaris before?"

Nyctasia wiped tears from her eyes. "Asye's blood! You don't mean to say they're *supposed* to burn like this?"

"If they don't, they're no good. *These* are good," Corson said with satisfaction, eating Nyctasia's other zhetari. "They're festival-food, for harvest time."

"Barbaric custom!" Nyctasia muttered, hastily drinking down a stoup of goat's milk offered by a shrewd milkmaid. In her gratitude, she paid the girl three times its worth.

2

"MAKE WAY, MAKE way there!" A troupe of tumblers dressed in gaudy tatters shouldered their way through the crowd, and succeeded in clearing a space.

To the beat of a painted tabor, they formed a ring and began to juggle brightly colored wooden balls, tossing them back and forth across the circle, while keeping several aloft at once.

The crowd shouted and clapped to the drumbeat as the dark-skinned jugglers performed an intricate dance, weaving in and out of the circle, never dropping even a single ball. Nyctasia strained her neck to watch them over the shoulders of the on-lookers. The drummer bowed, sweeping off his ribboned cap which he proffered to the audience for coins. Meanwhile, the two tallest of the tumblers stretched out a rope between them and a small, nimble woman hoisted herself up onto it.

The drummer took up a pair of charred wooden clubs, their tops smeared with tallow, and dramatically set them alight. He threw both to the rope-dancer, who caught one in each hand and began to juggle them. Soon she was juggling five flaming brands, while the other acrobats scrambled for coins on the ground before the beggar-children could snatch them up.

With a final flourish, the woman tossed the clubs, one by one, into a tub of water, and leapt to the ground, rolling into a somersault. Delighted, Nyctasia squeezed her way to the front and slipped some silver into the drummer's cap.

The crowd quickly dispersed, and Nyctasia looked around for Corson. She was not surprised to find her haggling with yet another merchant. This time an ivory hair-clasp had taken her fancy. Corson was vain of her waist-length, chestnut hair, though she wore it sensibly bound up in a braid.

"Did you see them?" Nyctasia asked eagerly. "It was inspiring—a perfect manifestation of the Principle of Balance!"

Corson concluded her purchase of the costly ornament. "What are you blathering about now?" she asked Nyctasia.

"The jugglers—their skill and grace—like outward signs of discipline and harmony of the spirit! If only—"

Corson was used to her friend's everlasting explanations of the mystical philosophy of the Vahnite faith. According to Nyctasia's beliefs, the *vahn,* the Indwelling Spirit, was the true source of a magician's powers. Nyctasia herself had invoked its Influences, and she was always willing to discourse at length upon the workings of her spells. Usually Corson paid no heed, or cut Nyctasia off with a curt jibe, but this time, to her astonishment, Nyctasia suddenly fell silent.

Corson turned to her in surprise, and saw her staring, speechless, as a line of people straggled past, chained together at the wrists and ankles.

Nyctasia's own ancestors had been responsible for the elimination of slavery in Rhostshyl, and she thought of it as an ancient and uncivilized custom. The sight of people being sold like livestock in the market square sickened her. "I knew such things went on, but—to see it—it's shameful," Nyctasia said in horror. "It shouldn't be allowed!"

Corson spat. She'd seen slave-traders before, in her travels, and she considered them lower than vermin. Having spent time in the army, Corson valued nothing above her freedom.

"It's a disgrace how little I know of the world outside Rhostshyl," said Nyctasia seriously.

"I never thought I'd hear you admit that there's something you don't know. I told you the countryside's crawling with slavers, and they're none too fussy about how they get their wares."

"Surely only criminals can be sold—or captives of war?"

"Oh, so says the law. But half the folk who are sold were waylaid on the road and smuggled to foreign markets. I could sell *you* here and now if I'd a mind to."

"Nonsense!"

A gleam of deviltry lit Corson's blue eyes. Seizing Nyctasia by the collar, she called out lustily, "Who'll buy a beautiful foreign princess, stolen from the courts of the coast?"

"Corson! You fool! Hold your tongue!" Nyctasia sputtered indignantly. She tried to kick Corson on the shins but Corson held her at arm's length, still describing her attractions to the crowd.

"Take note of her pale skin and delicate features. . . ."

"Let go of me, you stinking—"

". . . and grey eyes! You'll not see her like in the Midlands!"

"Bitch! You'll regret this!"

"She can read and write, too, and sing to the harp—a prize at two hundred crescents! Who'll buy?"

Nyctasia bit her, hard, and Corson hastily released her. "You venomous little snake!" she exclaimed, waving her wounded hand about. "You're poisonous as a viper! My hand'll turn black! I'll die. . . ." She was laughing too hard to go on.

Nyctasia regarded her coldly. "Corson, you go too far."

"I daresay you're right," said Corson, still gasping with laughter. "No one would pay two hundred crescents for a vicious little creature like you."

Nyctasia meant to say a great deal in reply, but she had barely begun to hold forth on the subject of Corson's behavior, when Corson interrupted her tirade.

"Nyc, look! That fellow over there—don't you remember him?"

"Where?" Nyctasia asked anxiously. Which of her enemies would pursue her so far?

Without answering, Corson suddenly darted across the square, shoving people out of her way. She seized an unsuspecting young man by the arm, shouting, "Where are my earrings, you thieving bastard?"

He tried to squirm away, protesting, but Corson threw him against a fruit barrow, sending apples flying. The crowd watched curiously as Corson continued to pummel the man with both fists, as though she meant to murder him. She could easily have done so, since he was only of average build and clearly not a fighter.

"Corson, stop—what are you doing? You'll kill him!" Nyctasia tried to pull her away, but was knocked roughly aside. She grabbed Corson by the belt, but someone dragged her back and held her fast.

The furious fruit vendor had summoned the city watch. It took three of them to deal with Corson.

3

OF THE MANY indignities Nyctasia had suffered in exile, this was the crowning outrage. It was past believing that she, a lady of the rank of Rhaicime, could be thrown into a prison-cell with the riffraff of the city. She was only thankful that it was too dark to see her filthy surroundings. Fastidious by nature, she hardly dared breathe the foul air.

Corson would have enjoyed Nyctasia's discomfiture if she had not been so wretched herself. She'd been in prison many times, during her frequently lawless career, but she could never resign herself to confinement. She paced back and forth, cursing, as the other prisoners scrambled to get out of her way. Helplessness always frightened Corson more than danger, and her fear took the form of unfocused rage.

The man she'd attacked had simply been thrown into the cell with them; no one had troubled to discover who was to blame for the brawl. He lay huddled in the dirty straw, and Nyctasia knelt over him, tending to his injuries. Fearing that his collarbone was broken, she unlaced his shirt and removed the leather pouch he wore around his neck, then felt gently along his shoulder. He groaned faintly without opening his eyes.

Looking at him, Corson remembered the time he'd robbed her

and Nyctasia just after their escape from Rhostshyl. He and his fellow thieves had not only taken Corson's prized golden earrings, but had taunted her with her helplessness as well. Corson had felt shamed at her defeat, though she knew she was hopelessly outnumbered. She did not have a forgiving nature, and she never forgot an injury. She would gladly have taken out her panic on the thief now, but he was plainly not fair game for a fight. She stood over him, glowering, and stifled a desire to kick him.

"Stay away from him, you stupid savage!" Nyctasia hissed. "I don't mean to be hanged for murder to satisfy your bloodlust. Let him be!"

"But—but that's the rutting whoreson who robbed us—he was the ringleader, you remember! They should hang *him*."

Nyctasia stared at her. *"That* is why you tried to beat him to death—for the loss of a few coins and some trumpery jewelry? That is why I am in this reeking dunghole?"

There was some whistling and jeering from the drunks and pickpockets who shared the cell with them.

"Make way for Her Ladyship—"

"Clean linen for Her Majesty here!"

Nyctasia clenched her teeth, her fine features hard with rage, but in a moment she had mastered her anger. It was not like her to give herself away. She stood and faced her fellow prisoners, suddenly seeming to become a completely different person. Corson had seen these masquerades of Nyctasia's before, but they always caught her unawares.

"Now I leave it to you!" Nyctasia cried. "This great lummox is supposed to perform feats of strength to draw a crowd, so I can pick their pockets—and what does she do but start a fight in the middle of the marketplace! And here we are! What's to be done with a dunce like that?" She ended her performance with a remarkably ill-bred laugh, which the others echoed.

"Cut her throat," someone offered.

"Get rid of the dolt—I'll go partners with you."

There were other suggestions of a coarser sort, but Corson was in no mood to bandy words. "I'll serve the next who laughs just as I served that one," she threatened, pointing at the hapless thief. No one took up her challenge.

She turned back to Nyctasia, who was once again kneeling beside the thief. "It may have been a few coins to a wealthy *lady,*" Corson muttered, "but it was a rutting fortune for the likes of me."

"However much it was, it's not worth hanging for!"

Corson looked uneasy. "He's not really like to die, is he?"

"No thanks to you if he doesn't. He has broken ribs."

"Well, why don't you use your witchery to heal him then?" said Corson, lowering her voice. "You always say that healing-spells are simple to do."

"They are simple, but they're not easy. To heal, you must first be whole yourself—"

Corson foresaw another of Nyctasia's learned lectures. "Don't explain it, just do it!"

"If you'd keep out of my way, I *could* get on with it! Keep everyone away from me!" She glared until Corson had retreated a few paces.

Leaning over the thief, Nyctasia laid her hand over his heart, murmuring something ceaselessly to herself. To Corson, she seemed to be somehow drawing ever farther away, though she remained still as a figure of carven stone. Corson knew that Nyctasia's trance would take her deep into the realm of the *vahn*. Watching her, Corson could almost feel that it was she herself who was stranded on the shore of a dream, while Nyctasia entered into the waking world.

Corson shook herself abruptly. Magic! she thought, and spat.

4

IT WAS A highly discontented party that took shelter for the night in a barn on a small farm near the Southern Trade Road. That morning, they'd been unceremoniously escorted to the city gates, fined for disturbing the peace of the fair, and sent on their way with a warning not to return.

The unfortunate thief was still with them. He'd been unable to travel on foot, and Nyctasia had agreed to let him ride with her, but even on horseback he had found the journey a grueling one. By the time they dismounted he was more stiff and sore than ever.

Nyctasia was almost as weak as he. The healing-spell had already sapped much of her strength, and the long day's ride left her exhausted. The barn was not noticeably cleaner than the jail had been, but she was so weary that even a pile of hay looked inviting.

Corson too felt that she'd been very hard used. What right had they to arrest her for capturing a thief, and how could Nyctasia take his part against her? Was that justice? She had ridden ahead of the others in sullen silence for most of the day.

But everyone was in better spirits after the hearty meal they bought at the farmhouse. They ate smoked ham, buttered oat-cakes, and fresh curds. There was plenty of brown ale, and a crock of new buttermilk for Nyctasia, whose Discipline discouraged the drinking of spirits.

After her night in prison and a day on horseback, Nyctasia longed for a bath, but she made do with a wash at the well. Spreading out her long cloak, she made herself a comfortable nest in the hay, then hung her harp on a peg in the wall. "As a child I was taught that a lady ought never to complain about her accommodations," she remarked. "But I'm sure my nurse never imagined me in lodgings like this."

"I admired the ladylike way you accepted your lot in prison last night," Corson sniggered.

"It's not surprising I forget myself in company with a lout like you. The wonder is that I have any manners left at all."

"I stand rebuked, Your Ladyship." Corson made a mocking bow, and threw herself down in the hay.

The thief looked from one to the other of them, trying to make them out, then gave it up and settled down near Nyctasia. He moved stiffly, grimacing as he lowered himself slowly onto the hay.

"You ought to stay here for a while and rest," Nyctasia said. "You're not really fit to travel."

"I know," he groaned. "Would you think it impertinent of me to ask why your friend tried to murder me?"

Corson was indignant. "You and your people robbed us in Rhostshyl Wood and took our horses! I told you I'd make you pay, you slinking weasel—maybe you remember that?"

"I remember those rutting horses! They broke loose and we nearly got trampled trying to catch them. They were such beauties, too," he said regretfully. "They'd have fetched a good price."

"They were hers," Corson said. "Thoroughbreds can be quite vicious."

"You were that crazy soldier, then," he mused, "but you were traveling with some prating little student. . . ."

"He's taken *your* measure, Nyc."

Nyctasia had made her escape from Rhostshyl disguised as a poor student. "Appearances may be misleading," she said, sounding amused. "I'm Nyc brenn Rhostshyl, and this is Corson brenn Torisk. And you?"

"I'm called Newt." He eyed Nyctasia suspiciously. "What are you really? A witch? A pickpocket?"

"A liar," Corson suggested.

"A healer," said Nyctasia firmly. "And if you'll take my advice, you'll get some sleep. You're not yet whole."

"I feel like a bone that's been gnawed by hounds." Newt lay back and started to loosen his tunic, then sat up again suddenly, wincing in pain. He searched about frantically. "My pouch—where is it? I had it round my neck. Did you take it?"

"Not I," said Corson lazily. "But if I thought you had anything of value, I'd surely take it, as my right. You robbed me of a fortune."

"What, this?" asked Nyctasia. "Here, I'd forgotten it." She tossed the small leather bag to Newt.

But Corson was at his side in a moment and snatched it from him. "Let's have a look at this."

"It's just a scrap of paper!" he protested. "Give it back!"

"I will," said Corson, "when you give me back my earrings." She opened the pouch and pulled out a much-folded page, but to her disappointment there was nothing else.

Impatiently, she shook it out, but it concealed no treasure. "What's all the row about *this?*" she muttered, examining it by the light of the flickering oil lamp. "Here, Nyc, you're partial to this sort of gibberish:

> Neither out of doors nor in,
> Begin.
>
> Within four walls and yet beneath the sky,
> I lie.
>
> Riddle's secret, and to mystery
> The key.
>
> All unhidden
> Though I be,
> No man or woman
> Doth see me.

And here's another—

> Here is a web to catch the wind
> And a loom to weave a lay.
> Riddles play on words, my friend—
> Play on these and play you may.

"What in the Hlann's name...?" Nyctasia reached for the paper. "I don't make much of the first one," she said after a moment, "but the other's simple enough. The answer's in plain sight." She pointed to her ebonwood harp.

"A harp?" said Newt, sounding disappointed. "Just a *harp?* Are you sure?"

"As I said, the answer's in plain sight—for those who can read it. H-A-R-P," she said, touching the first letter of each line.

Newt looked puzzled, "But... what does that part about the wind mean?"

"There's a sort of lyre called a wind-harp," Nyctasia explained. "You hang them in the trees and they're sounded by the wind. I had one in my garden at home."

"I like the clue about playing on them," said Corson. "Read us another."

Nyctasia peered at the page in the dim light. "Let's see... there's all sorts of riddles....

> Where is the hunter found
> Who hunts by night and morn
> But never wearied yet?
> Who keeps not hawk or hound,
> Who has not horse or horn,
> But slays without a sound,
> With but a silken net?

Well, that's easy, and here's a pair that spell out rhyming answers:

> Bird am I none. What thing am I,
> Ever soaring as I sing?
> Lifting up my voice on high,
> Lightly I fly, without a wing.

And:

> Where is there a tower found,
> Empty, planted underground,
> Like a tunnel turned on end?
> Look down to see the sky, my friend.

What else have we here? Rhymes . . . drawings of some kind, names . . . Ylna, Rowan, Leaf and Bough, Amron Therain, Jocelys, Vale—" She stopped abruptly and turned to Newt, fixing him with a cold and baneful stare. "No wonder you tried to keep this from us," she said grimly.

"Nyc, what is it?"

"My name is on this list. The fellow's an assassin. Am I to be hunted like a fugitive all my life? Who was it sent you? Lady Mhairestri? Ettasuan ar'n Teiryn?"

"You're *both* mad!" cried Newt. "I'm a thief, not a murderer —I've no dealings with lords and ladies!"

Nyctasia stood and drew her dagger. "We'll soon see. Corson, hold him fast." Experience had made Nyctasia a keen judge of character. She was certain that Newt could be frightened into speaking the truth.

"But—please—I tell you, I don't know who you are. I can't even read—I don't know what's on that paper! It's nothing to do with me!"

"Then how did you come by it?" Nyctasia demanded.

"I stole it, of course! Me and three others—we robbed a traveler near Ylna. . . ."

"Why would you steal a piece of paper that you can't read?"

"We didn't know what was in the pouch when we took it. We might have given the thing back, but he fought like a madman to keep it, so it must be valuable. And the mark of the Cymvelan Circle is at the bottom—look for yourself. Folk still talk of the Cymvelan treasure in these parts. That paper might be a clue!"

At the mention of treasure, Corson retrieved the paper from Nyctasia and scanned it eagerly, still keeping a firm grip on the distraught thief.

"And it was just chance that brought you to Osela, I suppose?" Nyctasia pursued.

"I hoped to sell that paper at the fair—I come to Osela every year. Most of us do."

"That's so," said Corson. "The fair draws thieves like flies to a honeypot."

"No doubt," said Nyctasia, "but I trust they're not all carrying my name about with them."

Newt was sweating. "But I didn't know—"

"It's not your proper name, Nyc," Corson broke in. "It says 'Edonaris,' not 'Nyctasia ar'n Edonaris.' I'll wager it means those other Edonaris—the vintners." She dropped Newt indifferently and showed the page to Nyctasia again. "Look here. That *is* the sign of the Cymvelan Circle," she said, pointing to an intricate, knotted design. "Their temple was in the Valleylands to the south, near Vale—it can't have been far from the Edonaris vineyards. And some of these riddles do talk about treasure—'Wealth beyond a lifetime's spending'!" The two of them bent over the paper, forgetting Newt, who sank to his knees in the hay and stared at them.

"Nyctasia ar'n Edonaris!" he gasped. "The witch? In Rhostshyl they say you're dead."

"It's unwise to believe everything you hear."

"To think we let you slip through our hands," said Newt dejectedly. "If we'd known who you were we could have made our fortunes—there was a reward of five hundred crescents for your capture. Five hundred crescents!"

"Don't plan on earning it now, my lad," said Nyctasia. "My kinsman Lord Thierran offered it, and he's dead."

"I saw to that," Corson added, slashing her finger across her throat. She smiled at Newt.

"I don't want any part of it," Newt said hastily. "I wouldn't go back to Rhostshyl now for any money—it's too dangerous. The city's divided. It's nothing but brawls and bloodshed between the Edonaris and the Teiryn. There'll be open war before long."

"Sure sign of war, when the rats and thieves leave a city," sneered Corson.

"We had to go our ways. The gentry there go about with armed escorts, and folk are too war-wary to be careless. What were we to do, steal from paupers? We'd have soon starved," he said indignantly. "But there were good gleanings to be had at the fair—and now I'm banned from Osela, thanks to you!"

"A most sad tale," said Corson. "Nyc, this wretch knows nothing about you. It's no use to question him. Let's go to sleep." She turned back to Newt. "Don't think to mend your fortunes by picking our pockets—I sleep lightly."

"I can barely move," Newt protested. "How could I make an escape? I'll not stir from this place till I'm healed, if I can beg my bread from these folk."

Nyctasia roused herself from thoughts of her city torn by civil war. Taking up the curious piece of paper, she folded it neatly and slipped it into her shirt. "I'll buy this from you—then you'll have more than enough to pay your keep. The Edonaris of Vale might be interested in this paper."

Newt sat up a bit straighter. "It might be worth a fortune," he said eagerly. "The treasure of the Cymvelan Circle—"

"Is a lot of moonshine," Corson scoffed. "There's nothing but rhymes and scribbles on that page. You'll take what you get and be glad of it." She stretched out on the hay and yawned. "We ought to just take the thing, Nyc," she grumbled, without much conviction. "You're too softhearted by half."

Nyctasia blew out the lamp. "Mercy is the mark of true nobility," she said drily. "Go to sleep."

Corson had the soldier's knack for falling asleep in an instant, but Nyctasia, despite her weariness, lay awake brooding over her own behavior. "A fine Vahnite!" she accused herself. "The moment you think yourself threatened, your scruples take wing like startled quail!"

It was no use to tell herself that no harm had been done. What steps would she have taken if Newt's answers hadn't satisfied her? This was the question that kept her awake and restless. She did not want to know what answer might lie within her.

Newt was not asleep either. He shifted from side to side in the hay, trying to find a less painful position, but however he lay, his chest and sides ached unbearably. He groaned aloud.

When Nyctasia approached him, he struggled to sit up, alarmed, for he now regarded her as the more dangerous of the two. She stood over him for a moment, indistinct in the darkness, then knelt beside him.

"Forgive me, Newt," she whispered. "I see my enemies everywhere. I am certain I left them in Rhostshyl, and yet I cannot escape them." It was perhaps the strangest adventure of her exile that she should bring herself to ask pardon of a common thief.

But Newt understood nothing of her confession. "I'm no spy, my lady," he said helplessly. "What do you want with me?"

"You forget that I'm a healer. And sometimes I forget as well. But I can give you sleep if you wish."

"Please," said Newt, then hesitated. "How . . . by a spell?"

"A simple charm. It's quite harmless." She relit the lamp, but hooded it so that only a single ray escaped.

Corson was now awake and watching. "Nyc, what . . . ?"

"Healing, what else? When you attack someone, you don't do it by halves."

"He deserved it," said Corson crossly, turning her back to the light and burrowing deeper into the hay.

"Be still, if you please. I need silence for this spell." Nyctasia drew from her pouch a faceted crystal on a silver chain. "Look well at this," she said to Newt. "You've never seen its like before."

Newt watched the stone swing gently to and fro before him, catching the lamplight on its polished planes. "Is it a real diamond?" he asked covetously.

"It's far more valuable than a diamond. This jewel holds the power of peace." Back and forth it swayed, and Nyctasia's voice with it in a low, melodious tone. "This is a stone that can ease all ills, heal all hurts, soothe all suffering. Watch it well, and you will feel its peace possess you. It will give rest to your spirit, it will shelter you beneath the wings of sleep." Her words grew ever slower and slower. "You feel its power even now, don't you, Newt?"

"I . . . feel it," said Newt with some difficulty.

"Already your eyes are heavy with sleep."

"Yes."

"You cannot hold them open any longer."

Newt's eyes were closed, his face finally relaxed in repose. Without his habitually wary expression, he seemed another person entirely.

"Now there is nothing but sweet sleep," murmured Nyctasia.

"No, nothing," he sighed.

"And there will be nothing but sleep, till the sun is high on the morrow."

Newt made no reply, and Nyctasia blew out the lamp once more and returned to her place, wrapping herself in her cloak.

"Nyc . . . ?"

"You needn't whisper. He'll not wake."

"If you have a stone that heals all ills, why didn't you use it when I was sick, in Lhestreq?"

Nyctasia laughed softly. "This stone couldn't cure hiccups, Corson. It's only a common crystal. Anything bright would have done as well. The spell's in the shining and the speaking, and the healing's all humbug. It gives sleep, no more."

"Is that why it didn't weaken you to do it?"

That all power has its price was the guiding Principle of Nyctasia's philosophy. More than once Corson had seen her drained of strength by a healing spell.

"No, this is a spell that draws its power from the one who is spellcast, not from the one who acts. That's why it can only be laid upon one who is willing. It's a very rare and significant Balance."

A snore interrupted her explanation. Corson questioned everything, but she listened to the answers only when she chose.

Now that Newt slept, Nyctasia could sleep as well—though even in slumber she could not rest. In her dreams she was again in Rhostshyl, her ancestral home, but the proud city was in ruins, ravaged by flames, its walls broken, its towers fallen. Fires still smoldered among the piles of debris.

Nyctasia wandered through the empty streets, so well known to her that she could have walked them blindfolded, until she stood before the remains of a house where she had hidden before fleeing the city. The iron gate still stood, protecting ashes and dust and broken stone. She slipped into the yard and found the fragments of her great mirror shining among the blackened timber. Her favorite harp, the Sparrow, was charred and useless. It crumbled in her hand when she lifted it from the rubble.

"Why, 'Tasia, I thought you didn't know how to weep."

At first Nyctasia thought it was her cousin Thierran who stood outside the gate, but she saw in a moment that it was his twin, Mescrisdan. When they'd last met he had urged his brother to kill her, but now Nyctasia went out willingly to meet him. He could do her no harm—he was dead, struck down by Corson on that very spot, where he and Thierran had lain in wait for her.

"I can weep for Rhostshyl," she told him, "if it is now the city of the dead."

He shrugged. "When the city was dying you ran away. Why should you mourn it now? Come along, everyone's waiting for you."

She accompanied him in silence, knowing without question that the palace of the Edonaris was their destination. Where else was there to go?

The battered gates and smashed windows of her home were like wounds in her own flesh. She had passed most of her life within these halls, the most splendid in the city. Now they lay open to the night, the great columns and arches supporting nothing, the magnificent windows gaping, fanged with shards of colored glass.

Nyctasia followed Mescrisdan through the stone-strewn corridors till he stood aside to allow her to precede him into the dining-hall. She was, after all, a Rhaicime, his superior in rank.

Lady Mhairestri, matriarch of the Edonaris, sat at the head of the table, a privilege due her great age rather than her rank. Nyctasia was surprised to see her there, for the matriarch was not dead, for all that she could remember. There were others of the living present, her elder brother Emeryc among them, though it seemed that his wife, a commoner, had not been invited.

Nyctasia's parents observed her entrance with the same indifference they'd shown her in life. She had been a sickly child—a disappointment to her mother, an iron-willed woman so impatient of weakness that, after safely giving birth to twins, she'd scorned her physicians' advice to rest, and had died as a result. The elderly, reserved nobleman she'd married out of duty had survived her by only a few years. Nyctasia had not often seen her father in life, and she hardly recognized him now, but she bowed dutifully to both her parents. Her father did not seem to know her, but her mother nodded coldly in reply.

"Late as usual, Nyctasia Selesq," said, Lady Mhairestri. "Take your seat. You have kept us waiting long enough."

"Your place is here, cousin, at my side," said Thierran. "Now that you are here at last, our wedding feast can begin. Only you would arrive late upon such an occasion, 'Tasia, but I forgive you, as always."

Thierran had been Nyctasia's bitterest enemy ever since she'd refused the marriage their family had planned for them. But now she faced him with composure. Him too she had seen lying dead at her feet, his throat slashed. She felt only regret as she stood beside him, looking into his pale, handsome face.

There was no malice in his eyes as he said, "You've taken a long way, only to return to me, 'Tasia. Would it not have been simpler to remain where you belonged?"

"Perhaps," she sighed. "But what choice had I, Thorn?" It was a childhood name she'd not used for him for many years. "I suppose we none of us had a choice."

How could she have helped falling in love with Erystalben ar'n Shiastred, who had seemed to her a twin spirit? And how could Thierran have helped his jealousy and, above all, his wounded pride? All the Edonaris were proud and willful.

Nyctasia might have honored the marriage alliance, to serve the family's interests, and kept Erystalben as her lover—an arrangement which was common enough among the high aristocracy. But Erystalben too had his pride, and the more he had tried to persuade Nyctasia to repudiate the betrothal, the more dangerous he had become to Edonaris ambition. The full power of the

house of Edonaris was brought to bear upon his kinfolk till he
was forced to flee the city to protect his people. In time, Nyctasia
had renounced her family and followed him into exile, but by
then it had been too late. . . .

Now she seemed to see this course of events clearly for the
first time. What could she have done to alter it? Who was to
blame? If she had been wiser, kinder, like the Vahnite she
claimed to be, would anything have been different?

And the maddening thing was that she did love Thierran,
could not but love him, in spite of everything. They had been
children together. Why had she not been able to explain—? Before the assembled company of ghosts and memories, she bent
down and kissed him. "I'm with you now," she said.

He took both her hands in his and drew her down beside him.
"A toast to our union!" he called.

A full wine glass stood at every place except Nyctasia's, as
was usual. But now the matriarch filled the gold chalice called
the Bride's Cup and handed it to her brother, Brethald, who bore
it formally to Nyctasia.

"Your affectation of Vahnite Principles must give way to tra-
dition for once," he said, presenting the goblet.

All glasses were raised, and everyone looked toward Nyctasia.

"To the bride and groom."

"To the House of Edonaris."

"To your homecoming, sister," said Emeryc.

It was for Nyctasia, as the guest of honor, to drink first, and
the others waited, watching her. At that moment she desired
above all to obey, to be accepted, finally, by her kin. She had
only to lift the wine to her lips and her exile would be at an end.

"Allow me, my lady."

She turned and saw her trusted henchman Sandor standing
guard behind her chair. Sandor, who had been killed while trying
to bring her warning of a plot against her. Now, like a monarch's
table-servant, he took up the goblet and tasted its contents before
Nyctasia could drink.

Without a word he put it down and turned it on its side, to
signify that the drink was dangerous. A crimson stain spread over
the damask tablecloth, seeming as though it would soak the
whole table. Nyctasia was seized with a sudden horror that it
would reach her, drench her, drown her. She clutched at the cup,

trying to right it and stop the endless tide of poison that threatened to flood the city. "Help me!" she cried.

"You are weak, weak!" said the matriarch sternly. "Only thus will the fires in the city be quenched." She stood and raised her glass. "To the everlasting destruction of our enemies! An end to the Teiryn line!" She smashed her glass on the hearth, and another spring of crimson welled from the spot, flowing across the floor. The others echoed her toast.

"No, don't! Stop! You're making it worse," Nyctasia pleaded. "We'll all be drowned!"

The company broke into laughter. "How could that be, when we are already dead?"

"But surely not the whole city," Nyctasia sobbed. "Not all! We must warn them!" She ran from the hall, down corridors haunted by her earliest memories, through courtyards where she had often gathered the hounds for the hunt, past gardens she had planted herself, now sere and withered.

The gates had always been guarded, but now they stood open, and Nyctasia raced out into the streets, seeking the living. Not till she reached the Market Square did she see another person, a man who sat at his ease on a fallen beam, as if waiting for her. She hurried to him eagerly, but when he turned to her she found herself facing another of her remembered dead.

"Fie, Nyctasia, and you a Vahnite!" said Rhavor ar'n Teiryn. "If you mean to break your Discipline, drink honest wine, not that foul brew."

Nyctasia realized that she was still clutching the golden goblet, and she threw it from her with disgust. "Ah, but it's your fault, Rhavor. If you'd married me, they'd not be able to wed me to Thierran."

They had once considered a political marriage between them, in hopes of uniting their warring families. Rhavor's death had put an end to the plan, but now he smiled and said, "It is not too late for that."

"It is too late to save a dead city."

"Rhostshyl dead? Nonsense, my dear girl!"

"Show me the living then! Where are they?"

"They are coming this way. Don't you hear them? Listen—"

At first there was only the heavy silence, but then a sound of horns and drums reached her, distant but drawing nearer.

"Hurry," Rhavor urged her, and she set out again, her heart leaping wildly to the drumbeat. The streets grew lighter as the music grew louder, until she turned a corner and met with a grand wedding procession in full regalia, bright with banners, colorful caparisons and gold trumpets splendid in the sudden sunshine.

Nyctasia was astonished to see the coats-of-arms of both the Houses of Edonaris and Teiryn among the heralds and standard-bearers. Together! Was it possible? But more bewildering still was the sight of the noble couple who led this festive throng. The bride was herself, but younger, hardly more than a girl, and the groom was not much older. But he was Rhavor ar'n Teiryn, Nyctasia saw, not her cousin Thierran. They rode side by side, solemn and unsmiling, she looking straight ahead, he down at the cobbled street.

Overcome with wonder and confusion, Nyctasia watched the procession pass. She had never known Rhavor as a youth—when she'd come of age he'd already been a grown man, a widower with a young son.

Perhaps he could explain this mystery. She turned back toward the Market Square, following the parade, and now she saw that the streets through which they had passed were whole again, the shops and houses restored. Behind them, folk flocked, cheering and shouting, but ahead of them the silent streets were still in twilight and in ruins.

Nyctasia fell behind, gazing all about her at the return of life and prosperity to the city she loved. Then suddenly she stopped in her tracks, forgetting all else as she caught sight of one man among the onlookers. He looked more haggard and careworn than she had ever seen him. His long black hair was unkempt, his clothing dirty and ragged. Even his fierce blue eyes seemed dulled and defeated. But Nyctasia knew at once, without doubt, that here was the lover ravished from her by a dark and desperate spell, lost beyond an unknown threshold of perilous magic.

"'Ben," she cried, "this way! I'm here!" But she could not make him hear. She struggled toward him through the crowd, calling his name again and again, but when at last she reached his side he looked past her without a sign of recognition or welcome, and kept on his way, unseeing. "No!" Nyctasia screamed. "'Ben, no—come back!"

I can't bear any more of this, she thought wildly, and woke.

It was day. Corson was already up and feeding the horses, but Newt still slept, while the farm folk gathered eggs and milked the cows, not far from where he lay.

"If Her Ladyship would deign to rise we might reach Ylna by

nightfall," Corson remarked. "The people here say it's a day's ride. I've been trying to rouse you since sunup—it's time enough you woke up!"

"It is indeed," said Nyctasia.

* * *

"Well, it was only a dream," Corson said sensibly.

It was easy to dismiss Nyctasia's fancies in the clear light of morning. As they rode south along the Southern Trade Road, they were greeted gaily by families traveling north to the fair. Corson joked with the passersby and accepted an apple, which she ate in three bites. "A fair day and good traveling," she observed with satisfaction. She had no misgivings or forbodings about the future.

But Nyctasia could not shake off the memory of her visions. "The *vahn* speaks to us through dreams, Corson."

"Not to me it doesn't."

"Very likely not. But I've had dreams before that later came to pass."

Corson was not impressed. "And for every one that did, a hundred that didn't—isn't that so?"

"Yes, but—"

"Dreaming of cabbage doesn't fill your belly," Corson said firmly.

"You don't understand," said Nyctasia, but she smiled, and for once she did not offer to explain. This time she preferred to think that Corson might be right.

5

THE VILLAGE OF Ylna was little more than a cluster of cottages and a wayside inn that depended on the Southern Trade Road for its custom. Corson and Nyctasia reached it in good time and might have pressed on, but the signboard of the Leaf and Bough caught Corson's eye.

"Nyc, wait. Let me see that foolish paper again. Yes, look, Ylna is on this list, and it says Rowan, Leaf and Bough." The Cymvelan treasure was still on Corson's mind.

Nyctasia shrugged. "We may as well stop here as go on. I'm ready for a rest, that's certain." What matter when she reached the Valleylands—one place was the same as another to her.

They gave their horses to the ostler and entered the public room of the inn, which was crowded with travelers on their way to the Osela fair. They paid their share, and sat at the long table, where folk were helping themselves to the common fare. The host scurried about, filling the mugs with foamy, dark ale, while the help brought more food from the kitchen.

Set before the company were platters of meat and roasted fowls, great loaves of bread, wheels of cheese, and basins of suet pudding. Bowls of boiled potatoes and onions were passed from hand to hand, and crocks of butter and honey stood at either end

26

of the table. Corson and Nyctasia fell to eagerly. Corson forgot
about treasure for the time being, and even Nyctasia found nothing in the meal to complain of. She had several helpings of sweet
bread-pudding with apples and raisins, floating in cream.

When the board was cleared, people gave their full attention
to drinking and exchanging news. Travelers from the south reported rumors of bandits and slavers prowling the countryside
and attacking solitary wayfarers. But most of the talk centered on
the harvest and farmers' concerns. Had there been enough rainfall in the Valleylands? What did a bushel of millet fetch in town?
Did the spring frost kill many lambs?

Should barley be planted during the new moon or the first
quarter? Believers in both traditions had their say, and the discussion was a lively one. Nyctasia, who had inherited a good deal of
farmland, had been raised to take an interest in such matters. But
she held her peace, unwilling to reveal her station to strangers.

Corson only interested herself in barley when it was brewed
and fermented, and she nursed her mug of stout, paying no attention to the talk. A group of students, as bored as she, looked
about for some amusement and caught sight of Nyctasia's harp.

"You, there, harper, give us a song!"

"The 'Song of the Bat'!"

"No, not that—something bawdy!"

Corson expected Nyctasia to resent their addressing her in this
manner, but instead she made them a bow and began to tune the
strings of her harp. "I fear the songs of this region are not known
to me," she said mildly. "I'll sing you one of my own."

"She's up to some trick," Corson thought.

Nyctasia winked at the students and sang:

> "O, I never was made
> To take heed of advice,
> I've gambled and played
> By the fall of the dice,
> And rambled and strayed
> All over creation,
> Beset by temptation
> And courted by vice.
>
> Each friend and relation
> Who knew me of old
> Often foretold

That I'd go to the bad.
By wall and by wold
I've rambled and wandered,
And gambled and squandered
The whole that I had,
To my last piece of gold.

Of all wisdom's students
'Twas I was the best,
But I never learned prudence
When put to the test.
For all of my lessons
I was no whit the wiser—
When I've lost my last crescents
Then I'll be a miser,
And if my last pence
Should follow the rest,
With virtue and sense
I shall feather my nest!"

Her performance was received with enthusiasm. The students cheered and threw coins, and even some of the other guests applauded. Corson made haste to gather up the money.

"Give us another, lass!"

Nyctasia smiled. "I believe I do know a song from this part of the world, after all," she said. "Perhaps someone here can explain it to me:

What has come before
Will return again,
Neither less nor more,
Neither now nor then.

Nothing that befalls
Comes about by chance.
The nurseling babe that crawls
Will soon join in the dance.

Stars are wheeling in the night,
Moments spinning into time,
Winter turning into spring.
Birds are circling in their flight,

Words are winding into rhyme,
Children dancing in a ring.

What has gone before
Will return again,
Neither less nor more,
Neither now nor then."

This time there was no clapping when Nyctasia finished. An uneasy silence had fallen on the crowd, and people turned away, avoiding one another's eyes. Corson recognized the song as one of the verses from the page of riddles.

"What do you mean singing that accursed thing in here?" shouted the landlord. "We're decent folk here. Take your trouble-making somewhere else!"

"I'm sure I didn't mean to give offense," Nyctasia said in a bewildered tone. "I heard a drunken man sing it at the fair."

He looked at her suspiciously. "You'd be wise to guard your tongue, minstrel," he muttered, and hurried off to the kitchen.

Nyctasia turned to the students. "Why all this fuss over a trifling verse?"

"Don't you know that's a song of the Cymvelan Circle?"

"Well, and what if it is? Who are they?"

"Don't blame her, she's an outlander," said Corson. "I've heard of them—sorcerers or demon-worshippers or some such, weren't they?"

"That's what people say. The Valleylanders rose against them during the great drought. In my father's time, it was. They slaughtered the lot of them and destroyed the temple."

"Not all of them were killed," said a local farmer. "Some of the children were spared, and *he*"—he jerked his thumb toward the kitchen—"was one of them, though he doesn't like folk to mention it. He thought you sang that song to bait him."

"I've heard it said that they had some great treasure hidden," Corson said cautiously.

"Superstition," said one of the students loftily. "Many a fool has wasted time hunting for it, and no one's so much as found a copper."

"That's all very well," said a traveler, "but I come from the valley, and I can tell you those ruins are haunted. Some who entered those walls never came out again, and their friends found no trace of them. You tell me what's become of them—that demon-brood may be dead, but they're not gone yet."

"They don't sound so very fearsome to me. *Cymvela* means 'peace' in Old Eswraine," said another student, showing off his learning.

Nyctasia, who prided herself on her scholarship, winced at his mispronunciation of the word. *Cymvela* was a word with several levels of meaning in Ancient Eswraine, and it was with difficulty that she restrained herself from explaining them all at length, from "the harmony of Creation" through "the conciliation of the Spirit." But a tavern-songster would hardly know such things, so she held her tongue.

One of the villagers stood. "You ought not to name them," he warned. "It's bad luck even to speak of them. I'll not hear it— you'll bring their vengeance on us!" He and his neighbors hastily took their leave.

"I seem to have shaken down a wasps' nest," said Nyctasia apologetically.

"Never mind those ignorant peasants," said the student. "Now they're gone, we shan't have to hear about tilling and toiling. Let's have another song!"

"Oh, I daren't," Nyctasia demurred. "I don't know what's like to displease these folk—"

"What of the 'Bird in the Bush'?" someone suggested with a leer. "Will anyone quarrel with *that?*"

There were no complaints.

6

CORSON AWOKE AND lay stiffly in bed, listening carefully. What had roused her? Nyctasia lay beside her, her breathing steady and peaceful. A tree branch tapped against the shutters, and there were all the random noises that plagued old houses—creaks and groans as timbers shifted like troubled sleepers.

As her eyes grew accustomed to the darkness, Corson looked into every corner of the room, trying to spot something odd or out of place. But the shadows all resolved themselves into the clumsy furniture of a country inn, and the shaft of moonlight sneaking in between the shutters revealed no prowler lurking nearby.

Yet Corson would not go back to sleep. Her intuitions had saved her too often for her to ignore them now. She slid softly from the bed, without waking Nyctasia, and padded silently to the door.

Had she heard a sound outside, and then another, following too evenly to be a settling board or loose panel? Her right hand stole to the latch and paused there for a moment. Suddenly she yanked the door wide, lunged over the sill and grabbed something with her left hand, throwing it into the room.

Nyctasia started up and was faced with the sight of Corson

31

bending back the leg of a rather short, plump fellow, and then sitting on him.

"Corson, what in the name of all that's reasonable—!"

"It's the landlord," said Corson. "*I* don't know why. Ask *him*, why don't you?"

Nyctasia shook her head. Wrapping the blanket around her with a regal air, she got out of bed and ambled over to Corson and her prisoner. She sat down on the floor beside the man, looked at him with drowsy disapproval, and yawned.

"It's not yet dawn," she pointed out.

"Good of you to wake up, my lady," said Corson.

"Dealing with the rabble is your job. And I'd really much prefer you to do it outside in future, if you don't mind. I need my sleep." She turned her attention to their host. "Explain yourself! How dare you come in here unbidden?"

"I know why you're here," he gasped, "and I've come to tell you I want no part in it!"

Corson and Nyctasia looked at each other. "Why *are* we here?" Corson asked. Nyctasia shrugged.

Corson relinquished her hold on the indignant landlord and sat down next to Nyctasia. They both looked at him expectantly.

"It wasn't by chance you sang that song here," he accused. "You meant it as a sign to me."

"Well . . ." said Nyctasia slowly, "we meant it as a sign to *someone. . . .*"

"Garast told me you'd come, but you're wasting your time. I'm not one of you. It'll be the ruin of me if folk learn you've been here!"

"We're not C—" Corson began, but Nyctasia cut her words short.

"Then why is your name on this list?" she demanded, fetching the page of riddles. "You're Rowan, are you not?"

"This is Garast's," he cried. "He wouldn't have given it up— how did you get it? What have you done with him?" The man's face was ashen in the moonlight.

Nyctasia sighed. Was she so soon to break faith with her Principles again? "We mean you no harm," she said gently. "We are not Cymvelans—we bought this paper from a thief. I only want to know why it says Edonaris here."

"*I* want to know why it says treasure," Corson put in.

"You're only treasure-hunters, then?" Rowan asked hopefully.

"I am an Edonaris," said Nyctasia in a haughty tone that unmistakably proclaimed her rank and station. "I wish to know why our name is listed here. What has the Cymvelan Circle to do with us?"

Though he had seen her playing the minstrel, and now saw her sitting on the floor, wearing only a threadbare blanket, Rowan did not doubt Nyctasia's claim to belong to a distinguished family. Her manner simply did not admit of doubt. "Garast heard that the Edonaris had bought the land the temple stood on—it was no more than that," he explained, much relieved. "He thought he'd need their—er, your—leave to search the ruins."

"Ah, yes, well it's possible," said Nyctasia coolly. "But it is hardly a matter for common gossip."

"Of course not, madame. By no means—"

"And who's this Garast? One of the Circle?"

"No! We were only children when the Circle was overthrown —Garast, Jocelys and I. We never knew that there were other survivors. We even shunned one another, the better to forget our evil lineage. But this past spring Garast visited me, to warn me that they were looking for the three of us. Somehow, a few of the elders escaped the attack on the temple, and now, after a score of years, they would bid us return to the Circle! Garast refused them, of course. When you turned up tonight, I was sure they'd sent you. I suppose they'll find me sooner or later, but they'll get the same answer from me." He seemed glad to be able to tell the tale to someone.

Nyctasia frowned down at the page of Cymvelan rhymes. "If Garast spurned their offer, what did he want with this?"

"He took a notion that they meant to go back for the treasure, and he thought to outfox them, the fool. The three of us were to recall all we could of our childhood lessons, according to his plan, and that would somehow lead us to the legendary treasure—"

"Then these *are* clues to the treasure," said Corson.

"These are rot," he said scornfully. "Mere rhymes for children. Garast's mad! There was never any treasure there that I saw, and no more did the rest—we lived like poor folk. If there'd been anything of value there it would have been found when the place was sacked."

Corson grabbed the list from Nyctasia. "What about this?" she insisted.

"Tales I have told, although I cannot speak.
Treasure I hold, enough for all who seek.
However many plunder me for gain
Yet will as much as ever still remain."

Rowan laughed. "Any half-wit could answer that riddle! What could it be but a book?"

Corson crumpled the paper in her fist and threw it into a corner. "Just my rutting luck! A lot of useless bookworms like you, Nyc. It's not fair!"

But Nyctasia retrieved the page, smoothed it out, and replaced it in her commonplace-book. "I believe that all our questions have been answered," she said calmly.

7

"WHAT DO YOU mean we're lost?" Nyctasia asked indignantly. It was growing dark, and there was a steady rain. "How can we be lost? We've not come half a league from the Trade Road."

"They said we'd pass fences and cottages soon—do *you* see any?"

"I can't see anything in this wretched rain. We should have kept to the road."

"We won't find your long-lost relatives that way."

"We're not finding them this way either," Nyctasia pointed out, and sneezed. "At least we might have found some shelter along the roadway. I'm drenched."

It had been raining all day, and neither of them was in a gracious temper. Water trickled down Corson's neck as she asked herself how Nyctasia contrived to make her feel personally responsible for the weather. Nyctasia sneezed again.

"If you were any rutting good as a sorceress you could make it stop raining," Corson said spitefully.

"That is not the purpose of the art."

"You can't do it, that's all."

"True. But if I had the power, I'd not use it so lightly as that.

35

It doesn't do to interfere with the Balance of the elements for frivolous purposes. The consequences can be—"

"No doubt," said Corson. "Tell me about them another time. I think there's some sort of building ahead—maybe it's those cottages. Come on."

But if it was a dwelling they came upon, it had long been abandoned. They climbed the broad stairs and crossed a roofed portico to peer into the open doorway, but it was too dark to see anything within. The place was altogether still, save for the sounds of the storm. It was not a welcoming spot, but it was dry, at least where the roof was still whole. They left the horses tethered to a pillar in the shelter of the porch, and settled themselves in the empty corridor just within the doorway. There was an inner door at their backs, and the corridor stretched away into the blackness to both sides of them.

Enough leaves and branches had blown into the porch for a small fire, and they tried to dry their clothes a little in its warmth. Nyctasia sneezed, in a way that clearly expressed her vexation with her present circumstances. Sleeping on the ground was nothing new to her, but sleeping in damp clothes on cold stone was, she felt, a grievous affront to her good breeding. She dutifully attempted to regard the situation as an opportunity to practice the Discipline of Toleration, but discomfort such as this lacked even the dignity of pain. And sneezing interrupted her concentration.

Corson had been unusually silent for a time, but at last she burst out angrily, "Why did you bring us here, Nyc? What's your game?"

"I? I've been following *you!*"

"This place feels like that spell-ridden Yth Forest you're so fond of. You can't deny there's magic here—anyone could tell!"

"On the contrary, anyone couldn't. I can, because I've studied magic and developed an awareness of it. But you, you sense its presence by instinct alone. That's a rare talent. I shouldn't wonder if you could be a magician yourself, Corson, with the right training."

"I'd rather be a swineherd!"

"Well, that's probably wise. But I suspect that your antipathy to magic is actually a result of your unusual sensitivity to it."

"What's 'antipathy'?"

"Loathing."

"Oh, *that's* just common sense. Magic's rutting dangerous."

Nyctasia laughed, incredulous. "You're a warrior, woman! What you do's not dangerous, I suppose?"

"That's different! What I do is straightforward, there's no pretense or cheat to it. A battle's a monster's bloody maw that'll chew you to shreds if it can, but if you know what you're doing, you'll be one of the teeth of battle, not the fodder."

"But that's what the magic of *yth* is like, you know. Safe enough for those skilled in its ways, but—"

"No, you don't see what I mean. War . . . war is *honest*. You can *see* that it's hideous and vicious, so at least you have a chance. It can destroy you, but it can't deceive you. It doesn't promise one thing and give you something else. . . ." Corson thought of the alluring and deadly denizens of Yth Forest, and of the mirror-spell that had shown her an unflattering reflection of her own spirit. "Magic!" she spat. "Magic's all lies—that's why *you* take to it."

"Lies . . ." Nyctasia mused. "Why, that's really quite profound, Corson."

"It is?" Nyctasia was a puzzle Corson could never quite make out. She might take furious offense at a chance remark, while a deliberate insult would only amuse her. "You're—" Corson began, but stopped suddenly. This time, she would not let herself be caught and lost in the web of Nyctasia's words. She'd have an answer! "Curse you, Nyc! I want to know what we're doing in this place!"

"But I don't know, I tell you. I only sensed it a little while ago, myself. I didn't say anything because I know you fear magic, and since we'd lost our way—"

"I don't fear it," Corson lied indignantly. "But I've wits enough to let it alone, and that's more than you can say. I don't believe you didn't lead us here."

"I know," sighed Nyctasia. "No one ever believes me when I tell the truth. But I swear it, on my honor as a Vahnite and an Edonaris. I don't even know where we are."

Corson shrugged, more or less convinced. Nyctasia had too much respect for her precious faith and her family name to take such an oath lightly. It would be no use arguing. It was never any use arguing with Nyctasia. She stood. "You won't mind if we move on, then. I think this must be part of the Cymvelan ruins, but I don't mean to fight with phantoms for that treasure, so I tell you."

"We'll go if you like. But I don't believe we're in danger here. The power in this place is potential, not actual."

"Oh, yes, that makes all the difference, of course," said Corson, with leaden sarcasm.

"Listen, I can explain. It's like a weapon—that sword of yours is potentially dangerous because you *could* draw it and kill someone—"

"I admit I'm sorely tempted, at times like this."

"—but so long as you don't, it isn't *actually* dangerous. This place isn't like Yth Wood. The power there is free, but here it's fettered. It cannot act unless it's invoked."

"Could you invoke it?" Corson asked suspiciously.

"Perhaps. But I'm not about to tamper with a power I know nothing about—one might as well try to bridle a dragon. This is a sleeping dragon, though, and it won't wake unless we step on its tail. We're safe enough if we let it be."

It was still raining, and Corson wanted to be convinced to stay within the warm shelter of the passageway. Her clothes were just beginning to dry, and there were the horses to consider, too. Nyc knew about such things, after all. . . . Nyctasia's suggestion that Corson was afraid to stay spurred her to prove her mettle, and if they stayed she could have a look for that treasure by daylight. That decided her, but she was not easy about sleeping with those dark, ill-rumored ruins at her back. "You might as well get some rest, then," she told Nyctasia. "I'll keep first watch."

Corson took a brand from the fire and set out to survey their campsite, to satisfy herself that all was secure. The building held too many hiding places to suit her, but all the rooms seemed to be deserted. They were laid out in a simple rectangle about a long inner yard where she found only rank greenery and an old stone well. Returning to the corridor, she stepped over Nyctasia and went out to the porch to see that all was well with the horses. The rain had slackened, and the night now seemed very still and desolate.

Just past the foot of the stairs was a round, ornamental pool, filled by the rain. Corson sat on the steps and tossed her torch into the water. From here she could see Nyctasia through the front doorway and keep an eye on the horses as well.

She watched her reflection, a darker shadow floating on the dark shadow of the pool, distorted by ripples. A few stars had pierced the cloudy sky and cast wavering reflections that danced before her eyes. One of them, she saw, gleamed brighter than all the rest, a star called by some the Crimson Empress because at its height it burned a deep red in the autumn sky.

But farmers, Corson knew, called it by the humbler name of the Reaper's Eye. Seeing it in the ascendant, they knew it was time to look to their barns and houses, to make sure they were fast against the cold winds that would soon be coming. The star was a signal to the wise that it was a time for putting by, and counting stores, for looking forward to the comforts of home and hearth.

And what of me? Corson thought discontentedly. Blown this way and that like a leaf in the wind. Where will I be when winter comes?

As always, when she was in this mood, her thoughts turned to the coast, and Steifann. She knew how he would answer such questions. She could almost hear him, reasonable as always, urging her to give up her wandering and stay with him. "This senseless roaming of yours has to end someday, Corson," he'd say. Steifann had raised himself from a penniless sailor to the owner of a thriving tavern. He was proud of the prosperous and secure life he'd made for himself, and he wanted Corson to share that life.

Corson knew that she'd be wise to accept Steifann's offer of a home and a comfortable living, but the restlessness that drove her from place to place would not let her stay anywhere for long— even with Steifann. Their arguments were always the same. At times his confidence and complacency made her hate him.

"What's so wonderful about a life of peeling potatoes and serving drunks?" she'd yell.

"It's good enough for me. But if you'd rather make your living murdering people, that's an end of the matter."

"You smug bastard! Just because I don't choose to stay pent up with you all the time and lose my mind from boredom!" It was a lie. She never grew bored with Steifann, and she was ashamed at saying it, all the more because she saw she'd hurt him.

"No one's keeping you here," he'd say coldly. "If you want to take to the road, and throw your life in the gutter, I can't stop you. Go ahead!"

Corson's pride made it hard for her to apologize, but losing Steifann would be far harder to bear than losing an argument. He had forgiven her for much worse things than insults—but what would she do if one day he was no longer willing to forgive her? "Oh, Steifann, I didn't mean . . ."

He shook his head, tossing the hair back from his brow, and grinned at her in the way she found irresistible. "Asye! You're nothing but an overgrown child who doesn't know what she wants. Do what you have to, Corson, but just don't think that I'll spend my days, or my nights, pining away for you while you're gone."

"Yes you will!" She threw her arms around his neck and pressed close to him, letting her hands travel slowly down his back. Nuzzling his bearded chin, she whispered, "You will, you'll long for me all the time, and don't you forget it."

All their arguments ended in the same way too.

Corson groaned. *Was* he longing for her? Probably not, the brazen breed-bull! She always imagined, when she was away, that Steifann was in bed with half the town of Chiastelm. Somehow she never thought of him doing anything but being unfaithful to her. Now, with a pang, she remembered the vision Nyctasia had conjured for her outside the Yth Forest.

Steifann had appeared to her in a mirror, worn and haggard-looking, working on his accounts long after he should have been asleep. Seeing how hard he had to work when she wasn't there to lend a hand with the heavy chores, Corson had felt guilty not only for spying on him, but for refusing to settle down in Chiastelm as well.

He needs me, she thought mournfully. What am I doing chasing all over the countryside when I could have the best home on the coast for the asking? What ails me? When I'm there for a season I long to be journeying again, and when I'm away I only want to go back! Once I see Nyc safe with these grape-growers I'll go straight back to Chiastelm for the winter. Searching for this treasure is nothing but hunting the will-o-the-wisp. There are other treasures in this world.

Steifann's good-natured laugh, his steadiness and generosity, his unequaled lovemaking. She closed her eyes and pictured his body stretched beneath hers, as her hands and mouth wandered along his broad, powerful chest toward his tender, yielding belly. "Sweet as honey from the comb," she sighed.

Corson knew it would be easy for him to find someone who'd gladly share his life—he reminded her of the fact often enough, curse him! Did he even think of her when she wasn't there? As she stared into the pool, taken up with her memories and jealousy, the words to Nyctasia's mirror-charm came back to her, unbidden. The spell promised to reveal the doings of friends or enemies, however far away they might be. Now she wondered, uneasily, was Nyctasia right that she, Corson, had magical skills of her own? She found that she remembered the whole of the spell perfectly.

The rain had ceased, and the surface of the pool lay still and smooth as a mirror, yet her reflection seemed to waver and dissolve in the water. Somehow, Corson was not surprised to see another image forming in its place—the taproom at the Jugged Hare, Steifann's tavern, as plain to see as though she were standing outside on a cloudy night, looking longingly in through a torchlit window. Even the familiar noises of the place, laughter and chatter, the clink of tankards, came to her from afar, seeming to form within her like the echoes of her own thoughts.

Steifann was sitting sprawled at one of the tables. Across from him was the smuggler Destiver, and it was clear that they both had had plenty to drink. "It was in Ochram," Destiver insisted, pounding the table with her fist. "It's just that every time we went there, you were too drunk to know where you were."

"I may have been drunk *then*," Steifann argued, "but I'm not *now*. I remember everything."

"That doesn't make a rutting bit of sense, and you're drunker than the ship's cat when she fell in the ale barrel. You're heeled over like a cog in a gale."

"Destiver, you haven't been sober since you could hoist a flagon, and it was in Cerrogh. You'd take that crooked alleyway behind the Red Dog Inn, then the little street on the other side of the ashpit. It was the third on the left, and you'd go . . ."

"The Red Dog is in Ochram."

". . . into the side door, the one in the alcove that you'd miss if you didn't know it was there." A broad grin spread across Steifann's face. "It was a wonderful place. There was nothing you wanted that you couldn't have."

"The House of One Hundred Delights," said Destiver dreamily. "Every room had something different, remember? If you liked what you saw . . . Ah, that little one, with her song . . .

> You fishers come back with the tide,
> You sailors come home from the sea,
> My port, it lies open and wide,
> My fish is as fresh as can be!

She was fine, that one. She'd shake all over like a leaf in the wind. What a little pearl."

Steifann snickered. "Here's to pearls," he said, emptying his mug.

"It is the jewel every woman is born with—rich or poor. Here's to them," Destiver agreed. "And to certain other jewels too. The more the better, eh, Steifann?"

He carefully poured out another mug of ale for Destiver, then one for himself. "Well, I like to be an obliging fellow. How can I refuse anyone, when no one else can do the job as well as I can?"

"You are handy, no mistake. No one threads the needle the way you do, old friend."

"Or churns the butter," Steifann suggested, grinning.

"Or rakes the hay."

"Or shakes the ashes."

They both collapsed in drunken laughter. Annin ambled over to their table, hips swaying under her full skirt. "You two make a merry crew," she said, setting down a trayful of dirty mugs, and taking a long pull of Destiver's ale.

Destiver reached around Annin's waist and pulled her down onto her knee. The chair creaked. "Here's a true pearl among women. Annin, my queen, when I make my fortune, I'll take you away from this rat-hole on a golden galleon." She buried her face in Annin's neck.

"My place is no rat-hole, you slattern," Steifann protested huffily. Both women ignored him.

Annin snorted. "You worthless water-rat, you'll make your fortune when the Empress peels potatoes in the kitchen. Why should I waste my time waiting for you when there's plenty who'll spend on me now?"

"You're a faithless wench. I love you better than them all."

"Hmmph! And what is it you're both braying about while I do all the work of the house?"

"Why, love again, my beauty," said Destiver, running her hands over Annin's bodice.

"Lechery, more like, if I know you and this one here," Annin retorted, jerking her head in Steifann's direction.

"And where's the difference?" Steifann asked, waxing philosophical. "It's love, even if it's only for the night. A cold and lonely bed's never made anyone the happier. It sours you, and turns you from the world." He gestured broadly, knocking over some of the mugs on the tray.

"You're a besotted fool." Annin took another drink and started to mop up some of the spilled ale with a cloth she wore at her waist.

Steifann began to sing:

> "Ah, once I caught a bird,
>   A sweet and lovely dove.
>   I said to her these words:
>   Come here and be my love.
>
>   Ah, doveling don't be shy,
>   Don't hide your head away.
>   I'll teach you how to fly
>   Though on the ground you'll stay.
>
>   Charm me with your eyes so bright,
>   Let me hear your song.
>   Kiss me once and hold me tight,
>   Here in the grass so long.
>
>   Into my arms the darling flew,
>   I kissed her downy breast,
>   And how that dove began to coo
>   When I entered her snug nest.
>
>   'Twas a deep and mossy valley,
>   And fit for any king.
>   In that nest long did I dally,
>   Till the bird and I did sing."

Annin and Destiver began to sing with him.

> "Ah, once I caught a bird,
>   A sweet and lov—"

"Corson, do you hear me? I'll take a turn at watch—why didn't you wake me?" Nyctasia called sleepily. "It's nearly dawn."

"Whore!" Corson shouted, throwing a rock into the pool. "You scum, wait till I get back to Chiastelm. I'll kill you, you and that stinking smuggler with you!"

Nyctasia was wide awake now. "Corson, what's the matter?"

Corson turned on her in outrage. "You and your filthy magic! Do you cast spells in your sleep?" She was astonished to see that the sky was already growing pale at the horizon. How long had she been in the grip of the vision?

"Perhaps, if it isn't asking too much, you'd be good enough to tell me what you're talking about," Nyctasia suggested. "What spells?"

"I saw him, in the pool."

"You saw whom in the pool, a merman?"

"Steifann—at the Hare—and Annin, and that bitch Destiver. 'Old friend'—I'll wring her scrawny neck for her! I was thinking about him, and then he was there. . . . He was drinking and singing and, and . . ."

"And not moping about, missing you?" Nyctasia guessed. Corson scowled at her. "But, Corson, it was probably just a dream."

"I never fall asleep on watch—I couldn't if I tried!" That was a weakness which had been beaten out of Corson in the army.

"All I know is, I could have been murdered in my bed while you were dreaming of your lusty lover—if I had a bed," she added ruefully.

"It wasn't a dream, I tell you!" Corson suddenly stiffened. "You may be murdered yet," she said tensely.

"Now, Corson, don't be so hasty—"

"Quiet, fool! There's someone over there. Draw your sword."

"Are you sure you're not still imagining things?" Nyctasia whispered, but she obeyed, nevertheless.

"Watch those trees," Corson breathed.

"It's too dark, I can't see any—"

Then three people stepped into the open, from the overgrown stand of trees, and strode toward them purposefully. As they emerged from the morning twilight, Corson could make out a man and two women, all armed, their long blades held at the ready.

"Good morrow, strangers," said one of the women. "Have you passed the night in this haunted place?"

"And if we have, what of it?" said Corson, making no attempt to hide her mistrust. "We've done no harm. We'll be on our way at once."

"Not so soon, I think," said the man, and rushed at her. One of the women followed his lead, while the other turned on Nyctasia.

Suddenly it seemed to Nyctasia that she was back at the inn-yard in Osela, with Corson shouting at her, "Don't hesitate, act! Move! Faster! Don't stop to think, there's no time for that. Think with your arm—that sword's alive! It's faster than you are, you can barely keep hold of it—grip it fast—don't let it get away from you—that's right—"

It was still too dark to see her opponent very clearly, but she could hear the woman's gasping breath, and she realized that she too was panting heavily. I suppose one of us will be killed," she thought dispassionately, watching her own arm in fascination. But then the woman dove in under her guard and knocked her legs from under her. Nyctasia's back struck the ground with a bone-jarring blow that forced the air from her chest and lit sparks before her eyes. She lay stunned as the woman knelt over her, pinioning her arms.

Yet a moment later, to Nyctasia's surprise, her assailant leapt to her feet again, called something to her companions, and ran off swiftly into the trees. The other woman too turned and fled, and the man hurled his sword at Corson and followed.

Corson hurried to Nyctasia and helped her to her feet. She was still dizzy and breathless, but otherwise unhurt. Reassured, Corson went in pursuit of their attackers, calling back, "Stay there, watch the horses. If you see anything, shout."

Shout? thought Nyctasia, I can't even breathe! She waited, worried, for Corson to return. As soon as she could draw breath well enough, she decided to go after Corson on horseback, lead-ing the other horse with her. But before she had mounted, she saw Corson returning, alone, and she seemed to have her cloak wrapped around her arm. Nyctasia ran to meet her. "Corson, are you wounded?"

"*Wounded?* Of course not." Corson took a last bite of juicy pear and tossed away the core. "I was just fetching us some breakfast. Those are all fruit trees in there! Here." She handed Nyctasia a ripe peach from the mound of fruit she carried wrapped in her cloak, in the crook of her arm.

"But what became of those people?"

Corson swallowed a mouthful of apple, and frowned. "I don't know—they just vanished. I couldn't find a trace of them. I don't like it. Probably spirits," she said glumly.

"They seemed all too substantial to me. What did they want, for *vahn*'s sake?"

"Us, of course. Why do you think that woman didn't cut your

throat? They're slavers, you can wager what you like on that, and we'd better get out of here before they come back with the rest of the band." She spat out seeds as if spitting in the faces of their would-be captors.

"By all means. We can't be far from Vale now, and I for one have no intention of spending another night in the open." Silently, they rolled up their blankets and saddled the horses. The rainclouds had passed with the night, and faint streaks of rose and misty grey were slowly drifting across the sky. There was lark-song in the old orchard; the sunrise already gave promise of a bright, hot day. Nyctasia, who was used to the cooler climes of the coast, wished above all for a bath.

"Do you mean to come back here to look for the treasure?" she asked Corson, as they rode back to the by-road.

"If it's guarded by spells, I'll do without it," Corson said, biting into another pear. She looked back, but in the early morning light the ruins didn't seem such an uncanny place after all. "Nyc, you never told me—was it real, all that about Steifann? Is that what he's doing now?"

"Well, I wouldn't say it's impossible, but—"

"Can't you ever give a simple answer to a simple question!"

"Corson, that is not a simple question. Tell me, did you say the spell?"

"Not aloud."

"That's no matter. . . . What were you thinking about before it happened?"

"I told you, I was thinking about Steifann."

"*What* were you thinking about Steifann?" Nyctasia asked with exaggerated patience. Corson gave her a sidelong look, and they both laughed. "Well, what *else* were you thinking about him?"

Corson sighed, trying to sort out the jumble of thoughts that had preceded the bothersome visitation. "I was . . . remembering all the arguments we've had . . . about the way I'm gone for months at a time. He always says I shouldn't expect to find him waiting for me when I get back. As if I care."

"So you were distressed, most like, and therefore susceptible," Nyctasia said thoughtfully.

"I was what?" Corson bridled, suspecting an insult.

"Defenseless against the Influences present in the place. What with your natural ability, and your rather perturbed state, it's not inconceivable that you did experience a manifestation of some sort."

"You prating parrot! Did it mean anything?"

"Of course it did. Everything means something. Everything we do, everything that happens to us, is part of the web that binds us to our past and our future, and links us each to each, whether we would or no. Our actions, our visions, our dreams—" She was silent for a moment, then shook herself abruptly. "As for what you saw, it may not have been what it seemed. There'd have to be a very powerful Influence at work to call forth a true Reflection. This was more likely a lesser magic that showed you only shadows—"

"Lies."

"—of your own fears."

Corson looked sullenly at the ground. "I'm not afraid—I could find another lover quick enough."

"In the time I've known you, you've found no end of them, but you've always said that no one's as good as your bearded bedmate in Chiastelm." Nyctasia looked at her with real irritation. "If you don't care, and you're not afraid, what does it matter whether you really saw him or not? You can ask him yourself when you're back in Chiastelm. And all the man was doing was drinking and singing a few vulgar songs, according to you. Why do you want to kill him for that? I swear I've no patience with you! You know better!"

"He didn't even mention my name. He's not thinking about me at all, and it seems like I think about him all the time."

"It wouldn't seem that way to him, if *he* could spy out *your* doings," Nyctasia pointed out.

Corson had to smile. "He wouldn't stop yelling for a week," she admitted. "But it's more than that. . . ." She struggled to explain. "It's not just Destiver, it's—well, Steifann needs someone to help him at the Hare, but I can't stay locked up there all the time, like a beast in harness."

"Well, why should you?"

"Because if I won't, he might find himself someone else who will, the mangy cur! He cares more for that rutting tavern than for me."

"He'd be a fool if he didn't—it's his livelihood. He sounds a very sensible man. But that doesn't mean he doesn't care for you, Corson. Because you love your freedom best doesn't mean that you don't love him, does it? Look at the matter reasonably—"

Corson blushed. "Oh, what's the use of talking to you? I don't want a scholar's argument! You don't know what I'm talking about—you only understand what's in your moldy books."

Nyctasia did not answer, and her silence was a reproach to Corson. It wasn't Nyc's fault that Steifann didn't miss her. She'd meant to help in her maddening way. But the sense that she was in the wrong only made Corson more stubborn, and they continued on their way in silence till Nyctasia spoke again.

"It's a mistake to think that a lover can be a way of life. I do know what you feel, Corson, but I've no answer for you. How could I blame 'Ben for loving magic more than he loved me, when I had proved that I loved Rhostshyl more than I loved him? I *understand* that he could love me still, though he loved the Yth better—I *know* I loved him well though I loved my city more. But I am not comforted by that reasoning, and why should you be? There is no absolute union of spirits, no companion in eternity, no mirror of one's being. Each of us is one and separate and utterly alone. Is that simple enough for you?"

"No—it's a lot of blather about nothing. There's enough to fret about in this life without worrying over eternity too. What's the good of it?"

With one of her abrupt changes of humor, Nyctasia smiled and said, "You're a deep one, that's certain. You may well be right. Many great philosophers agree with you."

"Philosophy!" Corson snorted. "Antipathy! Plague take it, I want to know what Steifann's at with that hag Destiver. He'll see—two can play at that game. Maybe I will hunt out that treasure. Then I'll go back to Chiastelm with more money than he's ever seen, and—"

"Why wait? You're carrying quite a fortune with you as it is—how much do you need to impress him? The treasure's probably all moonshine anyway, you know."

Though she had made light of Corson's vision, Nyctasia was worried at the thought that Corson might return to the ruins. If the spell had been all that it seemed, then she had dangerously misjudged the power of the place. What sort of magic had the Cymvelans meddled with, to leave such Influences at work when they themselves were long gone? She had not put much stock in the tales of demon-worship and blood-sacrifice, but now . . . If Corson, who was no magician, could unwittingly draw upon it, then that power was too unbridled to be safe. She herself might control it, but Corson was hardly prepared for such an undertaking.

Nyctasia saw much in Corson that she knew to be true of herself. In Corson she recognized her own pride and passion, her deep fears and her love of power. But in Nyctasia they had been governed, by years of Discipline and denial, to serve her rather than rule her—or so Nyctasia hoped. She was a Vahnite. But Corson would be defenseless against a magic that promised to fulfill the darkest desires of the spirit . . . and did as it promised. Corson, with her curious gift for magic, would be its perfect prey.

"Besides," Nyctasia added, "I thought you were so eager to know about the carryings-on at Chiastelm."

Corson spat. "Drinking and screwing everyone in sight—I don't need sorcery to tell me that." She gave Nyctasia a shrewd look. "You won't get rid of me so easily as that. I'm not afraid of that place. And there's no such thing as enough money. If you weren't such a spoilt, rich little aristocrat you'd know that."

"Civilized," said Nyctasia, "is the word you want, not 'spoilt,' but I suppose I shouldn't expect your barbarian brain to grasp such fine distinctions."

Corson grinned wickedly. "That reminds me, I can't go back to Chiastelm just yet anyway. I was forgetting I owe you a few more lessons in swordfighting. You didn't do too badly against that clumsy fool, but you shouldn't have come out into the open. You had the advantage inside the porch there, among the pillars. When your opponent is bigger than you are—and that means anyone, for you—you should keep the fight in a tight place if you can, where the enemy will be hampered while you can move freely. You can't help being such a little speck of a thing, but at least you can put your size to use now and then. I might be able to make something of you if I work hard at it."

"I don't believe that you'll stay in Vale that long, even for the pleasure of cutting me to shreds. Don't you have to go west from here to reach the river at Amron Therain?"

"The port's not a half day's ride from Vale," Corson assured her. "I've wasted so much time looking after you that another day or two won't matter. I'll have time enough to give you those lessons, don't you worry."

Nyctasia groaned. "I'd get more mercy from the brigands and slavers." She was glad enough to change the subject when they saw a team of ditchers hedging a field beside the road, not far ahead of them. "Now we'll find out where in the *vahn*'s name we are."

But at first the laborers only stared when Corson asked for directions to the Edonaris vineyards. Then one woman finally answered politely enough, "You've only to ride ahead as the road climbs, mistress, and take the east turn when you smell the grapes." The others stood as if struck dumb, but broke into excited talk as soon as Corson and Nyctasia had ridden on.

"I think they're still gaping after us," Nyctasia said uneasily, looking back.

Corson was used to being stared at. "They don't often see soldiers in these parts."

"Let alone soldiers tall as towers, eh?"

"Better than being a half-grown gnat with a title longer than my arm."

"They say one stinging gnat can drive an ox to frenzy."

"It's not the stinging I mind so much as the buzzing."

"Well, you needn't listen to it longer, you know."

"That's as may be—we'll see. You might decide to go on to Amron Therain with me. How do you know this Edonaris family will want anything to do with you? They might not even believe you *are* an Edonaris. Maybe they'll think you're an imposter claiming kinship with them because they're rich. That's an old game," Corson pointed out, clearly relishing the idea of the proud Lady Nyctasia being turned out of doors as a charlatan.

"And you mean to be there to see me humiliated, I take it?"

"I wouldn't miss it for all the diamond-fields of Tièrelon. Nyc, what *will* you do if they don't accept you as an Edonaris?"

"The possibility has occurred to me. I have my seal-ring, of course."

"You might have stolen it."

"Well, I know more of the family history than any outsider possibly could."

"But do they?"

"I suppose I'll find out—and soon, at that. This must be the east turning she meant." There could be no mistake. The scent of grapes was stronger with every breath they took. Nyctasia smiled ruefully. "You're right, you know—they probably won't believe me. If I *weren't* an Edonaris, I know I could convince them, but since it's the truth . . ."

"Then use your persuasive powers to convince them to let us search the rest of the ruins, since we've come all this way."

"Oh, come, you don't really believe there's a hidden treasure there?"

"No . . . ," Corson said reluctantly, "not much. But we're here, after all. And those moth-eaten riddles might mean something."

Nyctasia shrugged. "Possibly the Edonaris ought to see them, since their name's on that list, though it seems to be harmless enough. Let's ask the way to the house."

They were riding through grape-covered slopes now, where workers were busy pruning the vines and testing the ripeness of the fruit. Corson and Nyctasia dismounted and hailed a man who was walking toward them along the roadside, stopping at the edge of each row to examine the grape-leaves for harmful insects. When he saw Corson, he stuck his pruning-knife in his belt and strode up to her jauntily, with a welcoming smile.

"Probably an overseer," Corson thought, and started to ask about the Edonaris manor, but when she saw his face she only stood and stared, her question forgotten. He looked enough like Nyctasia to be her twin brother.

"Nyc," she said finally, "I don't think you'll have trouble convincing them that you're an Edonaris, after all."

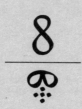

8

BUT THE MAN ignored Nyctasia and swept a low bow to Corson, gallantly kissing her hand. "A harvest goddess, come to bless the vines!" he declared, then, turning to Nyctasia, he demanded, "What ails you? Why don't you introduce me to this vision of heartbreaking beauty?"

Corson grinned at her. "I like this branch of your family better than the other," she said.

"This is Corson brenn Torisk," Nyctasia told him, laughing, "but who am I, for the *vahn*'s sake?"

He glanced at her quizzically. "Are you really ailing, 'Deisha? You do look pale."

Nyctasia took off her hat to allow him a better look at her face. Her grey eyes met his, and she smiled at his start of astonishment. "I've always been pale," she said.

He took a step toward her but stopped, shaking his head as if to deny that she stood before him. "You're not—I took you for —but, who are you?" he whispered.

Nyctasia bowed. "Nyctasia of Rhostshyl, cousin."

"An Edonaris of Rhostshyl, of course. You'd have to be. What do you want here, Rhostshylid?"

Nyctasia's manner stiffened. "Hospitality," she said, "is what we expected. If we're not welcome here, we'll seek it else-where."

"All strangers are welcome at harvest time," he said resign-edly. "Forgive me—I am Raphistain ar'n Edonaris. But since when do the nobles of Rhostshyl own us as kin? What sort of welcome would any of us receive at court?"

"A fairer one than I, I fear," Nyctasia sighed. "I myself am banished from the city."

"Then you are not here as an emissary?"

"By no means. Rather as a fugitive."

"Why, that's another matter altogether! The others must hear of this. Come with me, the rest won't be back till dinner. You'll have time to refresh yourselves from your journey." Now that he knew who Nyctasia was, he became the courteous host, but he was no longer certain how to address Corson. Was she only a guard? Was it fitting for him to flirt with her?

Corson saw his curious look, and decided to make it clear that she was not Nyctasia's servant. "You can blame me that we're here," she said. "I told Nyc there were Edonaris at Vale. She'd never heard of you."

Raphistain abandoned his scruples. *"You* would be welcome in any company," he assured her, with a meaning smile. "But how did you hear of us? Isn't Torisk one of the Maritime cities, then?" All coastal accents sounded alike to a Midlander.

"Torisk's a swamp, in the south. But I've traveled about the Midlands a good deal, and heard praise of Edonaris wine. I've never tasted it, though," she hinted.

"What a tragedy! Fortunately, that can easily be remedied, now that you're here. I shall see to it myself."

They followed him on foot, leading their horses, till a stable-boy came running from the yard and took the reins. He gave Nyctasia a puzzled look, but Raphistain sent him about his business at once and hurried them on to the manor house. It was a sprawling stone manse which had obviously been added to many times, as more space was needed. The newer wings and turrets were joined to the main body of the house at all possible angles, but the ivy climbing over the whole facade seemed to bind its parts together and make them one. The walls were alive with song-sparrows, invisible in the ivy vines, chirping and rustling restlessly, never still. Nyctasia saw the coat-of-arms of the Edon-aris carved into the arch of stone above the main portal, half-hid-den by leaves.

The great, dim hall was almost chill after the late-summer heat of the countryside. The walls of thick stone allowed little of the sun's power to penetrate, and the windows were high and small here in the oldest part of the house. The doors stood open to admit more light, and Nyctasia could not but compare them to the portals of the palace of the Edonaris at Rhostshyl—defended by a portcullis and armed guards, fortified with great bars and bolts of iron. What must it be like to have no enemies?

Their host led them quickly through the confusing maze of corridors and stairways, but he could not altogether avoid the curious stares of the few servants they passed. He stopped before the open door of an old, book-lined room where a sharp-featured woman of middle age sat bent over the household accounts. A great ring of keys at her belt clinked when she turned to face them.

"What are you doing here?" she demanded. "Dinner's not for hours. 'Deisha, why aren't you at the calving?"

Nyctasia had been examining the backs of the books, all of which, she noticed, were dusty from neglect. She started guiltily. "But I'm not—" she began.

"What mischief are you two about now? And at harvest time too! Who's *that* great creature?" she continued, noticing Corson.

When Raphistain could get in a word, he bowed and said, "Aunt, allow me to present our guests. Mesthelde brenn Vale ar'n Edonaris—Corson brenn Torisk and Nyctasia brenn Rhostshyl ar'n Edonaris."

She frowned. "What nonsense is this? We've no time for games and foolery. What have you done to yourself, 'Deisha? You look like a ghost!" She approached Nyctasia as if she intended to take her by the collar and drag her off to wash her face and hands.

"Madame, I—" said Nyctasia. "Permit me—"

The woman peered at her, squinting, then stepped back suddenly, setting the keys jangling. "Sacred Name of Creation! Who is this?"

"But I've just told you, my good aunt," said Raphistain, enjoying the scene. "Our cousin Nyctasia has come all the way from Rhostshyl to pay us a visit. And you greet her with a scolding—what will she think of us?"

Ignoring him, Mesthelde sat down again, still staring. At last she said, "Have you sent word to your father, Raphe?"

"Not yet. I only just—"

"Then go fetch him, boy! He'll be at the coopers' yet. Don't waste time. I'll see to our guests."

He sighed. "Very well, I suppose it will be best if I go myself. I shall see you all at dinner, I trust. Mind, Aunt, you're not to frighten them away."

Mesthelde looked them up and down with obvious suspicion. "Well, if it must be, it must. Come along. As you're here, you might as well be comfortable. You'll need some fresh clothes. 'Deisha's are sure to fit you," she said to Nyctasia in a tone which implied that the resemblance was a piece of wanton deceit. "But I'm sure I don't know what we'll find for *you*." She looked up at Corson and shook her head in disapproval of such immoderate height. Nyctasia endured this treatment with unaccustomed forbearance. Corson had rarely seen her so abashed and silent.

Their hostess showed them to spacious rooms in the newer part of the mansion, promising to send maids to see to their needs and fetch them to dinner. Her manner made it clear that they were not expected to show themselves before they were summoned to the evening meal.

Corson was pleased with the chamber allotted to her. It was large and well furnished, but simple enough to make her feel at home. She was accustomed to sharing servants' quarters or the crowded barracks where guards were housed. So this was what it meant to be a guest, not a mere hireling. But then, these Edonaris were vintners and tradesfolk—the local gentry, perhaps, but not of the highest aristocracy like the Edonaris of Rhostshyl—not too proud to treat a common swordswoman as a guest in their home.

There was therefore no reason, Corson assured herself, to worry about how she should conduct herself here. . . . But . . . what did one do with ladies' maids? She wished Nyctasia were with her. What would *she* do?

As soon as she had asked herself this, Corson knew exactly what to do. When two girls arrived, one bearing bed-linens, the other a tray of grapes and cheese, Corson instructed them to prepare her bath, quite as if she had been giving orders to domestics all her life.

But she did not know that the maids would stay until they were dismissed. It never occurred to her to say, "That will be all," and as a result she was attended with every possible service while she bathed. The ladies' maids washed her hair and feet, scrubbed her back, fetched more water, and stood about waiting to rub her dry, then wrapped her in a capacious robe. When they took away the tub, Corson thought she was rid of them at last, but one soon came back to dress her hair for her. Corson managed not to show her surprise, but she was glad she had the fine silver comb and brush Nyctasia had given her, which were fit for any lady.

The maid exclaimed over her long, glorious hair, and Corson began to feel more comfortable with her new station in life. As she was enjoying the rare luxury of having her hair brushed, an older woman entered and looked at her critically. "Oh, it'll have to be the gold, no question," she said, and went out again, leaving Corson mystified.

"The gold what?" she asked the girl, before she could remember not to display her ignorance.

"It's the cloth she means, mistress—we're to make you a gown straightaway. There's a length of gold silk from Liruvath that's long enough."

Corson was appalled. A gown—! She'd never worn such a thing in her life. Perhaps she should go find Nyctasia and ask her how she ought to behave, after all.

Nyctasia dismissed the maids as soon as her bath was ready. She had always preferred privacy to constant attendance, and she had much to think about.

I oughtn't to have come here, she brooded. I knew better. I was a fool to imagine for a moment that I might find a welcome among strangers simply because they bear my name. These folk want no part of me, and I can't blame them—they must have heard what poison we are, we Rhostshylid.

She pressed the water from her sleek, close-cropped hair and felt it trickle down her face like tears, making her somehow sadder. I'll leave them in peace, she decided. I'll ask nothing of them but a night's lodging, and say that we came because of that strange Cymvelan paper. The thought of the list was comforting —she had, after all, some legitimate reason to be here. She quickly dressed in the elegant clothes the maids had laid out for her, meaning to go at once to look for Corson, but just then the girls returned to tell her that the Lady Nocharis had summoned her.

She was shown to a tapestried drawing-room where the family was gathered, obviously to discuss what to do about her. "But if she's come on her own account—" she heard, before they fell silent at her entrance. Only a few gasps of astonishment greeted her appearance, and she too was taken aback at the uncanny resemblances to some of her near relations in Rhostshyl.

Raphistain performed introductions, but Nyctasia soon lost track of the names and the web of kinship. She gathered that the grey-haired Diastor was Raphistain's father and Mesthelde's brother by marriage, that Leclairin was away on business, and that Tepicacia was someone's younger sister. She met Mesthelde's cousin Nesanye, his wife Ancelin and their son Nicorin. There was a Great Uncle Anseth and an elderly cousin by marriage named Heronice, but Diastor and Mesthelde seemed to be the heads of the household.

"I was told that Lady Nocharis wished to see me," said Nyctasia, puzzled.

"So she shall," said Diastor, "but you'll hear what we have to say, first."

"Willingly, sir." She gratefully sank into the chair that Raphistain placed for her.

Diastor frowned. "For generations the Edonaris of Rhostshyl have refused to acknowledge us because we dealt in trade. All of our advances to them were met with threats or with silence, and the family gave up the attempt long ago, before my time."

"I know nothing of that," said Nyctasia. "I was never told that there was another branch of the family. Perhaps my parents didn't even know it."

"Nevertheless," he continued, "we hear news of the coast from time to time, through travelers' tales. We know that the House of Edonaris is at war with the Teiryn, and we'll have no part in it, mark me well. You'll find no allies here for your blood-feud. If we're not good enough to mix with the noble Edonaris of Rhostshyl, we'll not send our young folk there to die for them!"

"That's for us to say!" One of the younger men spoke out boldly. "Some of us want to see Rhostshyl once in our lives. We've the right—it's our heritage. Rhostshyl's our homeland as much as the valley is."

"Oh, but—" gasped Nyctasia.

" 'Corin's right," said a girl who looked no older than sixteen. "We've no call to turn our backs on our kin just because their ancestors scorned our ancestors. It's our duty to defend the House of Edonaris, with our blood if we must!"

"Nonsense!" thundered Diastor. "Children's notions! Hold your tongue, 'Cacia, you know nothing about it."

"You youngsters only want some excitement," Mesthelde said witheringly. "You think you can be lords and ladies and live at court instead of doing honest work in your own home. But you'll only make fools of yourselves, if you're lucky, and get yourselves killed if you're not—all for a lot of strangers who care nothing for you!"

Nyctasia was aghast. "But I'd never—"

"Why didn't you send her away before they heard about her?" Diastor demanded of Mesthelde.

"Too late for that, others had already seen her. And what was to keep her from coming back? It's best to have it out now and be done with it."

"True," he said, glaring at Nyctasia. Everyone was now looking at her. Raphistain caught her eye and grimaced ruefully.

Nyctasia took a deep breath. "You mistake me, I assure you. Never would I counsel you to take part in the madness that afflicts Rhostshyl! I myself am in exile because I opposed the feud." She turned to the youth who'd spoken before. "Believe me, the Teiryn are not the enemy—it's the feud itself that will destroy the House of Edonaris, and the city with it. You must have nothing to do with it, I beg you!" Her voice trembled with undisguised passion.

There was a stunned silence on all sides, but at last Diastor said, "Come, it's time you met the Lady Nocharis."

9

A GIRL SAT sewing in an alcove window, while a young child crawled at her feet, playing with a wooden horse. But when Nyctasia and the others entered, she picked up the baby and quietly left.

Lady Nocharis received them sitting up in bed. As the eldest in the family, she held the purely ceremonial title of matriarch. She was a small, frail woman, almost ghostly with her pale skin and stark white hair, but the warmth of her smile and the wisdom of her clear grey eyes dispelled all suggestion of lifelessness.

Nyctasia bowed respectfully and kissed her hand. "Madame," she said, "you do me honor."

The old woman smiled, amused at Nyctasia's stately courtesy, which seemed quaint and old-fashioned to her. "What pretty manners you have in Rhostshyl," she murmured.

Nyctasia realized her mistake at once. This was not the court. "We're a formal lot, I'm afraid," she apologized, "but I mean to leave that behind me now." She bent and kissed Lady Nocharis on the cheek instead. The others withdrew, leaving them alone, and the matriarch patted the edge of the bed, inviting Nyctasia to sit near her.

"So you've come to stay with us, instead of taking us away with you?" she asked gently. But it was not truly a question.

Until this moment, Nyctasia had not dared to think seriously of settling here in the valley, but suddenly it seemed to her to be possible. To one of her station, kindred was all-important, and the bonds of blood were the hardest to break. "I hardly know why I've come," she said slowly. "It matters little where I go, since I cannot go home. When I heard there were Edonaris here, I was curious to know whether they were kin to me. It was no more than that."

"And now you know."

"Yes indeed. You resemble my great-aunt, the matriarch Mhairestri."

"And you, truly it is remarkable, child. You could be one of my own daughters."

Nyctasia smiled sadly. "I wish I could," she said.

"That place is still in your heart. But you were in danger there, I think."

Nyctasia looked away. "Yes . . . ," she said, faintly disturbed by a shadowy memory she could not quite capture. Why did she feel that Lady Nocharis's words held a warning for her? Did these folk know more about her than she had supposed? She shook her head, impatient with herself. What did it matter? They had every right and reason to be wary of her—but she must trust them, if she was ever to learn to trust anyone. She had not come away from Rhostshyl only to continue in her devious and suspicious ways.

"Yes, grave danger," she said simply, "and the greatest of all was the danger to my spirit." For the first time, Nyctasia saw that the true danger had never been that she might be killed, but that she might live to become more and more like Lady Mhairestri with every passing year. She shuddered.

Lady Nocharis stroked her hand. "My poor child, I think you had best stay here for the time, don't you?"

"If you'll have me," said Nyctasia, with unwonted humility. She felt close to tears, but instead she returned the old woman's smile. A Vahnite ought never to weep.

Raphistain arrived to escort Nyctasia to dinner, and the serving-girl followed with a tray. Lady Nocharis, who was lame, and bedridden much of the time, often did not dine with the rest.

"You must come and chat with me again, my dear. Perhaps between us we can discover what our degree of kinship is."

"I shall," said Nyctasia. "I'd like that."

She felt unusually carefree and lighthearted, as if relieved of a crushing burden. At last she truly believed that she had been right to leave Rhostshyl, whatever the cost. It seemed a long time since she'd known such well-being and freedom from doubt.

Raphistain too was relieved. If Mother 'Charis accepted Nyctasia, the others would be satisfied. He led her on a tour of the parts of the house she'd not seen before, and Nyctasia was pleased with everything she saw.

"Nyctasia, I . . ."

"Please, call me Nyc."

"With pleasure. And I'm Raphe, if you will. Nyc, I must apologize for the reception you've had here. You see, ever since we learned of the feud in Rhostshyl, there's been mad talk among the youngsters of going to the defense of the House of Edonaris. And now the rumors of war are wilder than ever, so when you appeared everyone was sure you'd been sent to make allies of us. I *did* suggest to my father that we might ask you your intentions, but the day he heeds my advice will be the day it rains roast potatoes. I hope we've not offended you beyond redress."

Nyctasia laughed. "We trust no one, and we don't expect to be trusted. I quite sympathize with your suspicions, I assure you, and I share your apprehensions as well. I'll do all I can to discourage your young folk from running off to Rhostshyl."

"For that my elders will call you daughter—but I fear my young cousins may call you traitor."

"I'm accustomed to that. My own family called me so, because I wanted to settle the feud by treaty."

He shook his head. "They want us to muster an army and march to the coast, all to prove to our Rhostshylid relations that we've true Edonaris blood in our veins."

"I fear they are right about that, at least, cousin. In Rhostshyl they say that all the Edonaris are crazy."

Corson's gown was really no more than a long, straight sheath that fell to her ankles and gathered at her waist with a sash. Nothing more elaborate could be stitched together in so short a time, even with the seamstress and two maids all working together. But the richness of the heavy, cream-gold silk was shown off all the better for the simplicity of the garment. No sleeves were needed in the late-summer weather, but an edge of the cloth was draped in graceful folds over Corson's wide, proud shoulders. The maids insisted that she leave her hair down, though they fastened it back with the ivory clasp and wove it with ribbons cut from the same gold material.

Corson accepted a pair of sandals that laced up above her ankles, and she strapped a small knife to her calf, among the leather thongs. She could not very well wear her sword-belt, but the gown would hide the knife from sight. The thought of going about almost unarmed made her uneasy, but she reminded herself firmly that she was a guest, not a guard. She need not hold herself ready to attack or be attacked at the blink of an eye.

When she was summoned to dinner, Corson found it almost as hard to leave behind her money-pouch as her weapons. In the sorts of lodgings she was accustomed to, she would never have let it out of her sight for a moment. But to carry it with her would look like mistrust, and she had been long enough with Nyctasia to know that these folk would take it amiss. "Well, if I'm robbed, *someone* will pay for it," she thought grimly. "I wish this wretched rag had some pockets!"

She dropped her belongings in the chest with feigned indifference and strode to the door, but her swaggering gait was much hampered by the long skirt. Before she could catch her balance, she fell heavily to the floor and lay sprawled in a tangle of honey-colored silk.

Corson forgot her fine manners. "Curse this rutting cocoon and the dung-worms that spun it and the bitch's whelp who wove it!" she stormed, struggling to her feet. She glared at the waiting-maids. "Laugh at me and I'll tear your tongues out!"

"Oh, no indeed, mistress," said one respectfully. "Are you hurt? Let me just tidy your hair."

"There, the seam's not torn a bit," said the other with satisfaction, straightening the folds of the gown.

"Don't fuss at me!" Corson growled. She felt pinioned and harried and defenseless, but she took a deep breath, drew herself up to her full height, and said with dignity, "I'm ready, lead the way. I mustn't keep everyone waiting." She proceeded down the corridor at a rather more restrained and ladylike pace.

10

THE WHOLE COMPANY rose to its feet when Corson made her
entrance, though most of them had no idea who she was. Even
Nyctasia did not recognize her, for a moment, in her finery and
her dignity. The elegant cut of the gown gave her height new
stateliness, and the pale gold silk perfectly graced her dark gold
skin and the red-gold glow of her hair. The golden earrings she
always wore might have been meant for just this occasion. By
torchlight and candlelight Corson was a glorious golden candle
herself, and all who saw her rose instinctively to do her honor.

She was absolutely terrified.

How was she to acknowledge this unexpected reception?
Should she curtsy? How? It was all she could do to *walk* in this
dress without falling on her face! Petrified, she looked desperately to Nyctasia, who came forward at once to her rescue.
"Allow me to present my companion," she said, taking Corson's
hand. "Corson brenn Torisk, the most beautiful mercenary on the
coast, and the most dangerous."

"Most beautiful in the Midlands as well!" someone called
from the foot of the table.

"Most dangerous too—she has conquered me without striking
a blow."

Nyctasia led her to the table, and Raphistain made room for her to sit between them. "I saw her first and am already captive to her charms. You are too late," he declared, winking at Corson.

"Indeed, we all surrender," said Diastor. He bowed to Corson, and the company resumed their seats, still showering her with welcome and flattery.

Corson began to feel much more at her ease.

Then another latecomer suddenly claimed their attention. She came dashing into the dining-hall, shouting, "Listen, Cloud's had *twin* calves—two beautiful little heifers! It must be a sign. We'll see marvels this season!" Two large dogs had run in with her and were racing around the table eagerly, thrashing their huge tails and greeting the family with noisy enthusiasm.

"'Deisha, take those creatures out of here at once," snapped Mesthelde. "And go get yourself washed. You're late already, and you stink of the barnyard."

"At once, Aunt," laughed 'Deisha, "but first I must see the mysterious visitor everyone's talking about. Where—" She stopped short and gazed at Nyctasia, openmouthed.

Nyctasia too stared, forgetting everything else. The two were identical, save that Nyctasia's skin was ivory-pale, 'Deisha's dark from the sun. And 'Deisha's hair was not cut short but plaited in a long, untidy braid.

"My sister Frondescine," said Raphe. "'Deisha, this is our cousin Nyctasia from Rhostshyl."

"*Vahn*, as if 'Deisha weren't trouble enough, now we have two of them," someone groaned.

"And she's a 'Tasia, too. We'll go mad."

"Why, call me Nyc, then," said Nyctasia. She rose and turned to 'Deisha, smiling. The dogs sniffed her and Corson and barked, excited by the unfamiliar scents. One tried to climb into Corson's lap, which it was much too large to do, and only succeeded in sweeping a few things off the table with its wildly wagging tail. The other reared up on its hind legs and planted its paws on Nyctasia's shoulders, almost knocking her over, and thrust its great muzzle affectionately into her face.

"Be quiet, you curs! Get down!" Raphe pushed them away, and 'Deisha swatted each on the nose sharply, ordering them to lie down and be still. They collapsed to the floor at once, tails thumping, and looked up worshipfully for her approval.

Blushing brightly, 'Deisha faced Nyctasia, stammering apologies. "They're very well-behaved as a rule. . . ."

"They're nothing of the sort, they're wild beasts!" said Mesthelde indignantly. "I've told you dozens of times not to bring them in—you can take your meals in the kennels in future, if you can't bear to be parted from them."

"Just the place for her," agreed one of the older men. "The little mongrel's not properly house-trained."

The youngsters were delighted. "She-wolf, you mean," one shouted.

"What he means's bi—"

"Enough! We've guests at table!" roared Diastor, slamming his fist on the table.

Nyctasia stifled her laughter. "But they're beautiful animals!" she cried, holding out her hands to the disconcerted 'Deisha. "I used to raise hounds myself."

'Deisha approached her, but then, seeing her own grimy hands, she thrust them behind her and mumbled, "I must go wash, I'm filthy, excuse me. I won't be a moment. . . ." She fled, abashed, with the dogs galloping after her. Mesthelde sighed and signaled the servants to bring in the dinner.

Corson decided that her manners would be quite adequate to the occasion, and enjoyed her meal thoroughly, though many of the dishes were strange to her. She was accustomed to much plainer fare, but it was not difficult to appreciate the rich sauces of cream and wine, the fowls stuffed with sausage and berries, or the pork baked with plums. She felt that she could easily get used to food like this, and it was a simple matter to imitate the way the others used their tableware. Corson took note that one only picked up a bone to gnaw at it after cutting away the meat that could be reached with knife and fork. And one wiped one's mouth with a napkin afterward.

Nyctasia too followed her hosts' manners—it wouldn't do to show that her own were considerably more refined. These folk would never learn from her that their behavior would be thought low-bred at court.

A very rare old vintage wine was served in their honor, from a lot laid down by the Edonaris lord who'd come from Rhostshyl long ago to settle in the valley. But its subtle savor was wasted on the guests, for neither Nyctasia nor Corson had a taste for fine wines. Corson heard Nyctasia's hissed whisper, *"Sip it slowly!"* in time to prevent her from emptying her glass at a gulp, but she found the drink bland and tasteless compared to the cheap, harsh wine served in taverns. "I've never had wine like this," she said quite truthfully, wishing she had a strong ale instead.

Nyctasia, in accordance with Vahnite Discipline, rarely drank spirits at all. One wine was the same as another to her, and plain water would have suited her better. But she smiled and declared the vintage "worthy of the name of Edonaris," much to the satisfaction of the household.

They did not guess how shamed Nyctasia felt, to think of her family's name sullied by commerce, branded on kegs that anyone might buy—as if the House of Edonaris were no better than a dramshop. But she pushed away such thoughts and forced herself to ask her newfound kin about their Edonaris ancestor.

It was he, Mesthelde told her, who had begun the winery. When he'd married into the family they had been merchants who dealt in fine wines and other luxury goods. But with the wealth he'd brought from Rhostshyl he had purchased land, and persuaded some of his bride's family that it would be more profitable to produce and market their own wares. Nyctasia understood his actions perfectly. A nobleman would naturally feel that he must live on his own land, establish a domain. She would have done the same, even if it had meant taking part in trade.

"He was Raphistain Elwys Jhaice brenn Rhostshyl ar'n Edonaris," Mesthelde continued. "Raphe's named for him, of course, because he has the look—we get a few in every generation who look like you. Both my sisters have the Edonaris features, though not so much as Raphe and 'Deisha. No, you don't see them here. Andelsy lives at Tezroth with her husband's kin, and Leclairin's away at Osela. But my mother looked much like 'Deisha, they say, when she was a girl."

"It's Lady Nocharis you mean?" asked Nyctasia, trying to remember who was whose child.

"Yes, the title's come down to her. I was her first child, so I'll inherit, and 'Deisha's the oldest girl of the next generation."

Corson was puzzled. "Why won't it come to Raphe? Was it a woman's title before the first Raphistain received it?"

"The title of Jhaice doesn't descend strictly in the male or female line," Nyctasia explained. "Now that a woman holds it, it will stay in the motherline so long as there's a girl in the next generation—daughter or niece. But if it passes to the fatherline, it will stay there until there's no son or nephew to inherit. It *is* rather confusing."

"What of your own title? Does it work the same way?"

"No, a Rhaicimate must remain in the original line as long as possible, even if it must pass to a sibling or cousin instead of descending to the next generation. If I'd no daughter or niece, my title would go to my sister, even if I had a son. But if there were no female heir, and a man succeeded to the Rhaicimate, it would have to revert to the female line in the next generation to produce a female heir."

Corson had lost interest by this time, but the others were more attentive than ever to Nyctasia's words. They had not suspected that she held such a high rank, and even Diastor was awed at first to learn that they had a Rhaicime in their midst. If they had been willing to have her settle among them before, they now became eager for her to do so.

Unsealing another carafe of wine, Diastor called for a toast, first to a bountiful harvest, as was customary, and then to the guests of the house.

Raphe seconded him. "To the irresistible slayer of hearts," he said, bowing to Corson. Then he turned and raised his glass to Nyctasia. "To your homecoming, cousin."

At his words, the festive, firelit scene seemed suddenly unreal to Nyctasia, like a painted mask hiding the features of an enemy. Now she saw that the tapestries hung in blackened tatters from the roofless walls. Mhairestri, not Mesthelde, sat at the far end of the table, and it was her brother Emeryc who proposed the toast. Her hand trembled as she lifted her glass, spilling a few dark drops of wine on the snowy table linen.

11

THE SPELL WAS broken by the return of 'Deisha, without the dogs, her face glowing from repeated scrubbing, her hair still damp and shiny, twisted into a neat wreath. She wore a colorful blouse embroidered with vines and blossoms, and a full flowing skirt over green hose and sandals with golden buckles. "Have you saved me anything to eat?" she asked, laughing, quite recovered from her earlier dismay. She hastily kissed her father, and swatted one of her younger brothers in passing, in payment for his previous remarks. Crowding in beside Nyctasia, she helped herself plentifully to goose, then proceeded to dominate Nyctasia's attention throughout the rest of the meal, clearly enamored with her elegant foreign cousin.

Seeing them together, no one who knew either woman could have long mistaken one of them for the other. 'Deisha, radiant with warmth and good spirits, made Nyctasia seem cold and distant by contrast, her words restrained, her very movements deliberate, as if she were somehow less alive than the impulsive, affectionate 'Deisha. Though life often amused Nyctasia, she had never known what it was to abandon herself fully to present pleasures, untouched by regret for the past or anxiety for the future. There was a faint air of weariness about her that made her seem older than her inexperienced cousin, though she was actually several months the younger. 'Deisha much admired her polish and breeding, while Nyctasia was drawn to 'Deisha's frank and vital nature. Before dinner was over, they had discussed everything from fine needlework to recipes for curing mange.

At the end of the meal, servants cleared the board and brought out bowls of chopped apples, raisins and nutmeats. Nyctasia had a weakness for sweets, and she praised the large, succulent, yellow raisins especially. "I've never seen raisins this color. Are they made from your own grapes?"

"Ah, those are Raphe's affair," said Diastor. "A southern strain of golden grapes he's been nursing for a new wine. We'll be opening the first casks of it soon."

"I have great hopes for it," Raphe said earnestly. "It should be a rough wine, rather sweet. I left the skin on while it aged, to give it a dark gold color. Come and see the vines—it's a fine evening, I'll show you over the grounds as well." He rose and offered his arm to Corson.

'Deisha caught at Nyctasia's hand and jumped up. "Yes, and come see my new heifers! One's white with black patches, and the other's black with white ones."

"We'll name them Day and Night, then," one of the children called out. "Day for you, 'Deisha, and Night for Nyc there."

The suggestion met with general approval, and Corson was particularly satisfied with it. "I always said you were a mooncalf, Nyc," she declared, and her wit was much applauded.

To 'Deisha and Raphe's disgust, their younger brothers and several cousins invited themselves along for the walk through the fields. Jenisorn, one of the brothers, offered to serve as Nyctasia's escort. "You'll need protection from the twins," he told her, with a grin. "They've no doubt laid a wager already to see who'll seduce you first."

Nyctasia smiled. "I'd say it's Corson who's caught Raphe's eye."

"Oh, I meant the both of you, of course, but your friend looks well able to defend herself."

"So she is," said Nyctasia, "and so am I." But she did need to be rescued soon, not from the amorous designs of Raphe or 'Deisha, but from the endless questions of the younger ones. Strangers were a welcome change in the valley, and foreigners from the coast were especially rare. But Nyctasia—an exiled noblewoman from far-off Rhostshyl—was an unheard-of figure of glamor and romance to her young kinsfolk.

They'd heard of Rhostshyl all their lives, as the ancestral home of the Edonaris, a city of palaces and wide, paved thoroughfares, noble courts, jeweled swords and deadly duels. It had always seemed to them a place half-mythical, like a city of legend, but now a real Rhostshylid had come among them, and they meant to make the most of the marvel. Their curiosity was boundless. Had Nyctasia not been the image of 'Deisha, they might have been less forward with her, held in check by her lofty rank, but she looked too much like one of themselves to inspire them with much diffidence.

"Nyc, do they hunt with hawks in Rhostshyl?"

"Sometimes," said Nyctasia, who never had enough of hunting. "But I prefer hounds." She showed them the faint scar on her temple from a *graika*'s talons.

"Have you been on a sailing ship?"

"Once. I was seasick for days. I desperately wanted to die."

"Did you ever fight a duel?"

"When I was younger, and very foolish."

"Why were you banished from the city?"

"For asking impertinent questions!" snapped 'Deisha, rounding on them fiercely, and displaying a marked family likeness to Mesthelde. "Let Nyc be, and stop making a nuisance of yourselves. You've the manners of wild swine!"

"You're a fine one to talk of others' manners, 'Deisha. *We* didn't set the dogs on her!"

"My dogs are better trained than the lot of you." 'Deisha drove them off at last, with threats, and led the way through the barn to the calves' stall. The others fell behind, indifferent, as Nyctasia and 'Deisha engaged in a serious discussion of the merits of different kinds of feed grains. The Rhaicime was a disappointment, but they were better satisfied when they joined the cluster of questioners around Corson.

Warriors too were a novelty in the Valleylands, and everyone was eager for accounts of Corson's prowess in battle. Some, indeed, hoped that she'd teach them to fight with sword and shield, though they knew that their elders would never permit it. Corson, for her part, was more than willing to boast of her daring exploits. She'd drunk a good deal of wine at dinner—wine far stronger than she'd suspected from the mellow smoothness of it—and under its inspiration she held her listeners spellbound

with bloodthirsty stories till Nyctasia and 'Deisha returned from
the dairy.

"If you've finished boring the Lady Nyctasia with your barnyard lore," Raphe said, "we might get on to the vineyards before
dark."

"You must excuse him," 'Deisha told Nyctasia, in tones of
pity and tolerance. "He's incapable of taking an interest in anything but grapes. It's exceedingly dull, I know, but he can't help
it. The poor fellow has no use for living creatures, though grapes
can do nothing but grow, and have no use except at table."

"My dear sister, you have admirably expressed my exact sen-
timents about livestock. What is more, the very air we breathe
contradicts you." He gestured toward the vine-covered slopes
they were approaching. "Compare that aroma"—the fragrance of
the grapes was intoxicating—"to the stench of the stable and the
barn, the sheepfold and the fowl-yard."

"You see . . . ?" Jenisorn whispered in Nyctasia's ear. "The
both of them showing off for your benefit."

"Charming," murmured Nyctasia discreetly.

"The grapes," Raphe concluded, "are pure and unsullied, fit
for human hands to hold, not stinking of their own filth and
crawling with lice!"

'Deisha objected vehemently to this description of the animals
she raised, which, she protested, were clean and well-groomed
creatures, every one of them. But she was outnumbered. Winemaking was the chosen profession and the passion of most of her
kinsfolk. Even those who longed to see something of the world
outside the valley could not really imagine a life without the
seasonal rhythm of budbreak, berryset, ripening, harvest and
frost.

"Anyone could see that this land's meant for grapes, not graz-
ing," said Nicorin. "You know it well, 'Deisha." They had
climbed a hillside which gave a striking view of the surrounding
vales and three of the valley's many small lakes.

"I never denied it," 'Deisha countered. "Oh, it's country for
grapes, right enough. The best there is." The pride in her voice
was unmistakable. Though she spent most of her time tending the
animals of the estate, 'Deisha too had winemaking in her blood.

"Why is that?" asked Nyctasia. "I thought it was sunshine and
rainfall that made the difference."

"They do, but grapes need slopes like these as well," 'Deisha
explained, "to let the damp and cold flow away. And breezes on

the heights keep the fruit dry." Nyctasia was already making notes in her commonplace-book, while Corson made a polite effort to look interested. Most of the others drifted away again.

"And warm air blows off the lakes, you see," Raphe added. "Protection from frost. Everything needed is here—the soil is rich, and these hills are riddled with caves that are perfect for aging and storing the wine. We've rarely had to dig cellars for it. . . . Ah, here's what I wanted to show you." He cut a small bunch of ripe grapes from the vine for Corson and Nyctasia. The plants on either side were heavy with purple-black fruit, but these were the color of sunstruck amber with a frosty bloom, glowing among the dark clusters that grew from the same vines.

"I brought these from the south, from Esthairon," Raphe said proudly. "They're too delicate to grow by themselves in colder climes, but I've grafted them to a hardier rootstock, and now they're thriving here. I think they're really doing better here than in their native soil. I suspect that an old strain may sometimes be improved when it's joined to a flourishing new stock."

Nyctasia knew that Raphe meant these words for her. She smiled at him and sampled a few of the golden grapes he'd given her. They were warm from the sun, and piercingly sweet.

"I've been playing about with different changeling stocks for years," he remarked, "but there was never space enough to plant a whole crop of them until we acquired the Cymvelan lands."

And it was only then that Nyctasia remembered the reason she'd meant to give for her visit to the valley.

12

WHEN THE OTHERS turned back to the house, Corson lingered in the darkening garden, to let the cool night air clear her head. She was still lightheaded from the wine—which was not unpleasant, but it made her feel restless and somehow unsatisfied. "I *won't* think about Steifann," she swore, tossing her head like a skittish filly and nearly falling over a low stone bench.

Impatiently gathering up her skirt, she sat down on the bench and closed her eyes, savoring the sweet smell of the ripening grapes. She was not much surprised when Raphistain came back to join her.

"How does my fair guest?" he asked, bowing.

"Well, good sir," Corson replied, amused at his courtly speech, and at her own mimicry. As he bent over her, she was struck again by his resemblance to Nyctasia. He was taller, of course, and darker, his skin weathered from years spent working out of doors. His rugged, broad-shouldered frame was nothing like Nyctasia's slight figure either, and Corson noted with approval that his limbs looked strong and well muscled. It was his features that revealed the Edonaris blood, and the Edonaris were a handsome lot. She suddenly found it easier not to think of Steifann.

Raphistain sat down beside her. "Does what you see please you, my harvest queen?"

Corson pretended to admire the view of the fertile hills and fields. "It seems a lush and inviting land, though I speak as a stranger," she said innocently, though there was no mistaking her meaning.

"You must become more familiar with it. I would have you feel at home here, and learn all there is to know."

"It has always been my delight to find new countries to explore. But no land holds me for very long."

"I too, though I have spent all my life in the valley, am a keen explorer. Let me tell you my theories about how it should be done."

"You are Nyc's kinsman, and no mistake," Corson said drily.

"You flatter me. I am but a tiller of the soil, and she is, in her own place, a ruler of the highest rank."

"Blood will tell, they say. You've many of the same ways about you." It seemed to her that he preened himself a bit at this last remark. What strutting peacocks these provincial gentry are, she thought. They're worse than the true nobility any day.

"Mind what I say, Corson," said Raphistain. "We were speaking of exploration. Now, my question is, if one were to travel this whole world of ours, what would be the best way to go about it?"

"I think you have an answer to your own question."

"But I want your advice. You have so much more experience than I. First, I think, it would be well to start in the northernmost climes—what are said to be the coldest places." He stroked her hair softly.

"It sounds as good a plan as any other."

"Just so. Then, one would be wise to travel southward, but slowly. It would be a shame to miss any of the sights, and subtler delights do not reveal themselves to the hasty voyager."

"That I agree with, to be sure."

He smiled. "It heartens me that my ideas find favor with you."

"I think you know what you're about."

Raphistain took her hand. "Perhaps that is because the lands I now want to explore seem fairer to me than any I've ever imagined."

"We're still in the north," Corson reminded him.

"So we are. Now, it has also been my experience that as we go southward, the climes begin to grow warmer."

"Then the southernmost point is the hottest?"

"No . . . In fact, I believe that the central regions are the most torrid."

"So I have found," said Corson, who was beginning to grow bored with the game.

"But I mustn't let you think that I would neglect what lies to the east and the west. If one is to be a daring adventurer, all the extremities must be explored. Therefore, though the general direction is southward, there should be many pleasant excursions to see what is to be found on either side."

"It sounds like a lovely journey," said Corson, yawning. She stood up suddenly, and pulled Raphe to his feet. "Yes, there's no doubt that you're a true Edonaris, my friend. Nothing but talk, everlasting talk!"

Raphe was so startled at Corson's challenge that he dropped his pose of detached amusement and looked her directly in the face. "Corson, you're the most desirable creature I've ever met," he said with ardent sincerity, and clasped his arms around her waist, drawing her close. Corson kissed him, and he responded with passion, pressing her to him as if afraid she might escape, caressing her silk-clad body with hungry hands.

"He tastes of the grapes," Corson thought, biting at his lip gently. She whispered, half singing:

> "He who would be my mate
> Must be of the roving kind,
> And follow, to find his fate,
> Where the wandering roadways wind."

They both laughed. Then, with their arms about each other's waists, they walked back to the house in silence.

* * *

Nyctasia was dismayed to discover that there was no bar for the door to her room. Watchdogs guarded the yard, and of course the main gates and portals were barred at night, but there was no reason to sleep behind locked doors. No doubt a maid would come in at dawn to rekindle the fire, before Nyctasia was awake. In a great stone house like this, mornings would be chill all the year around.

Nyctasia understood this well enough, but she was accustomed not only to a locked room, but to having armed guards on duty while she slept, to keep watch for her enemies. Though there was no danger here, she could not help feeling uneasy and vulnerable in this undefended chamber.

But for her, as a guest, to request a bar for her door would be to imply mistrust of her hosts, and etiquette forbade that she commit such a breach of courtesy. The *vahn* knows I do trust them, Nyctasia thought, as she tossed restlessly about in the canopied feather-bed. This is absurd. I've nothing to fear here. But she could not bring herself to draw the curtains around the bed and hide the unguarded door from view. She slid her dagger under the pillows, feeling like a fool, but still she did not sleep.

Would she ever feel secure enough, she wondered, to go about unarmed, as the Edonaris of Vale did? They carried knives, yes, but useful knives sharpened on one edge only—tools for cutting, not weapons for stabbing. A dagger, with its double edge, was highly impractical for anything but murder.

Finally, Nyctasia rose and wrapped herself in the white pearl-silk robe—'Deisha's, no doubt—that she'd found neatly folded on the bed. She would spend the night in Corson's room, she decided. With Corson at hand she'd feel safe sleeping in an open field. Corson took up most of any bed, she pulled away the bed-clothes, and she snored like a wild boar, but she was an exceptionally reliable bodyguard.

But outside Corson's door she hesitated. Had she heard voices within? If Corson was not alone, she'd hardly welcome another visitor. Nyctasia peered through a crack in the door and smiled at the genial firelit scene that greeted her.

Corson, still in the golden gown, was sitting on the edge of a bed piled high with feather mattresses and colorful quilts. Raphistain knelt at her feet, unlacing her sandle, and both were laughing quietly.

"I thought you said the north was the ideal starting place," said Corson, lazily stretching out one bare foot to touch his hair.

"Under a strange sky, one cannot steer by the stars, madame. North depends on how you lie. Is not this as good a point of departure as any other?" He kissed the arch of her foot, then her ankle, and lightly caressed the back of her calf.

Corson lay back on the bed and said a little huskily, "Mind you don't lose your way, friend—"

"No fear," whispered Raphe, sliding the silk dress up above her knees.

Nyctasia stole away noiselessly and returned to her own room.

Good breeding prevented her from spying any longer at Corson's door.

Back in her bed, she resolutely refused to lie staring at the unbolted door. She had nearly succeeded in falling asleep at last when a faint sound from the threshold suddenly woke her again. Heart racing, she groped under the pillows for her dagger. It was not merely her fancy this time—the door *was* being pushed softly open.

13

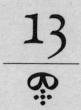

"NYC," WHISPERED 'DEISHA, "are you asleep? May I come in?"

Nyctasia began to breathe again. "By all means," she said shakily, "as long as you haven't brought your dogs."

'Deisha chuckled and crossed the room quickly on bare feet, to perch on Nyctasia's bed. "I couldn't sleep for thinking about you. I never had you to myself all day. You must keep that robe —it suits you far better than me. Aunt Mesthelde says it's a waste to put fine clothes on me, and she's quite right." 'Deisha wore only a threadbare night-dress of what had once been delicate layers of lace. Her long hair was loose and wild, and she looked altogether enchanting. Brushing the shimmering silk at Nyctasia's wrist, she went on dreamily, "But you're like the Lady of the Moon in it. . . . Your skin's so fair and smooth I can hardly tell where the silk leaves off." She stroked Nyctasia's arm lightly.

What a brazen flirt, thought Nyctasia, amused. Jenisorn had certainly been right. "I was thinking of you too," she lied gallantly. "I've dreamed of having a twin all my life. There are always twins in the Edonaris line. My younger sister and brother are a pair." There was no need to mention Thierran and Mescrisdan.

"Like Raphe and me. I used to wish Raphe was a girl—four

78

brothers, after all! But now I have you for a sister I'm quite satisfied," 'Deisha said with a most winsome and alluring smile.

Nyctasia refrained from asking, "And is it the custom in these parts to seduce one's sisters?" and remarked instead, "It's as well Raphe was a boy, perhaps. There might have been dreadful confusion over succession to the Jhaicery."

"I never thought of that. Nyc, the others say that you're a *Rhaicime*—is it true?"

"Alas, yes. If I weren't of Rhaicime rank, I wouldn't have so many enemies in Rhostshyl."

"Well, I'm glad of it, if it's brought you here. Now I've found you I shan't let you go back to Rhostshyl unless you take me with you. You know, you'll simply have to marry Raphe. Father would give anything to have another title in the family."

"Doesn't Raphe have a say in the matter? He might prefer to marry Corson."

"He's much taken with Corson, who wouldn't be? But it's you he'll pay court to, you'll see. He doesn't really mind that I'm to be Jhaice, and not he, but all the same I know he'd be pleased for a child of his to inherit the rank of Rhaicime. And you could do worse than Raphe," she added loyally.

"Do you promise he'll not murder me in childbed to let his firstborn succeed at once to the title?"

'Deisha grinned evilly at her. "What's your full formal title?" she demanded.

"Oh, no, not formally . . . ? That would be—let me think—Hlaven Nyctasia'v Teselesq Rhaicime AesTirre wys Gwethrad-Moir brenn Rhostshyl ar'n Edonaris, I believe." She paused for breath. "I rarely need to use it all. For the usual business of the Rhaicimate the standard form of address is sufficient."

"You'll have to teach me these things, Nyc. I thought I was to be Lady Frondescine Clairin Jhaice brenn Vale ar'n Edonaris. Isn't that right?"

"Yes, but Formal Address is different. For one thing, the Old Eswraine word is used—'Hlaven,' not 'Lady.' And since the title doesn't descend from your mother—her name is Leclairin?"

'Deisha nodded, fascinated.

"Then you'll be Hlaven Frondescine Leclairina'v Mesthelde Jhaice brenn Vale ar'n Edonaris, do you see? Of course I'd have to study your family records to be certain. There may be further distinctions."

"*Vahn*, I hope not. It's difficult enough as it is."

"Your aunt could style herself Lady Mesthelde now, if she liked, since she's the heir apparent."

"I know, but you mustn't call her that, it only annoys her. She says it's all foolishness and won't get the eggs to market."

Nyctasia smiled. "I've not heard that old saying for years. She's a wise woman."

"Oh, the household would run to ruin without her. My mother and Uncle Aldrichas only want to travel and trade at the market fairs, and Father's had to take on most of the duties of the vintnery since Great Aunt Heladis died. Raphe and Nesanye help, of course, and I—"

"Look after the livestock," Nyctasia supplied, wondering where she herself could fit into this design. She knew a good deal about farming, and the other responsibilities of an estate, but she had never thought to devote her life to such duties. Was there work for her here? And would she really be satisfied to abandon her scholarly pursuits and live as lady of a manor? She quite loved her new kin already, but could she ever be one of them?

"Well, no matter what Aunt Mesthelde says, I mean to learn a lady's ways from you, Nyc. I'll not have you shamed by my ignorance. We must seem like a clan of savages to you."

Nyctasia put aside her doubts as best she could, the better to enjoy 'Deisha's sly game. "I think you're a rogue and a flatterer, my girl," she retorted. "That's what I think, if you much want to know."

"Oh, but I—" wailed 'Deisha.

"Nor shall I try to make a lady of you," Nyctasia continued firmly. "I'd be better pleased if you could make a vintner of me. As for you, I think you're quite perfect just as you are."

Even 'Deisha was speechless at this—but not for long. She plucked at the tatters of lace at her throat, blushing. "Nyc . . . is Corson . . . are you and she . . . ? I mean, we could give you a large room together, if you'd rather."

"I thank you, but I'm very comfortable here indeed. And I'm sure that Corson has no complaints about her quarters. The hospitality of the house could not be faulted."

This was not what 'Deisha meant, and well Nyctasia knew it. 'Deisha looked down, at a loss, daunted by Nyctasia's mockery. "My grandmother made this quilt," she said at random.

"Lady Nocharis?" asked Nyctasia, interested.

'Deisha nodded, still not meeting her eyes. "For my mother. Look." She turned back a corner of the bedclothes to reveal the embroidered eye on the underside of the quilt, an old custom meant to protect the sleeper from evil spirits. "Nyc!" she gasped, "what do you want with this? Are you mad?" She had uncovered the dagger, which Nyctasia had hastily pushed out of sight at her entrance.

It was Nyctasia's turn to feel awkward and embarrassed. "It's foolish of me, I know, but I've not slept in an unlocked room for so long that I was fearful. When you came in, for a moment I took you for one of my enemies."

'Deisha leaped up from the bed, laughing. "Rogue I may be," she cried, "but no assassin! See for yourself, I haven't a weapon hidden anywhere about me—not so much as a pin." She pulled off the night-dress and tossed it away, holding out her bare arms to Nyctasia coaxingly. "There, you see, I'm not dangerous."

Nyctasia gave in. 'Deisha's brash charm was indeed irresistible. "I admit that you're unarmed," she said, "but I can't allow that you're not dangerous." She seized 'Deisha's strong, brown hands and pulled her back onto the bed.

'Deisha tumbled across Nyctasia's lap and lay looking up into her face, suddenly serious. They gazed long and silently, lost in wonder at each other's being. Their features were so similar that it was like looking into some mystical mirror that showed, not what one was, but what one might have been.

What grace of bearing she has, thought 'Deisha wistfully. So elegant and refined, exquisite . . . am I too old to learn some polish, so I won't bore her?

How frank and free she is, Nyctasia mused, as I've never dared to be. Not afraid to be trusting and unwary . . . Is it too late, I wonder?

'Deisha drew Nyctasia's face down to her own and lightly kissed her mouth and eyes. "I'm so very certain that you belong to me," she whispered, "I can't feel that I'm wronging Corson. Would she mind?"

Nyctasia laughed softly, leaning over 'Deisha and tracing her lips with one finger. "I'm very fond of Corson, but she's a wanderer. She'll be on her way soon, and I daresay I'll never see her again. And unless I much mistake, she has your handsome twin in her bed right now. I passed her door not long ago, and heard them laughing. That's another reason to lock one's room at night, you see—not only for protection but for privacy."

"You'll not want for protection here, Nyc. My dogs guard the grounds all night, and I'll watch over you while you sleep." As she spoke, 'Deisha loosened the sash of Nyctasia's robe and slid it from her shoulders, letting her hands glide down Nyctasia's arms and over her white thighs. Pulling Nyctasia down beside her, she pressed against her and drew the bedclothes over them both. "And you know nothing can harm you under Mother 'Charis's quilt."

'Deisha did want to protect her delicate, gently bred cousin. Nyctasia had spoken little of her past, but 'Deisha knew that she'd been wounded by sorrows, and she longed to heal those wounds, to shield Nyctasia from all further suffering. She held her as tenderly as if she were some fragile spray of blossoms, liable to bruise. Her own work-hardened hands seemed to her unfit to touch Nyctasia's milky skin. Lying naked side by side, they were more than ever like mirror images of one another— identical, yet opposite. 'Deisha kissed Nyctasia's soft palms, and her smooth throat. "My polished, pale reflection," she murmured.

Nyctasia smiled to herself, in the darkness.

> "See in this enchanted mirror
> Images reversed, but clearer.
> Seek your nature and your kind,
> But beware of what you find,"

she recited, nuzzling 'Deisha's ear. She too felt protective toward her bewitching twin, who seemed sheltered and ingenuous to her. 'Deisha was trusting because she had never known betrayal, bold because she had never known despair. Nor would she ever know them, if Nyctasia could do anything to prevent it.

Their kisses were soft and lingering at first, their caresses slow and dreamlike. They drifted in a haze of sweet, trembling contentment, then grew more ardent and playful, each knowing from her own pleasure what would please the other. 'Deisha pillowed Nyctasia's head between her breasts and wrapped her arms and legs around her tightly. "Now do you feel safe, sweet cousin?" she teased.

Nyctasia was seized with a sudden fit of giggles. "How could I not feel safe," she gasped, "in the very bosom of my family?"

'Deisha yelped in outrage and began to pummel Nyctasia with a pillow. Nyctasia tickled her under the ribs, where she herself was most ticklish, and they rolled about the bed wrestling and swearing till they both lay spent and shaken with laughter. But then Nyctasia crushed 'Deisha to her in a fierce, hungry embrace, half-sobbing, "Yes, protect me, 'Deisha—protect me from myself! Don't let me go back, don't let me go on as I am!"

'Deisha cradled Nyctasia in her arms, astonished at her distress. She did not understand a word of her desperate plea, but she promised, nevertheless, not to let her go.

14

"WHERE ARE YOU going?" Corson complained, as Raphe climbed out of her bed at dawn, waking her up. "Now the bed's cold."

He was already pulling on his clothes, but he paused to bend over Corson and lift a long lock of her hair to his lips. "Good morrow, fair guest."

"Morrow yourself. It's still night."

"Nothing of the sort. It's nearly light, see for yourself." He crossed to the window and pulled back the draperies and shutters to reveal the transparent darkness of early dawn.

Corson groaned and pulled the bedclothes up around her ears. "Nearly light! Do you take me for a dairymaid? Close that window or I'll throw you out of it. I'm half frozen as it is."

"Poor lamb. Never mind, there'll be hot weather today, by the look of it, and a good thing too. The grapes need it." He took a last, satisfied look at the clearing sky, then came back to sit on the bed and put his boots on.

Corson toyed with the hair at the back of his neck, then let her fingers trail slowly down his bare spine. "If you were a good host, you'd stay here and help me get warm," she chided him. "Surely your first duty is to the comfort of your guests."

"The duties of hospitality are sacred," Raphe agreed, leaning back to kiss her arm. "In fact, I can think of no duty I would so willingly fulfill, if work did not call me away. I want to have half the pruning done before the sun's high. By midday it will be too hot, I hope and trust. All that heavy rain's had me worried, I can tell you. Too much water can make the fruit split and spoil, but if today's fair all will be well." As he finished dressing, he told Corson a great deal more about the perils of rot and mold to the ripening grapes, but she fell asleep again before she learned much.

Nyctasia had been lying awake for some time, trying to remember what it was that she'd dreamt that night. The words of a song echoed in her memory, just out of reach . . . had there been something about a tower . . . ?

'Deisha rose, stretching, and slipped into her night-dress again, then sat on the edge of the bed, braiding her hair quickly and carelessly. When she bound the end of the thick plait and tossed it over her shoulder, Nyctasia snatched it and tugged gently, pulling 'Deisha back down and into her arms.

"I didn't mean to wake you, sweet cousin," said 'Deisha, snuggling against her.

Nyctasia kissed her invitingly. "I've been waiting for you to wake, my dear."

"Alas that I must go and see to the cows now."

"That *is* a pity. But we can wait, and cows can't. I'll go with you."

"Oh, no, stay here and rest, Nyc. I'd no right to keep you awake half the night, and you tired from your journey."

But Nyctasia pushed back the covers and reached for her robe. "I couldn't sleep more. There's so much I want to see. The kennels, for one, and the stables. And all the land—field and forest. I hope there's good hunting." She threw wide the window and drew a deep breath of the cool, grape-scented morning air.

Before her stretched a splendid view of the surrounding hills, their crests still wreathed in mist. The distant foothills of the Spine Mountains had begun to show the golden and scarlet hues of autumn, while the nearby slopes were carpeted with vines. Small children were running up and down between the grape-rows, clattering wooden noisemakers and shouting, to keep the birds away. "Do you know what I've seen from my windows all my life?" Nyctasia asked quietly. "Walls. The walls of the palace, and beyond them the walls of the courtyard, and beyond those the city walls. But the mountains are your fortifications here. The valley is protected, but you are not the prisoners of your own barricades and bulwarks."

To 'Deisha, who hoped to see its towering ramparts one day, the walled city sounded mysterious and exciting, but she said only, "You've come at a good time to see the hills at their best. Soon the colors will be glorious." She joined Nyctasia at the window and took her hand. "And you've brought us luck too— the weather's turned at last. We were afraid the rain would ruin the harvest, but yesterday you and Corson appeared and brought the sun with you. Today will be clear and bright, the damp's burning off already. There's a fine crop of mist."

She pointed to a newly tilled field in the distance, where the tall plumes of fog rising from the fresh-turned furrows did look rather like rows of ghostly grain. A crop of mist...thought Nyctasia, frowning. It was a local turn of phrase that pleased her, but it reminded her again of the dream and the song she had tried in vain to recall. The mists of morning...? Was that a part of it? 'But it wasn't quite right. And surely there was a bell—

"'Deisha," she said abruptly, "where's the land that belonged to the Cymvelan Circle? Can we see it from here?"

"We could if not for the mist. The temple was on top of Honeycomb Hill, over there. Most of the roof has fallen, and some of the walls, but when it's clear you can see the remains. And the bell tower's still standing. Nyc, what is it?"

Nyctasia had suddenly left her side and hastened to seize her harp, which hung from a sconce on the wall near the bed. "Wait —it's come to me," she said excitedly, snatching up her pouch and spilling out its contents. 'Deisha looked on in amazement as Nyctasia scattered a fortune in jewels and gold across the lid of a chest and picked out the silver tuning-key. She tightened a few strings then slipped the key around her neck on its silver chain, leaving the other things where they lay. To a ripple of high, icy notes, she sang:

> "White mists veil the fields at dawn
> In the pale, pearl, early hour.
> Shall I seek for peace or power?
> Shall I stay or journey on?

Sunlight warms the fields at noon.
Will the bell, high in the tower,
Peal for peace or peal for power?
Has the midday come so soon?

Dews fall on the fields at eve,
Whispering without surcease,
'Peace or power? Power or peace?
Will you linger? Will you leave?'

Or was it, 'travel on'?" Nyctasia said doubtfully. She sounded disappointed.

"Nyc, what is that song? What in the *vahn's* name does it mean?"

"Not a great deal, I'm afraid," sighed Nyctasia, "but I'd best make note of it anyway. One can never be certain of these things." She swept her valuables back into her pouch and tossed it into the chest. From her satchel she fetched a flask of ink and a quill, and began to record the song in her commonplace-book. She seemed to have forgotten 'Deisha's presence completely.

'Deisha leaned over her shoulder. "How beautifully you write!" she exclaimed, admiring the evenness of Nyctasia's quill-strokes. "Like a trained scribe. I can write, after a fashion, but I always finish with more ink on myself than on the page."

"I've had considerable practice," said Nyctasia absently. "I daresay you haven't."

What had Nyctasia had to write that she wouldn't trust to scribes, 'Deisha wondered. She felt again like a callow farm girl. "Nyc, will you teach me to play the harp?"

Without looking up, Nyctasia replied, "If you like. It's not difficult."

"Well, I'd best go look to my cows. . . ." There was no response. "Will I see you at breakfast?"

"Oh, yes, certainly," said Nyctasia, still intent on her task. When she finished, she read over her work carefully, weighing each word, then shook her head doubtfully and put away her book and writing utensils. She returned to the window and looked out over the landscape again, but the sun was just breaking over the horizon, and the hilltops were still hidden in mist. Suddenly feeling weary to the bone, Nyctasia went back to bed and slept soundly till a maid came to summon her to breakfast.

* * *

Raphe was gone by the time a maid came in, bringing Corson a basin of warm water to wash with. Corson ignored her and sank into sleep once more, to be awakened for the third time by Nyctasia splashing the now cooled water on her face.

"Idiot! If I'd had a weapon at hand I'd have cut you in two before I half woke."

"I know. I made sure there was none handy. Get out of bed, you indolent lout."

"Why should I? I don't have to answer to anyone here." She stretched slowly and settled back with her hands behind her head. Her long, thick hair lay in sleep-tousled waves about her.

Nyctasia threw her clothes at her. "It's discourteous not to come down to breakfast on the first morning of a visit, unless you know your hosts well."

"I know *one* of them well," said Corson, grinning. "Intimately, you might say." But the thought of breakfast moved her to rise and dress.

"And I thought you were pining for that faithless fellow in Chiastelm."

"He's not thinking of *me*," Corson said angrily, jerking on her sword-belt. "Why should I worry about him? Raphe wants me to stay for the Harvest Festival. Maybe I will, maybe I won't. I'll go back to Chiastelm when I please, and not before."

Corson's bluffing was so obvious that Nyctasia turned away to the window to hide her amusement. Pulling open the shutters, she leaned out to admire the bright, serene morning again. In the yard below, two children were twirling a skipping-rope while a third jumped over it tirelessly. Gradually, Nyctasia made out the words of the rhyme they were chanting together.

> "*On* the *hill* top *stands* a *tow*er,
>   *Strike* the *bell* and *sound* the *hour:*
>   One, two, three, four . . ."

So much for my premonitions, Nyctasia thought, smiling to herself. I must have heard them in my sleep.

The sunlight was already bright and powerful, and the mist had lifted from the highlands. On the crest of a nearby hill, the remains of stone walls were now visible, and a tall stone tower stood stark against the pale morning sky.

Corson finished braiding her hair and pinned it up with the ivory clasp. "Besides," she continued, "as long as we're here, I'd not mind just having a look for that treasure."

15

"I TRUST YOU didn't pay too dearly for this," said Diastor with a smile, handing the page of riddles back to Nyctasia. "I fear you were tricked. Treasure-hunters have combed the place for years, and nothing's ever been found. Outlanders will still buy treasure maps, though. It's an old game."

"No, it wasn't costly," Nyctasia said. "Newt hadn't much choice but to sell it to us."

"You think he knew it was worthless, then?" Corson broke in. "By the Hlann, I'll wring his scrawny neck if I see him again! But what of the innkeeper at Ylna? He recognized the thing."

Diastor shrugged. "He was probably party to the scheme. If there's a fortune to be had, it's in convincing others that there's a fortune to be had, believe me. I'd wager there never was a treasure. The Cymvelans weren't rich—they lived on the land, never even ate meat, from what I've heard."

"I've always heard they were bloodthirsty wizards who sacrificed to demons," Corson remarked, helping herself to sausage.

"It's easy enough to say such things," said Nyctasia, who'd been called much the same in her day.

"They were a peaceful, scholarly lot," one of the older men said firmly. "My uncle was sent to them for lessons when he was a boy. They were known as great teachers who'd never turn away a pupil, peasant or noble. The attack on the Circle was a disgrace."

"What made folk turn on them, then?"

"Well . . . some do say that the talk against them was started by lords of the great Saetarrin estates, during the drought. The crops had failed and folk were desperate for food. They knew the Saetarrin had reserves of grain, and in time they'd have torn down the storehouses—and maybe put torch to the manor-houses as well. The nobles feared for their lives."

"If the grain had been given out, as it should have been, they'd not have gone in fear of their own people," said Mesthelde. "You can't hoard corn while folk are starving."

"They preferred to sacrifice the Circle—so it's said. I daresay it was easy to persuade people that the Cymvelans caused the drought—they were foreigners and their ways were strange. It was even rumored that some of their gardens were still green while all others were withered. With the blame laid to them, the Saetarrin were left in peace."

"And it was the Lord Saetarrin who'd sold them the land, when they first came to Vale," Jenisorn put in. "And after the massacre his heirs reclaimed it. They said there was no proper record of the sale, and who was there to contradict them? If there was ever a treasure the Saetarrin made off with it before they sold us the place!"

"Idle talk," said Diastor, with a warning look at Jenisorn. "Lady Saetarrin gave us the land at a good price because it's thought to be unlucky now, and it's hard to find folk enough to work it."

"The land was unlucky long before the Cymvelans came," said the elderly Heronice. "It's always been an ill place. But Avareth ar'n Saetarrin was glad to be quit of it because she knows how her grandsire recovered it. We all know that." Diastor frowned, but did not contradict her.

"Well, it's been lucky enough for me," said Raphe complacently. "The ghosts haven't troubled my grafted vines. But I'll pour them an offering of the first lot of new wine, to appease them."

"Stop that sort of talk," said Mesthelde sharply. "It's no joke. People have disappeared in those ruins, even in my day. Wise folk still shun them." She made a sign to ward off evil, which was repeated by several of the others.

The youngsters, who had all explored the ruins, against their elders' orders, grinned and winked at each other.

"All the same, I mean to have a look at the place," said Corson, "with your permission, of course."

"By all means," said Raphe, "I'll take you there. But I warn you, there, *is* danger. Since the fire, much of the timbering's given way. There's not much roof left to fall, but the flooring's not solid underfoot, in places. You could fall through if you're not careful where you step. With all respect to my Lady Aunt, that is probably what became of those who've disappeared there."

"Then why weren't they found? And what of the screams folk have heard there, and nobody to be seen? It's those who perished in the fire, mark my words. Oh, I know it's no use talking to you young fools—you'll please yourselves anyway."

"I'd like to see the temple myself—and the tower," Nyctasia admitted. "I'm curious, I confess."

Diastor nodded assent. "I shouldn't put too much stock in that paper of yours, though," he cautioned. "You'll be disappointed."

"I never did believe in it. Not in the story of treasure, that is. It was the name Edonaris that concerned me. I didn't know you owned the land, you see. Even so, it might be interesting to see. We'll be very careful."

Mesthelde only sniffed in disapproval, her expression clearly declaring that they would have only themselves to blame when disaster befell. "And what hole has swallowed up your sister this morning?" she asked Raphe. "It's no more like her to be late for breakfast than to be on time for dinner. She's always up before us all to tend to her flocks."

"Perhaps she didn't sleep well last night," said Jenisorn, looking mischievously at Nyctasia from beneath half-lowered lashes.

"She said she'd be in to breakfast," Nyctasia volunteered, and then reddened, realizing that she'd just confirmed the surmises of most of those present. Jenisorn looked away pointedly, and bit into a piece of bread and honey, smacking his lips. Nyctasia reminded herself to strangle him at the earliest opportunity.

She was relieved when one of the children spoke up. "I saw her come in from the yard when I brought in the eggs."

"She must still be washing, then," said Mesthelde. "Remarkable! It appears that you have a civilizing influence on her, my dear Nyctasia."

"At last we agree on something, Aunt!" said 'Deisha, hurrying into the room and seizing a honey-roll in each hand. *"Vahn,* I'm hungry! Arrow's shoulder is much better, where the boar gored him."

The family greeted her appearance with stunned silence, too occupied with staring even to reply. The reason for her tardy arrival at breakfast was now apparent. She had cut off her hair, cropped it as short as Nyctasia's. Her wide brow, high cheekbones and slender neck now showed to full advantage, and she and Nyctasia were more alike than ever.

"I must say, it suits you," Raphe said at last. "But of course you knew it would. You'd only to look at Nyc."

"And it will be far less trouble this way," 'Deisha said, through a mouthful of ham. "I can't think why I didn't do it long ago."

Clearly a gesture on Nyctasia's part was called for, and she was not one to neglect a duty. She took off one of her silver earrings—Erystalben's gift—and gave it to 'Deisha, whose obvious delight reconciled her to its loss.

The proposed visit to the Cymvelan temple also met with 'Deisha's approval. "We might go today," she suggested, "if you're not needed here, Raphe. It must be soon, you know, before the crush."

He nodded. "In fact, I have to go up that way, as it happens. The golden grapes seem to be ripening a little earlier this year."

"The crush?" queried Nyctasia. "That sounds ominous."

"When the bulk of the grapes are brought in to be pressed," 'Deisha explained. "The different strains ripen at different times, but when the first are ready the rest don't wait long."

"It's a backbreaking job to keep up with them," said Nesanye glumly. "Once they reach the perfect flavor they have to be gathered then and there. They're tested every hour, day and night, for ripeness. Even a few hours' delay can affect the taste of the wine."

"And then you have to press 'em right away, too!" a small child chimed in from the foot of the table, proud of knowing something that a big person like Nyctasia didn't. "Else they lose their flavor!"

"That's right, 'Lorin," said Nesanye, and turning to Nyctasia, added, "The crush should begin at any time now, and once it does there'll be no rest for anyone."

Several of the others groaned in agreement, but the younger

folk asserted that the crush was the best time of the year, more fun than a fair or festival.

"It's exciting," insisted 'Cacia, "everyone racing around, and all the confusion and noise—"

"And lights burning all night."

". . . dinner outside, at all hours . . ."

"It sounds like preparation for a siege," said Corson, without enthusiasm.

"So it is," laughed Diastor, "defense against the invasion of time and decay. We guard a golden moment of perfection, safely sealed in, deep in the cellars. Time may hammer at the casks, but cannot despoil the wine, only improve it. We not only wage war with time, we conquer, and make time serve us! Who can make that boast but a vintner?"

This speech was met with cheers by young and old alike. On certain things all the Edonaris of Vale could always agree.

16

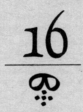

HALFWAY UP HONEYCOMB HILL, Nyctasia demanded a rest and collapsed on a stone ledge, panting and exhausted. She prided herself on her stamina, but she had never tried to ascend such a steep slope on foot before.

'Deisha offered her a drink from the waterskin at her waist, and Raphe brought her some of the golden grapes to refresh her. The entire hillside was terraced with his grafted vines.

Corson grinned down at her. "Shall I carry you the rest of the way, milady?"

"We can't all be muscle-bound monstrosities," Nyctasia said serenely.

"Oh, like 'Deisha here?"

"I've climbed these hills all my life!" 'Deisha flared. "Nyc's a scholar, she—"

But both Corson and Nyctasia were laughing now. "Don't mind Corson, love," Nyctasia chuckled. "She just likes to put me in my place. And furthermore, she's right, though I hate to encourage her effrontery by saying so." Nyctasia's tone became more serious. "I *ought* to be able to climb this hill as well as you can—it's a violation of the Balance—"

"Oh no," said Corson, "I've started her off. I should have known better."

"—between the Dwelling and the Indwelling," Nyctasia continued. "That I should be so weak shows that I haven't done my duty to this Dwelling." As she spoke, she made the Vahnite sign for the body, touching both hands quickly to her heart and crossing them on her breast. "Look at those people, some of them twice my age and more, and no whit wearied by this climb. It shames me!" She pointed to a group of vine-workers who'd walked straight from their encampment at the foot of the hill to the top rows of vines without pausing, only waving a greeting as they passed. The harvesters camped near the crops at this season, pruning and weeding and keeping off the birds, but mainly waiting to be at hand, ready for the crush.

One of the overseers approached to confer with Raphe, and they drew aside to talk undisturbed. 'Deisha, meanwhile, attempted to apologize to Corson for her sharpness, but Corson only laughed. "Nyc may be weak, but she needs no champion in an argument," she assured 'Deisha. "Her tongue's as able as anyone's."

Corson was in a fine humor that morning. She'd made an excellent breakfast in good company, the prospect of a treasure-hunt was still before her, and Raphe's continued attentions were a source of satisfaction to her as well. He was a rich man, after all, and if not titled himself, he was at least brother to a future Jhaice. She'd show Steifann that she was welcome under other roofs than his! When she returned to Chiastelm she'd let him know that she found favor with the gentry—even Rhaicimes pursued her. . . .

Raphe returned, and they began their climb again, only halting now and then as he pointed out to the workers where the trellis-cords needed tightening or where bushy new shoots near the ground should be trimmed.

"Ansen says there have been more thefts," he reported to 'Deisha. "A hen is missing now, and some coils of rope." He sounded worried. "And of course they say it's the ghosts' doing."

"Is she sure it was someone from outside the camp?"

"Well, so she says, and we've always found her honest."

'Deisha sighed. "Very well, I'll send them a hen—and a good watchdog to guard the encampment. That should put a stop to this business."

"Thanks, that would be best, I think. We daren't take chances, so close to crush." He turned to Corson and Nyctasia, explaining,

"We must keep these people satisfied, you see. It's hard to find harvesters enough to work this hill—most folk won't venture so near to those cursed ruins. I'm glad you suggested this expedition, Corson. It may give them confidence to see us going there."

"But we needn't worry about ghosts and demons while Nyc is with us," Corson said wickedly. "She knows all about such things."

Nyctasia winced. Not only was she secretive, from force of habit, but it was not always wise to let it be known that one was familiar with spellcraft. There were many lands where all magicians were regarded with distrust. "I have made a study of thaumaturgy," she conceded stiffly, "but I've also made a study of philosophy, astronomy, history and botany. Corson makes a point of it because she has a superstitious dislike of magic."

"Ha!" Corson snorted, "she got us both thrown out of an inn in Hlasven because she threatened to raise a demon. Take care she doesn't change you both to—"

"Don't let folk hear you talk like that, even in jest," Raphe cautioned, looking about uneasily. "Not here."

"Well, she did," Corson said, in a lowered tone.

"Corson, I would gladly turn you into a wild ass, if some other wizard had not been beforehand at it."

"Ah, mind what you say, Nyc. You've convinced your kin here that you've a sweet temper. It won't do to let them see what an evil-tongued shrew you really are."

"The gentlest nature would lose patience with your insupportable insolence!"

"Enlighten me, I beg you," Raphe interrupted. "However did the pair of you travel all the way from the coast together without murdering one another?"

"Through the grace of the *vahn*," said Nyctasia.

"By luck," said Corson, at the same time.

They sat on the remaining stones of a fallen wall and ate the grapes they'd brought with them, enjoying the cool breezes on the heights. From the summit of the hill they could see most of the valley, the vine-covered slopes, the neat golden squares that were fields of grain, the pale, light green stretches of cornfields and the dark black-green masses of woodland. Through this varied landscape wound the Southern Trade Road, and glimpses of the lakes shone a clear blue between the hills, reflecting the sky.

Nyctasia leaned back to look up at the great bell-tower looming over them. Most of the doors and lower windows had been boarded over. "Is the bell ever rung?"

Raphe shook his head. "Never since the fire. I expect the rope's rotted through by now. The whole structure's none too steady—a high wind rocks it."

Nyctasia was surprised. "But the walls are so thick. Look." She pointed to one of the high windows. "It ought to be sturdy enough. We couldn't climb it, I suppose?"

"No," said the twins together, and 'Deisha continued, "Mother 'Charis says she climbed it as a child, and saw all the way from the mountains to the river. But it's said to be far too dangerous now."

Corson, who hated heights, quickly changed the subject. "How much of this land belonged to the Circle?"

Raphe pointed down the hillside and across the intervening fields. "Those were their living quarters and kitchens, down there, across the way. There's not much left to see of them, just some tumbledown halls and an old well. There were cornfields and wheatfields in between—they were torched—and greengardens. And this was the temple, of course. There's an open courtyard inside that must have been beautiful once."

"Where was the library?" Nyctasia asked. "Here, or near the living-quarters?"

"Library? I don't know—do you, 'Deisha?"

"I've never heard tell of one."

"There must have been a library of some sort, if they were scholars and teachers," Nyctasia said, disappointed. The neglected and fragmentary library of the Edonaris household was yet another thing that made her feel out of place there. Her newfound family had little leisure or inclination for study.

"Wherever it was, it's sure to have been burned."

"Of course," sighed Nyctasia.

"Those orchards were theirs as well," Raphe continued. "I mean to have those trees looked after, next year, if I can find the time. I want to try to press some of the fruit for wine, or blend the juices with grape. The family think the idea's an outrage, of course, but I can't see why other fruits besides grapes shouldn't make a good wine—apples, say, or pears."

"Peaches," said Nyctasia. "They grew peach trees here somewhere."

"Yes, but how did you know that?"

"We spent a night in those ruins on the way here," Corson

explained, "and helped ourselves to some of your fruit for our breakfast."

"Why, of course—that's where we must have been," said Nyctasia. "But I was thinking of this." She took out the worn paper and read aloud:

> "Wholesome is my fruit and sweet,
>   Fit for nourishment at need,
>   But within the savory meat
>   Ever hides the deadly seed.

What could that be but a peach? You can brew a mortal poison from the pith of a peach-stone."

"You *would* know a thing like that," said Corson.

'Deisha was studying the paper now, with Raphe looking over her shoulder. "Do you think this might really have to do with the Cymvelans, then?" she asked in surprise.

"There's a riddle about the bell-tower too," Corson pointed out.

Raphe remained doubtful. "What of this one? It's senseless, listen—

> Builder, brewer, confectioner, chanter, chandler,
> Ever-armed guardian of garden's golden guerdon,
> Envy of alchemy, apothecary, artisan and architect.

Now what does that mean, I ask you?"

Corson glanced at the riddle. "The answer's in plain sight, for anyone who can read," she gloated, in a creditable imitation of Nyctasia. "It's about bees."

Nyctasia gave her a withering look, and explained the key to the riddle to Raphe and 'Deisha.

"'Ever-armed' I see," mused Raphe, "but why 'chandler'?"

"Beeswax candles," suggested 'Deisha.

"And 'apothecary'?"

"Honey's used in the preparation of certain medicaments," Nyctasia offered.

"'Brewer'?"

"Mead," said Corson promptly.

"And I suppose 'envy of alchemy' means that bees create gold from baser elements, if we allow honey to be gold? Rather far-fetched, if you ask me."

"It's not particularly profound, I agree," said Nyctasia. "In fact, it's a poor effort altogether—I suspect that it's more an exercise in composition than a true attempt at verse."

"Because it doesn't rhyme properly?" 'Deisha hazarded.

"No, actually it follows a highly complex pattern of consonance. You see, the vowels have alliterative value as well as—"

Corson recognized the absorbed, pensive tone of voice that always foretold one of Nyctasia's learned discourses. Privately, she thought of these as 'fits.' "It's one of her fits coming on," she said gloomily. "Don't pay her any mind or she'll go nattering on like that for hours. What I want to know is, did they keep bees here or didn't they?"

"I've no idea," said 'Deisha, but Raphe nodded. "There are hives at the far edge of the orchard. I saw them once when I was looking over the fruit trees."

"And were there, by any chance, wind-harps in any of the trees?"

Raphe stared at her, then looked back at the page. "Harp . . . !" he breathed, "and the well's here, too. 'Deisha, look at this—'Within four walls and yet beneath the sky'!"

"Why of course!" cried 'Deisha.

"What is it?" asked Corson and Nyctasia together.

'Deisha was already on her feet. "The inner courtyard, this way!"

Raphe grabbed her. "Not so hasty—the floor's liable to give way in there, you know. Mind where you walk."

The two led the way through a gap in the wall, where there had once been a doorway. The room beyond might have served well enough as answer to the riddle, for the wooden roof had completely burned and fallen in. They picked their way cautiously over beams and around the building-stones that littered the tesselated floor. Where the pattern of tiles was intact, it showed parts of the sign of the Cymvela, the interlaced circular design here set into a great four-pointed star that reached to the four corners of the room. "Only step where the tiles are whole," Raphe cautioned.

Nyctasia stopped and looked closely at the tiles. "The pattern is scuffed. I think they must have danced here." Mesmerized, she began to walk around the design, trying to find the path through the maze. "A right, then another, then . . . no, wait . . ." she murmured. "Did I turn this way yet? Left . . ."

Corson watched her uneasily, trying to imagine the room filled with people, dancing and singing. What had they been like? Probably no better, or no worse, than the rest of us, she decided, for whatever that's worth. And no more deserving of such a cruel end than anyone else. Hlann preserve us from the fate we deserve. Surprised at her own thoughts, she shrugged them off and bent to peer through a hole in the floor. "Have the cellars been searched?" she asked.

"Time and again," said 'Deisha, passing through an archway to an inner chamber, and beckoning for the others to follow.

The next room was smaller and narrower, also roofless, but with more of its walls standing, still displaying bright mural-work on their cracked and blistered plastering. Some of the paintings had been scarred by fire, but their colors were still rich and unfaded, and the figures seemed to leap out at the viewer, alive and vivid. Astonished, Corson and Nyctasia walked all around the room, stopping first at one scene, then at another.

One that held them both depicted a dance of sorts. Men and women had joined hands in a ring, and they circled around a great tree burdened with golden fruit. Their wide, uplifted eyes gazed at the branches, which were intertwined to form the mark of the Cymvelan Circle. The roots were also drawn clearly, gnarled and twisted, but they did not seem to form any pattern. The dancers who faced outward were all drawn alike, and their expression was solemn and severe.

Many of the drawings were renderings of the maze, drawn in all sorts of fanciful ways. One that Corson especially liked showed a flock of long-tailed birds wheeling in the sky. Standing back from it a bit, she saw plainly that their flight traced out the labyrinth.

"Mazes are a common sign of the devious paths we follow in our search for experience," Nyctasia pondered. "Many peoples have used them to represent the difficulties and confusions that beset wayfarers on the perilous journey we all make—"

Raphe winked at Corson, who snickered lustily.

"The spiritual journey," Nyctasia amended, "that *some* of us make, from ignorance to knowledge." She crossed the room to examine the painting on the opposite wall.

Nyctasia stood long before this last picture. The others had awed her with their beauty, but this one was different, and disturbing. It seemed to be an older drawing than the others, more crudely drawn, its colors duller—but it was not the less arresting for that. It too depicted a dance, but instead of the stately figures portrayed in the first painting, this one showed creatures half-human, half-bestial, shambling around the body of a slain animal.

The naked dancers were men and women below the waist, but their hands were taloned like hawks' feet, and their mouths were long, cruel snouts. Nyctasia paced back and forth between the two paintings, silently comparing them. *What has gone before will return again . . .* she thought, frowning to herself. *It is so. We do not live only in the present.*

There were doorways on all four sides of the room, and 'Deisha pointed out the one across from the entrance. "The courtyard is through there," she said impatiently. "You can look at these moldering paintings another time." She had pulled Nyctasia away from the grim scene and toward the door, when Corson stopped her and motioned the others to wait.

"Listen—" she whispered, "music. There's someone in there."

17

THE FOUNTAIN, BEING of brass, had been blackened by the fire but not destroyed, and its beauty was still quite evident. Around the rim of the broad, shallow basin was a ring of slender stems of brass, curving gracefully inward then arching back toward the edge, each crowned with a pendant brazen lily. Two inner circles of stalks rose above the first, the innermost arching high over the heads of the four viewers. A tracery of delicately crafted reeds and leaves wove between the tall flowers, complementing the stark grace of the design.

But it was not only the beauty of the fountain that made it unique. More remarkable still was the haunting melody that filled the air when the wind blew through the open courtyard. Each bronze flower was a bell that chimed gently, stirred by the breeze, and flutelike tones of varying pitches rose and fell as air was forced through holes bored in the hollow stems.

"I believe there'd be some sound even when water flowed through it," said Raphe. "But in winter they'd have stopped the water, and then they must have heard it like this—a wind fountain."

"And during the drought," said 'Deisha solemnly.

"Yes, and ever since the fire—giving rise to tales of ghosts here in the temple. A storm or high wind would probably produce quite shrill, piercing notes, and that, I suspect, is what accounts for the shrieks heard here, though I wouldn't dare tell Aunt Mesthelde so."

Nyctasia slipped between two of the stalks in the outer ring to admire the workmanship of one of the swaying lilies in the middle row, which reached almost to the height of her heart. The floral bell hung down at a natural angle, opening slightly outward, and the veins of each petal had been carefully molded by the sculptor. Nyctasia fit one small hand within the bell and found that even the inside of the flower had been reproduced in some detail. Beneath the back of the stamen-shaped clapper, she felt the opening to the hollow stem. "So the water came right from the throats of the flowers," she guessed, imagining the interlocking arcs of bright water leaping and crossing in the sunlight to fall and fill the dry, dirty pool at her feet. "We have some fine fountains at home, but nothing like so complex as this. It must have been magnificent."

"I'd like to have it repaired," said Raphe, "but we'd have to send to the Imperial City of Celys for artisans with such skills. There'll never be money enough for a thing like that."

"There would be, if we found the treasure," Corson reminded the others impatiently. She had tested the fountain in several places, with the edge of her knife, and found the metal all too hard to be gold. "Here we are, neither out of doors nor in, and what are we supposed to find? There's nothing here but that rut—wretched, tricksy fountain, and it's only brass. Is that the whole of the mystery?"

"It wouldn't seem so," said Nyctasia. "We can all see the fountain. What is it that's in plain sight that we can't see?"

They all looked about them in bewilderment. The courtyard was empty save for the fountain and a scorched dead tree. The ground was unpaved, overgrown with weeds and tall, rippling grasses.

An idea occurred to Corson, a solution so hideously fitting that she groaned aloud. "Not 'in plain sight,' but *'unhidden,'* " she said in deep disgust. "It's nothing but the *wind!* It's found in here because the fountain makes it known, but no one can see it. I might have guessed the treasure would be something worthless. Curse the Cymvelans and their rutting riddles! Stop laughing, Nyc, you bitch!"

Nyctasia tried to oblige, but without much success, for Raphe and 'Deisha had joined in the merriment. "Sorry, Corson," she gasped, "but I'm afraid you're right. Rowan told us these were rhymes for children—but it should console you to know that you're the cleverest child of us all."

A gust of wind set all the chimes jangling melodiously, and even Corson smiled, if rather sourly. "I'd be more consoled by the 'wealth beyond a lifetime's spending.' Let's see the rest of this fool place, since we've come all this way." She ducked through one of the other doors and disappeared into an adjoining chamber.

"Wait for us," called Raphe.

The rest followed, still chuckling. "'A web to catch the wind,'" said Nyctasia. "I begin to like these Cymvelans."

* * *

'Deisha read:

> "Neither in the open air
> Neither in a dwelling
> Seek, if so be that you dare,
> Riches perilous and rare
> Danger beyond telling,
> Where the earth doth secrets keep
> For the wellspring's weal lies deep.
> Wealth beyond a lifetime's spending
> Power beyond measure
> Everlasting, never-ending
> Treachery or treasure.

"That's all there is," said 'Deisha. "It sounds like the court-yard again."

"It's bound to be something else that's not worth a straw," Corson predicted. "Fire, I daresay—or more likely water. There was plenty of water in that courtyard once. Those two riddles are a pair, mark my words, wind and water. They both have to do with the fountain."

"That's probably it," Raphe agreed. "Water is a never-ending source of power. Waterwheels turn most of the mills in the valley, along the River Sheivoln."

"And it can be treacherous, especially at spring thaw," 'Deisha said thoughtfully. "When there's too much rain and melting ice at once, the river can overflow its banks, and the valley fills up like a bowl. There have been seasons of flooding that carried off homes, and drowned people and livestock. . . . Drought or flood, there's always danger of both. Every spring, year after year, folk worry—will there be enough rain? Will there be too much? Most years all goes well, but the danger is always there. I think Corson's right—water."

"Winter turning into spring, children dancing in a ring," recited Nyctasia. "And here we are, back where we began." For the temple itself was round, a ring of rooms about the inner courtyard. All the doors led either to the center or, finally, back to the entranceway.

The rest of the rooms had been a disappointment, empty and littered with debris. In the last room they passed through they discovered the remains of a fire, and the bones and feathers of a hen. "It seems that the ghost who haunts the harvesters' encampment has a healthy appetite," said 'Deisha.

"That one would be a ghost soon enough if I had my way," Raphe vowed. "Alarming the workers at a time like this! Well, we can tell Ansen that the mystery is solved—it was only some vagabond, after all."

"By all means, let's have no more mysteries," said Nyctasia. "We're all agreed about the final riddle, thank the *vahn*. I only hope we're right about it."

"I don't," said Corson.

"I know, but I didn't care for the threatening sound of the thing. All that about danger and treachery—it hardly seemed the kind of search one would set for children. But if it's only water . . . That solution has at least the virtue of safety."

Corson spat. "The real reason the Cymvelans were slaughtered was that folk grew sick of their stupid riddles! Let's get back down where there's some shade. Water isn't my idea of treasure, but I wouldn't mind having some just now."

"You shall have all you want," Raphe promised. "We'll go to Lake Teseren for a swim, if you like. It's barely an hour's ride."

"I don't hold with swimming," said Corson. "It's against nature. People have feet, not fins."

"As to that," said Nyctasia, "the earliest Eswraine myths say that people once lived in the water, like frogs. In fact, the word for 'ocean' and the word for 'womb' in Ancient Eswraine are very nearly—"

"But on a day like this," Corson interrupted, "I could soak in a stream with pleasure, I admit."

"All the children will want to come along," 'Deisha warned.

"Let them come," said her brother. "They can all swim well enough, even 'Lorin and Sparrow."

"I can't," said Nyctasia.

Raphe and 'Deisha stared at her. Raised on the lakes, they could hardly remember a time before they knew how to swim. "But you come from the coast!" 'Deisha protested.

"The borders of Rhostshyl are inland, a day's ride from the sea at best. We've made common cause with the Maritime cities, but we're not a port. Indeed, I've only seen the shore a few times in my life—I never had a reason to learn to swim."

"It's time you did then," cried 'Deisha, delighted at the opportunity to teach something to her accomplished cousin. "Fancy such ignorance, and you an Edonaris! Come along straightaway!"

* * *

The descent was not difficult, but the sun was directly overhead now, and beating down unmercifully. They were all glad to rest halfway down, in the shade of the same shelf of rock where Nyctasia had stopped before. Beneath the protruding stone a shallow recess cut into the hillside, one of the many caves that were common to the region. The chill, dark shelter was a welcome relief in the midday heat, and they crowded into it gratefully. The laborers had retreated to the shade of trees and tents at the foot of the hill for the long noon rest, not trusting the shelter of a cave on the haunted hill.

"No sun has struck here for a thousand years," said Raphe with satisfaction, reclining comfortably with his head in Corson's lap. "It would be perfect for a wine-keep if it were only deeper. We'll need more cellar-space in a few years if my plans bear fruit."

"What of the cellars at the temple?" Nyctasia suggested, leaning lazily against 'Deisha.

"They might do. I've not explored them properly. But I doubt we could find enough workers willing to set them to rights. It's hard even to get harvesters for the hill."

"Asye! If the place is so troublesome why don't you tear it down?" asked Corson.

There was a moment's shocked silence. "We couldn't do *that*. . . ." said 'Deisha.

"Why not?"

"It would be . . . disrespectful to destroy what's left of their sacred place. It would seem like defiance, as if we'd dared the Cymvelans to do their worst. Oh, I don't hold with the tales about the temple, but if something did happen we'd be blamed for it. Folk would say we'd brought down the wrath of the Circle, you see. It would be risky."

"I'd chance it," said Corson decidedly. "If you ask me, folk would thank you for ridding them of the bane. You lot are just like Nyc—you think too much. You dream up new troubles before you've done with the old. Sometimes it's action that's wanted, not ideas." She tweaked Raphe's nose spitefully. "Remember?"

He tried to bite her fingers. "That's all very well, my wild swan, but suppose we decided to raze the temple, where would we find people willing to do the work? No one in these parts would dare have a hand in it. So there we are."

"Aside from that," added 'Deisha, "think how distressed Aunt Mesthelde would be. She'd never know a moment's peace, waiting for ghostly vengeance to strike the family, foretelling disaster at every turn, warning folk away—there'd be no peace for the rest of us either."

"Now that is truly a terrifying notion," Corson acknowledged. "It would be a braver one than I who'd dare cross Lady Mesthelde's will. Let the temple stand!"

They all laughed, and no more was said of the matter, but Nyctasia wondered whether the twins had really explained their reluctance to tear down the temple. Beneath their glib arguments, had they in fact been frightened at the idea—and were they aware of it themselves? But, after all, what was there to fear?

As 'Deisha had foretold, their party increased in number appreciably before they set out for Lake Teseren that afternoon. Everyone who could be spared from the work in hand was in favor of the idea and hastened to fetch food and fishing nets and blankets for the outing. Those who were too little to ride alone were taken up behind the others or perched almost on the necks of the great patient workhorses ridden by the older children. Even 'Deisha's two favorite dogs came running alongside, barking and excited.

There were races along the way—which were strictly forbidden, of course—and halts to pick wild berries or to show some feature of the landscape to Corson and Nyctasia. Goats barred the path and had to be shooed away, a child was stung by a bee and comforted, but in time they reached a high bluff that divided the lake into two arms and sloped steeply to the shore on either side. Here they tethered the horses, and the children scrambled and slid down to the water's edge, disregarding the steps cut into the stone at intervals. The others followed more carefully, but Nyctasia lingered there, gazing out over the wide vista of rich green hills and bright water. The day was so clear that she could see the River Teseren and the towers of Amron Therain in the distance. All during the ride through the peaceful countryside, she had been possessed by a sense of heart's ease and contentment, kindled by a longing she could not put a name to. The delicate, dappled branches of young trees in the open meadows were patterned so perfectly against the dark mass of ancient woodland that they seemed to hold a message for her—a meaning that she might read if only she looked long and hard enough. Summer's infinite shades of green blended seamlessly, as far as the eye could see, illumined here and there by the red-gold flames of autumn's beginning, or haunted by the slender specter of a white birch. Nyctasia felt somehow both humbled and exalted by all that she saw.

"What has gone before, will return again," she sang softly, unheard. How could it be doubted that Harmony was the Governing Principle of life? Even flood, even drought, were part of the design. The deep, serene waters of the lake below reflected these truths to her more fully than her studies had ever done.

"Nyc? Aren't you coming?" asked 'Deisha anxiously.

Nyctasia smiled in reply, and they started down the steep stairs of rock together. "It is no wonder that the valley has known peace for so long," she said. "You Valleylanders live all your days in the midst of a vast manifestation of Balance."

"I've not been raised a very good Vahnite, I'm afraid," 'Deisha said apologetically. "I don't really understand the Principles of Foundation, much less the Balances and Influences and all the rest. My people have never taken the Discipline much to heart."

"You understand the Principles well enough, my dear," said Nyctasia. "You understand them better than I do."

Nyctasia was unfamiliar with the etiquette of a swimming party, but when she saw that the others simply stripped off all of their clothing and stepped into the water, she did the same with no hesitation or show of surprise. The only possible course of conduct for a lady to adopt, under the circumstances, was to behave as if she had been accustomed to such ways all her life. And the shock of discovering how ice-cold lake water could be on such a hot day soon drove all other considerations from her mind.

Everyone was interested in teaching her to swim, including the dogs, who ran along the shore barking wildly, then even swam out a way to watch and offer encouragement. The children demonstrated their skills with a great deal of shrieking and thrashing about, until 'Deisha chased them out of the way. They splashed her furiously and went off to hunt for water-lizards under the large, flat stones along the shore. The others made free with suggestions and advice while Corson stood by and watched critically.

Nyctasia was first taught to float on her back. "You can never sink so long as you do this," 'Deisha assured her. "Any time you're tired you've only to turn over and drift in to shore. I've never understood how people can possibly drown when all they have to do is float to stay above water."

"That's because you only know these calm valley lakes," said Corson. "If breakers are beating at you, or ocean currents dragging you under, you can't just drift to safety. You have to fight, and you'll probably lose. You can't trust wild waters."

"'Dangers beyond telling' indeed!" said 'Deisha. "But Teseren's not treacherous, I promise you—though you might be bitten by a turtle if you don't watch where you step."

Corson looked down hastily. The lake bed was mainly shale, and the water brilliantly clear. There were no turtles underfoot at the moment.

"And there are leeches out farther, where the water-weeds begin," Raphe said matter-of-factly, "but only quite small ones. They usually drop off if you douse them with vinegar."

"Or touch a live ember to them," someone else put in.

Corson was already striding toward the shallows. "People weren't meant to swim!" she declared. "It's against nature! I knew it was so!"

Raphe splashed after her, calling, "And beware of sea serpents too! Great scaled snakes with sawtooth fins and four rows of fangs!" Corson made a determined effort to drown him while 'Deisha showed Nyctasia how to tread water.

"Now if you just do the same thing, on your belly, you can

swim the way the dogs do, but it's a lot of work without getting very far. It's more practical to lie on your side and use your whole arm and leg, like this." She swam in a slow, graceful circle around Nyctasia, turning from side to side. "Now you try it. I'll hold you. You needn't keep your head up."

When Nyctasia had mastered the sidestroke after a clumsy fashion, 'Deisha said, "Now watch this," drew a deep breath, and dove under the surface, heading out into the deep water. Nyctasia followed with her eyes for a surprisingly long time before 'Deisha finally resurfaced for air and disappeared again. Underwater, she moved with a flowing silken ease, gliding effortlessly toward Nyctasia through the bright, sunlit lake to leap up beside her and drape her with an armful of white and golden water lilies.

"Teach me to swim like *that*," said Nyctasia eagerly.

But there was little to learn. Though she had never imagined that human eyes could look up through water to the light, it seemed perfectly natural now, like something she had done before. She was strangely surprised to find that she had to rise to the surface to draw breath. Small, sun-yellow fish darted away from her, and she felt as sleek and swift as they. All the while there was a pulsing roar in her ears, which she took for the sound of waves beating on the shore till she remembered how still and calm the lake was. Soothing and somehow familiar, the rhythm echoed in her blood, "The *well*spring's *weal* lies *deep* . . . Neither *less* nor *more,* neither *sea* nor *shore* . . . neither *earth* nor *air. . . ."

When she next came up to breathe, she was alarmed to find herself at such a distance from shore, and panic seized her like a strangling hand. She couldn't possibly swim back so far! She floundered helplessly for a moment that seemed an eternity, but 'Deisha was beside her, treading water, reminding her calmly, "Float if you're tired, *float.*"

Nyctasia at once fell onto her back, stretching out, balancing her weight, letting the water bear her up. She lay still, resting, only stirring her arms gently to propel herself slowly toward land. She drifted in lazy serenity, watching the crazed, crimson flames that the sunlight kindled behind her closed eyelids, and after a time she let herself drop down again and confidently made for shore. 'Deisha raced her and won, but not by much.

They surfaced together, gasping and laughing, to wade through the shallows with clusters of silver minnows tickling their ankles. Now it was the water that felt warm, and the air chill against wet skin. Nyctasia shivered and sneezed.

The younger children ran up to show them the shiny stones they'd collected, and the dogs galloped over to greet them and shake spray from their coats in all directions. Nyctasia stumbled painfully on the sharp stones underfoot. The others' feet were hardened from years of running barefoot, but every pebble seemed to cut Nyctasia cruelly. Finally she sat down on one of the great flat boulders, half in and half out of the water, and refused to take another step until someone fetched her sandals. The children scampered off to find them, each eager for the honor, with the dogs chasing after them. 'Deisha knelt in the water before Nyctasia to rub her bruised and aching feet. "A dainty, lady's foot, tender as a baby's," she said, smiling, and kissed it playfully. "We'll have to take better care of you."

"I shall have to adapt," said Nyctasia seriously.

"I think you're taking root very well," said Raphe, wading up to them in waist-deep water. "Come talk sense to Corson, she won't listen to me."

"No one can make Corson listen if she's not of a mind to," Nyctasia assured him, but she was glad to slip back into the lake and follow, drifting and swimming out to the rocky point of land where Corson was stretched out on the warm stone, sunning herself. Nyctasia held to a low boulder and pulled herself partway out of the water to reach up and splash Corson liberally. "Aren't you coming for a swim at all, you lazy great slug? The water's splendid here!"

Corson rolled over and looked down at her balefully. "You're welcome to it. I watched you—you might have drowned out there, fool!"

Nyctasia looked at her a moment, puzzled, then exclaimed in astonishment, "Why, you can't swim, Corson, can you?" At once she was sorry she'd spoken, knowing how Corson hated to ask for help or admit to any sort of weakness. But it was too late to recall her words.

Corson glared at her. "What of it?" she demanded. "I only know what I learned in the army. They thought it enough if we could fight on foot and on horseback. I wasn't trained for a fisher!"

"But this is sport, love," urged Raphe. "You'll enjoy it."

"We'll teach you—it's easy. Nyc's doing well already," 'Deisha said encouragingly.

But Corson would not be coaxed out into deeper water, and Nyctasia soon put a stop to their teasing. "Let her be," she said, climbing up beside Corson and waving to the children who were carrying all her things about in search of her. "Corson has a cat's nature, and hates the water. And I'm rather tired myself."

"Well, it is time we thought of getting back," said 'Deisha. "Nesanye's left already." She joined Nyctasia and shook herself like one of her dogs. "Let's see if any of the brats has been eaten by a pike." She surveyed the pack of children who soon surrounded them. "Where are Bean and 'Lorin?"

"Uncle N'sanye took Lorrie home," Sparrow volunteered, and someone else accounted for Bean to 'Deisha's satisfaction. Most of the the others had gone already, and the rest soon followed, rounding up the children and their own scattered clothes. Nyctasia found that she really was tired, though she had only said so to keep the twins from pressing Corson to swim. They had come too close to discovering what Nyctasia had realized only just in time —that Corson was deathly afraid of the water. She'd never forgive me if I'd given that away, Nyctasia thought soberly.

The afternoon of swimming, after the morning's hard climb, had taken its toll of Nyctasia's strength, and by the time they reached home she was fit for nothing more than collapsing across her bed in exhaustion. Her legs and arms ached to the bone, and there was a fierce, smarting pain across her shoulders.

When she failed to appear for dinner, both Corson and 'Deisha went in search of her. "It's discourteous to your hosts not to come to meals," Corson reminded her. "Get up, you indolent lout."

"Summon the guards," Nyctasia groaned. "Take this woman away, throw her in a dungeon, disembowel her, get her out of my sight. Let me die in peace."

"My poor Nyc, shall I bring you some dinner then?" cooed 'Deisha.

"Thank you, no. I'm not hungry. I can hardly move, I'm stiff as stone."

"Exercise is the best thing for that—up you get," said Corson cheerfully, grabbing her by the arm.

But Nyctasia shrieked so feelingly that Corson let go at once. "Sweet *vahn,* my back—!"

"What is it?" cried 'Deisha. "Let me see." She carefully pulled Nyctasia's shirt down over her shoulders and revealed the angry red-scorched skin. "Oh, no—how sunburnt you are! I should have thought of that, and you with that fair complexion. I'm so sorry, Nyc. Don't stir a finger, I'll fetch some unguent of arrowleaf right away."

Corson held a hand over Nyctasia's back and gave a whistle. "Hot as an oven! Is it very sore?"

"I feel as if I've been lashed with leather."

"No you don't," said Corson, who'd been flogged more than once in the army. "But it does look something nasty. Can't you heal a thing like that with your spells?"

"If I must. But arrowleaf will do it better. A burn will mend of its own accord. It's unwise to create an Influence where none is needed. Natural healing leaves one stronger, but spell-healing can weaken instead, if it's not used with caution. You ought to understand that, Corson, since you're such a champion of nature."

Corson shrugged. "No doubt you know best. I'd better be off. They expect me at table, and it doesn't do to keep one's hosts waiting. There's fresh lake trout with dinner, by the way."

"I hope you choke on a bone," Nyctasia muttered into her ‚pillow.

'Deisha returned with a clay pot sealed with wax and filled with a white salve. When she cut through the seal, a sharp, tangy fragrance pierced the air for a moment.

"That's mint, not arrowleaf," said Nyctasia.

"No, look." 'Deisha showed her the impression of narrow, pointed leaves that had been pressed into the side of the pot before the clay was baked. "It's only been scented with mint leaves to sweeten the smell. It was Aunt Mesthelde's notion."

"And a good one," said Nyctasia, with admiration. "I've never thought of it." It was the last thing she'd have expected from the tart, practical Mesthelde. No doubt there was a lesson in that, she thought.

"Oh, she's the clever one, to be sure. She makes most of our medicaments herself. This will soon put you to rights." 'Deisha began lightly to smooth the creamy ointment over Nyctasia's raw, stinging shoulders. It had a cold, tingling feel at first that soon gave way to a welcome numbness. 'Deisha worked with a gentle, circular motion of her fingertips that Nyctasia found restful and soothing.

"You have the touch of a healer, cousin."

"Oh, after tending to hurt animals, nursing a person's easy."

"Not always," said Nyctasia, remembering the days she'd spent with the ailing Corson in Lhestreq.

"I'll gladly nurse you anytime." 'Deisha leaned forward to kiss the nape of Nyctasia's blistered neck, very carefully. "Tomorrow your skin will peel off like a lizard's. Thank the stars you swam underwater much of the time."

"I thought Rhostshyl was a dangerous place," Nyctasia said sleepily, "but I'd no idea how hazardous the world outside the city was. The sea makes you ill, the sun flays you alive—it's a wonder anyone lives to an old age."

"We're a long-lived family."

"Unless we're murdered," Nyctasia agreed. It was true, the Edonaris often lived well past fourscore years, especially in the female line.

"To listen to you, one would think you did nothing at all but murder one another in Rhostshyl."

Something in her tone made Nyctasia ask sharply, "'Deisha, *you* don't think of going there?"

"Well, I don't mean to take part in a war, of course. . . . But I would like to see the city someday. I think we all would."

"So would I," murmured Nyctasia, "someday. . . ." She was silent for so long that 'Deisha thought she'd fallen asleep, and quietly slipped from the room, stepping softly and stealthily.

Nyctasia let her go. She was too tired for more talk, and 'Deisha must surely be starving for her dinner. She'll be late again, Nyctasia thought, smiling. Rousing herself sufficiently to sit up, she dipped her fingers into the salve, which 'Deisha had left at her bedside, and dabbed a little of it on her nose and cheekbones. She winced as she rubbed some into her collarbone, which felt scraped even by the touch of the pillow. But to her relief she found that she could now lie on her back, as long as she stayed quite still. Cautiously stretching out her arms, she let her weariness wash over her, and she felt that she was again floating languidly on the lake, warmed by the sun, cooled by the fresh water, and fearing no treachery from either. She could almost feel the gentle rippling of the waves beneath her, and the golden glare of sunshine again played in mad patterns upon her eyelids. She drifted into sleep, lulled by the ceaseless murmuring of the waters.

In her dreams a great iron bell was tolling a warning that grew louder and more urgent by the moment. Nyctasia ran weakly the rest of the way to the tower, exhausted by her climb but desperate to know what catastrophe had demanded the sounding of the tocsin after its years of silence. But then it was she herself who was

pulling with all her strength at the bell-rope, and she knew without question that it was her duty to warn those below of the
coming flood. Each swing of the heavy bell nearly lifted her off
her feet, and each time she brought down the rope a searing pain
racked her shoulders, but she dared not leave off. If the deluge
took the valley unawares the deaths of all its folk would be on her
hands. The bell swung ever more wildly overhead, tearing at the
rotted beams that held it aloft.

"Fool, it will fall and crush you! Come away!" a man shouted
from somewhere behind her.

The very foundations of the tower seemed to be shaking, but
Nyctasia grimly kept on with her task. "The fountain is working
again, doh't you see?" she cried. "None of our artisans knows
how to stem it at the source—the whole valley will be flooded!"

"Let be, the earth is parched," he called, and Mhairestri
agreed, "Only thus will the drought be quenched. . . ."

Nyctasia sobbed in pain and confusion. "But blood is as salt
as brine, it will kill the crops, all the young vines—" She woke
with a cry, her shoulders still throbbing with pain, the sound of
the bell still thundering in the air. She knew but a moment's relief
that she had only been dreaming, for she realized at once that a
warning bell *was* ringing loudly in the dead of night, somewhere
nearby. Her first waking thought was, *War!*

18

NYCTASIA SEIZED HER dagger and raced out into the corridor, where she found Corson, half-dressed and sword in hand, coming to meet her. There was a great deal of shouting and confusion below. "You're all right?" said Corson. "What—"

'Deisha burst upon them, still pulling on her shirt, and laughing in excitement. "Put away your arms!" she cried. "I thought you'd be alarmed, but there's nothing to fear. The Royal Crimson are ripe! The crush has begun! I *must* hurry—" She hugged Nyctasia wildly and darted away, not hearing her gasp of pain at this assault on her sunburned back. Corson and Nyctasia stared at each other and started to laugh.

"I suppose they need every able hand," sighed Corson, "but you'd think it could wait till morning . . . !"

"They'll not expect you to join in the work, Corson, you're a guest. No one would think the worse of you if you went back to bed."

"Who could sleep with that rutting bell ringing, and all the carryings-on? I might as well be in the thick of it."

"Well, it's good of you, but please come rub some more salve on me before you go, will you? I shan't be joining you, not tonight. My back's a blazing brand!"

* * *

Nyctasia woke toward noon to find that she seemed to be completely alone in the house. It was not difficult, however, to follow the sound of voices to the courtyard, where long tables had been set up in the open and covered with food and drink. No one was seated at them, though. The harvesters—the Edonaris and their hirelings alike—came and went in a steady stream, standing about long enough to wolf down a quick meal, then hurrying back to their labors. Nyctasia saw that most of the food had been prepared beforehand, to spare even the kitchen workers for the all-important task of bringing in the grapes for pressing. There were huge platters of smoked meats, bowls of pickled vegetables, pots of preserves and mounds of dried fruits, along with rounds of cheese as big as cart-wheels. But the bread was fresh and plentiful, and immense casks of ale stood at either end of the main table, to wash down the smoked meat and salted fish.

As soon as the platters were emptied, they were snatched away to the kitchens to be loaded again and returned, often by children who looked to Nyctasia much too small to carry them. Mesthelde was everywhere at once, filling pitchers, carving meat, giving orders and supervising all other activities at once. She nodded curtly to Nyctasia and said, "Have something to eat, and keep out of the way or you'll be trampled. And stay out of the sun."

"I thought I'd go help with the harvesting," said Nyctasia rather diffidently. She was still stiff and sore, but now that she'd rested she felt well enough to take part in the work somehow. But could she really do anything to help?

"Nonsense, you'd not last half an hour at the gathering. If you want to be of some use, cut up this joint." She waved a sharp carving knife in Nyctasia's direction and stalked off to attend to something else.

Nyctasia was by now feeling the lack of her last night's dinner. She chopped a thick slice from a warm loaf and poured honey on it, fresh from the comb. It tasted better than anything she'd ever eaten.

Between bites, she began energetically to slice the meats and loaves so that the harvesters could snatch up their food all the more quickly and carry it off with them. There were no mealtimes, it seemed, or any of the regular rhythms of daily life. Though the harvesting was in fact a carefully ordered and harmonious effort, it had all the appearance of chaos, nonetheless, and it was easy to see why the children looked forward to it every year.

As she worked, someone handed her one of the wide-brimmed straw hats they all wore, to keep the sun from her face. Nyctasia found that there was plenty for her to do. She fetched food, she helped look after the smaller children, she carried water to the workers, she scrubbed platters and bowls at the well with the other scullions. No one would have asked a Rhaicime to perform such menial tasks, but finding her willing to set her hand to anything, the others accepted her as one of themselves and treated her accordingly.

Nyctasia had never done the sort of labor that not only required no thought, but indeed kept her too busy to think, and she threw herself into it gladly, for there was much that she didn't wish to think about. Caught up in the frantic whirl of activity, she laughed and chatted with the rest, encouraging the pickers and speculating about the success of the crop. She soon lost all track of time, of days, often working far into the night, for the harvesting and pressing would not stop for a moment till the last of the juice had been sealed in casks. Everyone slept in snatches, and Nyctasia heard some of the harvesters boast that they could pick grapes in their sleep without missing a single one.

"Aunt Nyc!" One of the children stood tugging at her sleeve as she poured out mugs of ale in a row. It was one of 'Deisha's nephews, who had decided that Nyctasia too must be an aunt, since she looked so much like 'Deisha.

"Hungry, little one?" Nyctasia offered him a peach, which he accepted readily, but instead of running off he stayed at her side, still demanding her attention. She must come with him, he insisted, dragging at her arm. Mama Nona wanted her.

No one else seemed to be looking after the child, so Nyctasia allowed him to lead her away, out of the courtyard and up a flight of stone steps to one of the upper terraces, where he said Mama Nona was waiting.

"You're getting so brown, my dear, soon we won't know you from 'Deisha."

"Lady Nocharis! Fool that I am, I didn't realize it was you he meant. How good to see you." She offered her hands to the old woman, who was seated in the shade of a tall flowering tree at the edge of the terrace. At her feet were a few of the children, busily braiding together strands of straw to be woven into more of the light sun-hats. Lady Nocharis had a half-finished hat on her lap, and she went on twining and turning it as she spoke.

"You must call me Mother 'Charis like the others. How are you getting on? Let me look at you—you seem rather peaked, I think."

"Oh, I'm very well. I've never felt so well. Is there anything I can fetch you?"

"I'm excellently looked after, I assure you. Just sit down and rest for a little, and bear me company. I've watched you slaving away at ten things at once, like Mesthelde. You'll wear yourself to a shadow if we let you."

"The others all worker harder, I think." But Nyctasia obediently sat down on the stone balustrade and began to try plaiting a few pieces of straw. From here she could see many of the slopes, the main courtyard, and even the yard, around the corner of the house, where the immense barrel-presses had been set up. Grapes were being loaded into them constantly out of the carts filled by the pickers, and the dark, almost black, juice flowed out steadily through the spaces between the lower slats of the great barrel, into the circular trough that surrounded it. From there it was scooped up with lipped vessels and emptied into waiting casks on a low wagon nearby. I could do that, Nyctasia thought, but she said only, "So you watch over all of us from here."

"During the crush, at least—one must feel a part of the harvesting somehow, you know. I've been watching you both. That is your friend, is it not, the giantess trying to turn a press all on her own?"

Atop each of the presses was a platform, reached by a tall ladder, where people walked in slow, endless circles on either side of the central shaft, pushing the cross-bar that turned it and lowered the press-wheel. Corson was not really trying to do this by herself, but she was alone on one side of the shaft, while there were two or three people on both sides of all the others.

Nyctasia laughed. "Yes indeed, that's Corson. She does like to show off. Do you know, I've always believed that people crushed grapes with their *feet?*"

"So they do, when there's only a small crop, to make wine for the household. It wouldn't be worthwhile to keep a large press for that. But it's far too slow for our ends, and too much fruit is wasted that way." She had finished the hat, which she now gave to one of the children. "You've done very nicely, 'Kadri. Run and put this with the rest now. And you 'Risha, tell Liss that I'll go in to rest soon. Then both of you go right to the kitchen for your milk, yes?"

"Yes, Nona," they chorused. When they had each kissed her and scampered off, she turned and beckoned to Nyctasia.

"And what am *I* to do, Mother?" Nyctasia asked, smiling. "I've had my milk this morning."

"You sit here by me, my dear, and tell me some more about this friend of yours. We don't often see a sword-for-hire here. You trust this woman?"

"With my life," said Nyctasia without hesitation. So that was what the matriarch hadn't wished to say before the children. "I trust her absolutely, and I do not give my trust lightly."

"Ah." The old woman searched Nyctasia's face carefully. "So she is not dangerous? Mesthelde swears she'll cut all our throats one night and make off with everything of value in the house, but Raphe, now, declares that she's a lamb." She smiled as she spoke, but Nyctasia knew that the question was asked in earnest.

"She is most certainly dangerous," she answered promptly, "and I daresay she's no stranger to brigandry, but this household has nothing to fear from her." She gestured toward the yard where the presses were turning steadily. "That same pride that makes her flaunt her strength thus would never let her betray the trust of those who've befriended her. Perhaps she does not know herself how honest she is, but I stand warrant for her, upon my own honor. Would you have me speak of this to Lady Mesthelde? Will she be satisfied with my word?"

"I am satisfied. Leave Mesthelde to me. Indeed, now that she's seen how hard this cutthroat is working, I daresay she'll be better disposed to her."

"Unless I mistake, Corson will soon be on her way, at all events. She wants to get back to her people at Chiastelm before winter."

"Then she's given up her quest for the treasure?"

The matriarch obviously knew everything that was said or done in the household. "Poor Corson! She wasn't such a fool as to have much hope for that treasure, but still it does seem hard on her." Nyctasia recited some of the riddles for Lady Nocharis, and related their disappointing solutions.

"The fountain, how well I remember it. What a marvel—I often played in it as a child, and I believed it was magic that made it sing. The water was always fresh and cold, like well-water. The source, I think, must have been a spring deep within the hill. . . ."

"Did you go there for lessons? I'd like to hear about that one day."

"No, I was too young for lessons then. My older brother was sent there to learn his letters, and I went along to play. Children were always welcome there—the Cymvelans believed that children were sacred in some way, and rather spoiled them. The courtyard that you saw was just for the children to play in—there was a swing in the tree that *whistled* when it went fast, and a little tree-hut. . . ." She sighed. "All burned down now, of course."

"Play on these and play you may!" said Nyctasia softly.

"We envied the children who lived there, but they envied us as well, because we lived in a grand house and had fine clothes and servants. Well, they say that some of the children were spared, so perhaps they came to have those things at last, and no one regrets that enchanted garden but me. . . . Ah, there you are, Liss—"

Nyctasia recognized the girl she'd seen in Lady Nocharis's chamber at their first interview. "You wanted me, milady?"

"I'm going in to lie down for a little, and you shall sit at the window and spy out everyone's doings for me. Bring your festival dress, and I'll show you the wreath-stitch. Just hand me my stick, child. Your arm to lean on, Nyctasia my dear?"

"Do you want to take a turn at this, Nyc? I'll make room for you!" Corson shouted down mockingly from the platform of the press.

"No, ox's work suits you so well, I'll leave it to you," Nyctasia called back, then turned to watch the workers emptying the juice-trough. She had been breathing in the smell of the crushed fruit for days, but here it was so powerful she could almost taste it.

She drank a little of the foaming juice out of her cupped hands. It did not look at all like wine yet. The seeds and skins would be strained out of it later, Raphe had explained, after the color of the skins had set in the clear juice. But its flavor was already so rich and strong that Nyctasia could only sip it a bit at a time. She licked her fingers greedily then set to work, taking up one of the lading-vessels and copying the motions of the others. Her arms soon grew tired, but the Discipline of Toleration was one of the first precepts mastered by a Vahnite, and almost without trying, Nyctasia had soon withdrawn her will from the efforts

of her limbs. She fell into a rhythm of bending, lifting and turning, that had no beginning or end, but carried her along as the
water of Lake Teseren had carried her, floating, half-dreaming.

The work itself never stopped, only the workers changed.
When Nyctasia joined the laders, one of the others left to get a
meal, and when Raphe came looking for Corson he sent two
people up to the platform to replace her before calling her to
come down.

"Do you mind helping to harvest my Esthairon grapes? The
rest of them must be gathered now or they'll pass their prime on
the vines, but more pickers have refused to work near the ruins,
plague take them! There were more thefts, and now some silly
brat says he's seen lights in the temple at night. I've told them it
was only some vagabond thief's cooking fire, but it does no
good. I need everyone I can muster who's not afraid of a pile of
old stones—let the fools turn the presses."

Corson stretched her arms and back, cramped from bending to
the bar. "I told you you should have that heap torn down. But I
don't mind it—harvesting will be sport after this. Hey, Nyc,
come along with you! Raphe needs us to pick those yellow grapes
of his."

Nyctasia was startled, having noticed neither Raphe nor Corson. "What is it?" she asked, in a dazed tone.

"Asye! I just told you—Raphe needs harvesters for the
haunted hill. The ruin's scared his people away. Are you coming?"

"Oh. Yes, of course." She saw that no lading-vessels were
lying empty by the trough. "There are enough workers here without me."

"Well, it would be a help," Raphe said hesitantly. He hadn't
thought of Nyctasia as a possible harvester. "But you're not to do
more than one or two rows, Nyc. There's no shade on the slopes,
and you're not used to such strong sunlight."

The vines still to be harvested were those nearest the temple,
nearly at the crest of the hill, and Nyctasia was already worn out
by the time she reached the site, far behind the others. But she
was pleased to have made the climb without stopping to rest. The
track had not seemed quite as steep and strenuous as before.
When she had caught her breath, she took a hip-basket from the
pile and a newly whetted knife from the old man who sat by the
path all day sharpening the small, curved blades on a whetstone.

She watched the way the others lifted the heavy clusters of

grapes, sliced them neatly from the vines and dropped them into their baskets, all in one smooth motion, with no wasted effort. There was, she saw, a pattern to this too, not so different from the way she had been taught to pull an arrow from her quiver, nock it, pull back and release, without pause or hesitation. Nyctasia was quite a skilled archer, and she made up her mind now to become a skilled harvester. She chose an empty row and began to strip the vines, starting in the middle as she saw the others do, so as to be always working toward the carts waiting at both ends to take the grapes.

"Nyc, go easy!" 'Deisha called to her from a few rows away, with hardly a pause in her quick lifting and slashing motions.

There were several of the family among the harvesters, but most were hirelings—a mixed lot of all those bold or desperate enough to take work on unlucky land. Some were ragged and careworn and silent, others hearty and cheerful, singing as they worked. There were people who carried babies at their chests, or had small children trailing beside them, and some seemed to Nyctasia not much more than children themselves. Most were barefoot, and many worked stripped to the waist, men and women alike, but all wore the wide straw hats to shade their faces.

How, Nyctasia marveled, could they let this relentless sun beat down on their bare backs, or stand to have the rope basket-straps cut into their skin? Already the rope chafed Nyctasia's neck, even through her shirt. As the basket grew heavier, toward the end of the row, the shoulder that supported it ached fiercely, and sweat ran into her eyes and down her neck. The glare of the sun and the increasing weight of the basket made it harder and harder to concentrate on the rhythm of her work. The rope seemed to be digging a furrow in her collarbone, rubbing raw the skin newly healed from sunburn. It felt like an eternity before the waiting wagoner took the basket from her and emptied it. Nyctasia drank deeply from the barrel of water by the cart, and splashed some on her face.

"Hey, leave some for me, greedy beast!"

Nyctasia looked up, startled. There was certainly plenty of water for everyone. One of her young cousins handed over a heaping basket and bounded up to her, laughing, his shirt flapping behind him, knotted about his waist. Bare-chested and brown and graceful, he looked to Nyctasia like a young faun of the hillsides. But his grin faded when he approached and saw her face to face.

"Oh! Pardon me, Lady Nyctasia—I—I thought you were 'Deisha. I didn't mean—I was only joking—"

Nyctasia flicked drops of water at him. "I'm Nyc to my kin. Remind me, which one are you?"

He bowed. "Nicorin, son of Nesanye, and yours to command."

"Is that so? Then let me have the loan of your shirt, if you will."

He untied the sleeves at once and handed it to her. "Surely," he said, puzzled. "But you can't very well be cold—?"

"Alas, no. I can't remember what it is to be cold." She folded up the garment and stuffed it into the shoulder of her own shirt to pad the basket-strap. "Ah, many thanks, lad, that's what I need. I wasn't very well prepared. I didn't expect to be picking grapes today."

"I should hope not!" he exclaimed, indignant on her behalf. "It's a fine hospitality that makes a guest labor in the sun like a peasant!"

"It seems to me," said Nyctasia mildly, "that I'm laboring in the sun like an Edonaris." She shouldered her basket again and smiled. "And it's done me good, besides. My appetite's improved no end since I came here!"

Nicorin made a face, not at Nyctasia, but past her, in Raphe's direction. "I'd best get back to work too. Raphe's giving me a look that would turn wine to vinegar. And we've him to thank for this day's labor! We'd be through for the season if not for him and his outlandish new grapes."

They went together to the middle of a new row and worked side by side, gradually moving away in opposite directions. The basket was so much easier to carry that Nyctasia even found the sunshine more bearable. "So the crush is nearly over?" she asked, when they met in the middle of the next row. "Raphe's grapes are the last?" She was exhausted again, but still determined to keep pace with the others.

"Well, the harvesting's most done, not the pressing. And there's plenty to do after that, but it's not as urgent. We'll get a rest, and then we'll hold Harvest Festival—that's best of all. But after that we'll be back to the same dull chores again, every day." He sighed.

"Nicorin..." said Nyctasia thoughtfully, "you're one of the warmongers, aren't you?"

"I don't *want* to go to war," he insisted, "but I don't think it's right for us to stand by idly while our kin fight for the honor of our House, in Rhostshyl." He slashed fiercely at the vines with his harvesting-knife, as if they had refused to yield their fruit.

Nyctasia could not help smiling at the bored youth's notion of idleness. But she said only, "I hope you will go to Rhostshyl one day. I believe that the likes of you could well be the saving of the House of Edonaris." She paused to wipe her forehead with her sleeve, her shoulders sagging. "You *are* needed in Rhostshyl, but not to fight for the honor of the family—if it comes to war, Nicorin, it will not be to our honor, but to our shame. Oh, the Edonaris will win, you may be sure, with or without your help. We're stronger than the Teiryn, and everyone in the city knows it. But we've no more right to sole rule of Rhostshyl than they! Some of us would seize it semply because it lies within our grasp, no matter the cost to our honor, to the city—the lives lost, the law defiled." Nyctasia's voice shook, but she went on with her picking steadily, as if she were only passing on family gossip to her young kinsman.

But Nicorin had forgotten his work. "But... but, then, why—"

"For power, neither more nor less," said Nyctasia wearily. "My brother Emeryc would tell you it's for the good of the city, and I think he believes it. The matriarch Mhairestri claims it is the foreordained destiny of our House, and I know she believes it. Call it what you will, it's all the same—the lust for power that devours the spirit—that drives us to crimes against the *vahn*—I *know*..." She heard her own words tumbling out hysterically, uncontrolled, saying far more than she'd intended. *"Why?"* she whispered, turning to face the bewildered Nicorin. "Only because the Teiryn can't *prevent* us from taking power—that's why the Edonaris want war! Because we'd win—!" Her basket fell to the ground, spilling ripe grapes at her feet, and she clutched at a vine-pole for support.

"Nyc...? 'Deisha, 'Deisha! Nyc's sick, hurry!" Nicorin yelled, his voice cracking. He took Nyctasia's arm, and she grabbed him by the shoulders suddenly, shaking him and shouting.

"We'll win, never doubt it. We don't need you, but we might be willing to use you. We'll become the undisputed rulers of

Rhostshyl, and you might be allowed to share in that victory, but you'll also share in the disgrace—remember that!"

"Nyc, what is it? Are you all right?" 'Deisha asked anxiously, putting her arm around Nyctasia's waist.

Nyctasia staggered against her. "Yes, I . . . no . . . I'm sorry, I don't know what's come over me—"

"I do. You're sunstruck, dear, that's what ails you. Come with me."

"Here, give her to me." Corson easily lifted Nyctasia in her arms and carried her to the porch of the temple, where a bit of remaining roof gave some shade.

Nicorin brought a dipper of water, and 'Deisha bathed Nyctasia's face and wrists, even soaking her hair. While she sipped the rest, Nyctasia heard Raphe say wretchedly, "I told her not to do more than a row or two—"

"She oughtn't to have been here at all!" snapped 'Deisha. "And I shouldn't have let her stay."

"It's my fault," Corson began, "I brought her along—"

Nyctasia spoke up as firmly as she could. "It's my own fault, and no one else's. I wanted to come, but I'm only in the way here, only causing trouble . . . here you all are wasting time caring for me while the harvest . . . the grapes . . ."

"I don't care about the rutting grapes!" said Corson, whose anxiety, as usual, had quickly turned to anger, though she was not at all sure whom she was angry at. "I'm taking you back to the house now."

"No, I'm all right now, and you're needed here. I can go back with one of the carts."

Corson started to protest, but 'Deisha agreed with Nyctasia. "She's better off resting in the shade than carried in the sun, Corson. I don't even want her on a wagon till the sun's lower—they're too open. The best thing is to stay out of the light altogether for now. I'll stay with her, don't worry."

"Back to work, the lot of you!" said Nyctasia. "I won't be responsible for the loss of the crop. Away with you!"

They moved off unwillingly, Nicorin lingering with a guilty feeling that it was really his fault somehow. Shaken and ashenfaced, he looked much more ill than Nyctasia.

She smiled weakly at him. "Did I frighten you?"

He nodded mutely. He knew she was not referring only to her attack of sunstroke.

"Good. Then perhaps I've done my work here after all."

"That . . . that was all true then? You meant what you said about the Edonaris?"

"I didn't mean to say it all, but it was true, I'm sorry to say. And, Nicorin, I feel far worse about it than you do, believe me."

"Well, at least I understand now why you were banished from Rhostshyl," he said ruefully, and they both laughed.

"You go along, too, 'Deisha," said Nyctasia, gently pushing her away. "I'm fine now. I only feel bad that I can't help to save Raphe's grapes, but I'll feel worse if I keep you from it as well. I'll wait here if you like, but there's no need for you to stay."

'Deisha agreed reluctantly. "Very well, but mind, Nyc, you're not to move. Keep to the shade here."

I'll keep an eye on her, 'Deisha thought. And when she next came to empty her laden basket, she took another dipper of water up to the temple for Nyctasia—but she was gone.

* * *

Nyctasia did feel better, but before long she was unbearably thirsty, as much, it seemed, from the sweet juice she'd drunk as from the heat. She felt quite well enough to fetch herself more water, until she stood and took a few steps down the hill. Then a violent wave of dizziness struck her, and she stumbled back to lean against the temple wall, faint and dismayed. She certainly could not walk as far as the water barrel unaided, but she was determined not to give more trouble. If only she weren't so thirsty!

From within the temple the musical, purling ripple of flowing water reached her, and she thought with relief of the fountain. Hadn't Mother 'Charis said that its water was always fresh and cold? It wasn't far to the courtyard, and she needn't let go of the wall on the way.

At first she could see the water, but when she dropped down beside the fountain she found only an illusion woven of light and the swaying shadows of the brass bells, wavering on the polished marble basin. The bells chimed softly, like water striking stone, though there was hardly a hint of a breeze to relieve the heat.

Neither was there a hand's breadth of shade in the courtyard. Nyctasia forgot her thirst in her desperate desire to escape from the glaring sunlight that burned her eyes and maddened her senses. She could only think of the cave, halfway down the hill, where it was cool and dark. She could wait for the others there, if she could only reach it. But the sun seemed to bear down upon her bodily as she struggled to rise. When she gained her feet the dizziness was worse than before, and she fell heavily to her knees again. Formless, blurred shapes appeared and disappeared in the air before her, now dark, now dazzling.

Nyctasia rubbed at her eyes, and one of the cloudy shapes grew clearer and seemed to take on human form, but she could not make out who it was at the heart of that blinding light.

She reached feebly for the dark figure. "The cave—" she gasped.

"These hills are riddled with caves, riddled with caves, *riddled* with *caves...*" The voice echoed hollowly around the courtyard, seeming to come from everywhere and nowhere.

"Raphe...?"

"No riddle has only one answer."

"Why do you always keep your face hidden?" whispered Nyctasia.

"You who are Mistress of Ambiguities must know that."

"'Ben? 'Ben, I can't see, I can't stand—"

"No matter, 'Tasia, we've not far to go. I'll carry you."

"Yes, take me with you," Nyctasia cried, and fainted.

* * *

"Nyctasia! Nyc, where are you?" But there was no answer, and 'Deisha ran to question the carters. Finding that no one had taken Nyctasia downhill, she called to Corson, "I can't find Nyc, she's vanished! Do you know where she's gone?"

Raphe hastened to her and pulled her aside. "Keep your voice down, for *vahn*'s sake! I'll lose the rest of the pickers if they think people have started disappearing now."

Corson strode up to them, her half-loaded basket banging at her hip. "What do you mean she's vanished?" she demanded. "She was right there, she can't have gone far."

"Corson, not so loud, I beg you," said Raphe anxiously.

'Deisha turned on him furiously. "Will you think of something besides your precious grapes for once! Nyc's missing, don't you care?"

"Of course I do, fool! But there's no need to alarm everyone." The overseer Ansen stood to one side, listening. A few of the others had gathered behind her, talking among themselves and shaking their heads or making signs to ward off evil. Raphe turned to her and ordered, "Get these folk back to work, there's nothing to fear. The Lady Nyctasia was sunstruck, that's all, she hasn't vanished or anything of the sort."

"Perhaps if she were found and they could see her . . ." Ansen suggested uneasily.

"Then what are we standing about for?" said Corson.

"Aunt 'Deisha!"

"Not now, 'Lorin!"

"The lady," insisted 'Lorin, tugging at her hand, "the lady like you." Everyone stopped and looked at him.

"Did you see where she went?" 'Deisha demanded breathlessly.

The child nodded, filled with importance. "In where the golden spider is," he explained.

"Spider . . . ?" said Corson.

"Talk sense, 'Lorin!" said 'Deisha impatiently. "Where?"

Daunted, 'Lorin retreated to his mother's side and pointed toward the ruins. "In the middle," he whispered shyly.

'Deisha frowned. "The fountain? It is rather like a big spider, with those long stalks. But if Nyc were in there, she'd have heard me call."

"I'll go have a look anyway," said Corson. "She might have fallen into one of those cellar holes, curse her."

'Deisha hurried alongside, barely able to keep pace with the long-limbed Corson. "Why would she go in there?" she worried.

"Asye knows," said Corson. "Asye knows why Nyc does anything she does!"

19

CORSON AND 'DEISHA had been unable to rouse Nyctasia when they found her lying at the foot of the fountain, and this time they carried her home without delay. She did not wake on the way, nor even when 'Deisha bathed her face with cold well-water, and Mesthelde scorched feathers and pungent herbs under her nose.

Corson counseled them to let her be. "She'll come to herself when she's ready, and not before. That one knows what she's about, when it's a matter of healing—she's probably holding a pleasant little chat with the Indwelling Spirit right now, or something of that sort. Don't worry."

But 'Deisha fretted so much over Nyctasia that Mesthelde finally chased her from the sickroom. "Get out from underfoot, both of you," she ordered. "Go back to the harvesting where you can be of some use."

Raphe had stayed behind to rally his remaining workers, but when Corson and 'Deisha trudged back up the hill, he came to meet them and asked after Nyctasia, not meeting 'Deisha's eyes.

"She's not wakened yet," said 'Deisha heavily.

"But that's all to the good," Corson assured them. "Those healing-spells of hers seem to work best that way. I once saw her with a wound that I thought would be the death of her, and she healed it overnight. It would take more than sunstroke to do away with that one. I don't claim to understand the whole queer business, but she'll be well in no time, you'll see. Just don't ask her to explain it, whatever you do!"

Raphe nodded. "They say that secrecy is the source of a magician's power—that spells lose their might if they're spoken of. I daresay Nyc had to swear oaths not to reveal the workings of her spells."

"No such luck! She's more than willing to explain all about it to anyone who'll listen. And once that one starts in explaining, she won't stop for wind or wild weather."

Raphe smiled. "It must be an Edonaris failing. I'm like that myself, no?"

"We all are," said 'Deisha. "Headstrong, the lot of us."

Corson saw that they were speaking to each other more than to her, although neither had said a word directly to the other. She wisely decided to leave them alone to discuss their differences. "You're right," she said, taking up a new harvesting basket, "all the Edonaris I ever met were as stubborn as stone." As she walked off, she heard them both starting to speak at once.

While she worked, Corson pondered the morning's events. Why *had* Nyc gone into the temple? Had she merely been wandering, or was she still searching for something there? Corson looked over at the ruin and was surprised to see some of the children napping in the shade, with 'Deisha's two dogs keeping watch over them. If no one could be spared from the harvesting to look after them, why not send them home in one of the carts? Or was this the Edonarises' way of showing the other laborers how harmless the temple was after all?

Well, Corson still had a question or two about the temple herself. As soon as the harvesting was done she'd have another look at the place, she decided. There was yet one riddle not answered to her satisfaction.

Later in the afternoon, Raphe called her to join 'Deisha and Nicorin at one of the carts. When the wagoners had taken their baskets, Nicorin waved and trotted off down the path, whistling. Raphe picked out some of the freshly gathered grapes, offering them to 'Deisha and Corson to sample. They tasted perfect to Corson, but 'Deisha shook her head regretfully. "Too sweet. Sorry, love." There remained no trace of tension between the twins.

Raphe shrugged. "It's no great matter. The bulk of them have been pressed. I want another load of these for blending, and the rest can go for raisins—but there's no hurry now, so I won't need you two here any longer. I thought you might want to go see how Nyc's getting on."

'Deisha smiled at him. "I'll go down with the wagon. What about you, Corson? Have you had your fill of harvesting?"

"Nyc doesn't need me fretting over her. But there's time enough before dark for me to look through the temple again."

"Why? What is there to look for?"

"The golden spider," said Corson, and started off toward the ruins.

Raphe followed, curious. "Surely the fountain—"

"Maybe. But there was a bell for the bell-riddle, and bees for that riddle. Peaches. Harps. A well. Why haven't we found a spider somewhere? A picture or carving of some kind, I'd guess."

"There might have been one that was destroyed," Raphe pointed out.

"There might. But how would 'Lorin know about it then?"

"Hmmm. The riddle could refer to real spiders that nest in the courtyard garden, I suppose."

"Golden ones?" said Corson. She scooped up 'Lorin, who was painstakingly planting an orchard of twigs in the shade of the temple wall. Settling him on her shoulders, she suggested, "Let's go see the golden spider, sprat, shall we?"

'Lorin shrieked assent in Corson's ear, delighted to be up so high, taller than anyone in his family. They reached the courtyard without falling through the floor, despite 'Lorin's wriggling and tugging on Corson's braid. She was not sorry to set him down again. "Can you show me the spider?" she asked, with more patience than she felt.

To Corson's disappointment, 'Lorin pointed up at the fountain. "There!"

"This, do you mean?" said Raphe, touching one of the tall, overarching stalks.

"Is that its leg?" said Corson.

'Lorin looked disgusted at their stupidity. "Not *tree*," he said scornfully. "Spider, inna web! Right *there!*"

He pointed again, so confidently that Corson crouched down beside him, the better to follow his small, unwavering finger. After a moment she grinned and beckoned to Raphe. The brass spider in its web of delicate brazen threads was indeed in plain sight—from a child's-eye point of view—on the underside of a broad bronze leaf. From this vantage point, other details of the sculpture became visible—a butterfly clinging with folded wings beneath a blossom of brass, a tiny lizard climbing up the back of a thick stem—all waiting to be discovered by the children for whom the courtyard was created, though no man or woman was likely to see them.

But Corson was indifferent to these secret charms of the fountain. What claimed her interest was one of the hanging, flower-shaped bells. From below, she could see into its heart, and with a shout of triumph she seized the clapper and wrenched it out, holding it up to show Raphe. There was no possibility of doubt. What she had found was a large brass key.

Despite Corson's assurances, the family had been nonplussed at Nyctasia's quick recovery from sunstroke. Mesthelde had insisted that she rest in bed for another day, and Nyctasia had been quite willing to obey when she heard that the worst of the crush was over. But no amount of persuasion or dire warning could keep her from joining Corson on another climb up Honeycomb Hill on the following day.

There were regular meals once more, and during breakfast that morning everyone reasoned or remonstrated with her. "The clappers of all the other bells are shaped like stamens," Raphe argued. "We searched the whole fountain. There's nothing more to find."

"Oh, but—"

"You're mad, Nyc, to think of going out in the sun so soon, healer or no!" 'Deisha scolded, seconded by Mesthelde.

Nyctasia had to raise her voice to be heard. "But we're not going up to the temple, and I shan't be in the sun," she protested. "Our destination is that small cave on the hillside, where no sun has shone for a thousand years. I ought to be safe from sunstroke there."

"Nyc thinks the lock to this key may be there somewhere," Corson explained. "If the 'key to mystery' was really meant for a key, maybe the other riddle will yield some 'wealth beyond a lifetime's spending,' who knows?" It didn't seem very likely, even to Corson, but the key must unlock something, after all.

"Why the cave, though? How does that riddle go?"

"'Neither in the open air, neither in a dwelling,'" Nyctasia recited. "We all assumed that it meant the courtyard, but it could as well be a cave, and that's the nearest one—probably the only one the children were allowed to explore freely."

"Yes, but I know that cave—it's empty," Raphe objected. "It doesn't reach in much farther than you saw, and there's nothing there save rock and earth."

Corson and Nyctasia exchanged a knowing look. "The earth doth secrets keep," Nyctasia reminded him.

"'For the wellspring's weal lies deep,'" Corson added. "I'll wager you've never tried digging there, have you?"

20

THE OTHERS WERE still taken up with the harvest, but there were laborers enough for the remaining tasks, and the guests of the house could no longer be allowed to take part in the work. Corson and Nyctasia had the whole of Honeycomb Hill to themselves. They explored the interior of the cave with lanterns and candles, but found only the sign of the Cymvelan Circle, crudely scratched in stone. There were nothing for it but to dig.

The cave was too small to allow Corson to swing a pick, and she could barely stand upright to put her full weight behind a spade. There was not room for two to dig, but Nyctasia knelt and troweled the dirt and loose stones out of the way, sifting through them for clues. "Don't stay too long in one spot," she advised. "If there's anything here, it shouldn't be too well hidden. They expected children to find it."

"Probably *only* children can find it," Corson grunted. "I should have brought 'Lorin along instead of you."

It was slow work, but they had not been at it long when Corson's spade struck with a hollow thud against something unexpected. "Wait!" Nyctasia scraped a space around the edge of the spade. "This is wood."

They both set to, clearing the shallow layer of soil from the planks beneath.

"I think it's a chest."

"It's not a coffin, is it?"

It was neither. Before long they had uncovered most of the wooden flooring of the cave, and in the center was a small trap-door. When they tugged it open, a cold wind came rushing up from the blackness below to strike their faces with a disconcerting chill. A lantern lowered into the hole revealed stairs cut into the stone, leading down into darkness.

"It's a doorway for children, that's certain," said Nyctasia. "I might squeeze through, but you couldn't possibly."

For answer, Corson thrust the edge of her spade between two of the old boards and stamped it down with all her strength until the plank next to the open trapway began to break loose. Gripping the free side, she pulled up on the loosened board and tore it out with a crack of outraged joinery. Nyctasia stepped cautiously down the stairway far enough to push up on the next board while Corson wrenched it free from above. Corson tossed it aside and grinned down at her. "Now it's wide enough for someone of a decent size, eh?"

"Yes, and even for a monstrous creature like you." Nyctasia took up her lantern again and started slowly down the stairs.

Corson seized the other lamp and hastened to follow her. "Out of my way, mite, or I'll step on you."

21

THE PASSAGE WAS just wide enough for Corson and Nyctasia to walk abreast. They moved slowly, uncertain of their footing in the dim glow of the lanterns. Even their words were hushed by the dense gloom that stretched ahead of them endlessly, unbroken by any light or noise. They soon fell silent, listening, but heard only the sound of their boots scuffing the stone. They had not been walking long before the passage branched into two corridors, one continuing straight ahead but narrowing, the other angling off to the left. Corson turned into the roomier passage, but she soon regretted her choice.

It was clear that this part of the tunnel had served a definite purpose. On either side of them, long rectangular niches had been cut into the walls, some left empty, some closed over with clay tiles, their edges sealed with mortar. Although Corson had never seen their like before, she immediately knew that they were graves.

"'And we came to the city of the dead,'" Nyctasia recited, "'wandering long among those dark corridors, and past the innumerable and silent host that dwelt there. How humbled we were and awe-struck. What were all our travels but a path to this last, final journey before which all our adventures paled to country jaunts on a summer's day?'"

"What are you babbling about?"

"That's from the memoirs of the Lady Ghystralda. She was always going to one place or another, and then filling scores of books with her experiences and the old travelers' tales she heard. The woman had the most commonplace ideas, and she talked about them as if they were gems of learning and understanding, but when I was a child I thought them most profound. I read her works over and over, wishing I could run away from Rhostshyl and see the world. . . . This place is very similar to one she described, though, except that it was teeming with ghosts, according to her. It's interesting to see some of the same customs in such different parts of the world." She held her lantern close to one of the graves to study the tile, which was decorated with the sign of the Cymvela. Some of the tombs bore portraits of the departed, showing them sleeping serenely in a boat on calm waters, or reunited with their loved ones in a sunny garden. Others were ornamented with colored porcelain, brass medallions or terra-cotta lamps. There were even small crystal perfume flasks pushed into the mortar, and a sweet scent still lingered in the air, as faint and fragile as the memory of a long-faded flower.

"You don't suppose there really are ghosts here, do you?" Corson asked.

Nyctasia grinned at her. "'Who can say what restless spirits walk these shadow-haunted halls?'"

"Stop spouting bad verse at me!" Corson was glad of her rising anger, which made her forget how the place frightened her. "Here's one I'll wager you don't know," she said, and sang in a cracked, off-key voice:

"Sing hey, sing ho, if we will or no,
    To the worms below must our journeys go.
    If you can't pay, then you must owe,
    And death makes equal the high and the low.

"I learned that in the army. Write it down, why don't you?"

"I shall. Corson, if you want to go back—"

"No! Why should we? Let's see what there is to see." She wanted desperately to go back, but she would rather risk the ghosts than admit it to Nyctasia. The place seemed more eerie and unnatural to her with every step—and less likely to lead to any treasure. The ditty she had sung for Nyctasia ran through her head in a mocking refrain. Unbidden, images of death rose before her, not the peaceful death these tombs promised, but the cruel, bloody death of the battlefield. Her own ghosts haunted her, if no others.

"Corson, come look at these!" Nyctasia called.

"What now?" Corson demanded. "If it's not coin or loot I don't want to see it."

Nyctasia had come to the end of the passage, a smooth wall on which a remarkably realistic arched doorway had been painted. An inviting landscape of meadows and mountains lay beyond, and far in the distance a procession of men and women could be seen approaching. But Nyctasia was pointing to the ceiling of the crypt-chamber, which, Corson now saw, was also painted. "More of their cursed daubs," she snarled.

"These are different. They're much older, and I don't think they were done by the Cymvelans."

The drawings were of grotesque beasts, much like those in the temple, but even more vivid and alive. They were drawn in a helter-skelter fashion all over the ceiling, and each figure seemed absorbed in some private but violent dance. The light of the lanterns plucked the painted surfaces from the darkness and the distorted, wildly gyrating creatures appeared to move, as if they had come to life.

Nyctasia softly said, "The Cymvelans lived in the light, but it was the darkness that secretly nourished them. It was that they were trying to show in their temple paintings, I think. The tree was the sign of their belief, which was rooted in darkness but spread its crown wide under the sky, and throve in the sunlight. And all the while these crypts, with their prancing monsters, lay beneath the temple, and perhaps their rhythms were really the heart of the dance."

"I know which side I'd wager on," Corson said harshly, "in a contest between these"—she gestured toward the capering figures—"and those dancing poppets the Cymvelans painted. These speak for what's truly in the blood. The rest is just some sort of children's game, like your muzzy notions about the Indwelling Spirit. Suppose the Indwelling Spirit is really like one of these here?"

Nyctasia caught her breath. It hardly seemed to be Corson who spoke, but some malignant stranger who sought to turn her own deepest fears against her. Forcing herself to speak lightly, she said, "Well, now I'm frightened too, Corson. I hope you're satisfied."

"I'm not," said Corson. "Frightened, I mean. Or satisfied either, for that matter. I don't want the bones of idiot wizards, or the scrawls of lunatics—it's treasure I'm after. Let's quit this place and try the other tunnel. These lanterns are good yet for a while."

They began to retrace their steps, but just before they reached the main passageway, Corson stopped in her tracks and looked back. "Nyc, you don't think the treasure's buried back there, in one of those graves?"

Nyctasia hesitated. "I confess, the idea did occur to me, but I don't think it would have occurred to the Cymvelans. They had more respect for the dead than that. I think that burial chamber was a sacred place to them, not just a convenient spot to use as a treasury. And nothing in the riddles suggests it. But even if I thought it likely, nothing would induce me to open those tombs and look. You can do as you like, of course."

"Thanks," said Corson drily, "but you're probably right. Let's go on." They entered the narrower branch of the corridor, with Corson in the lead. Here they had to walk single-file. "Still, they wouldn't be the first, you know," Corson continued. "During the Battle of Aylrhui, they looted the tomb of one of the old kings. There were riches in there beyond anyone's belief. Plates of gold, chains of silver, jewels, all sorts of rich things." She ticked them off on her fingers like a householder's marketing.

"All part of the spoils of war, I suppose?"

"No. The robbers were caught and buried alive, as a sign of goodwill. That war was settled by truce, you see, since neither side looked like winning. It was all for nothing. A minor skirmish, they called it." She shook her head. "Scores of us were killed. But I've no right to complain. I was well-paid. . . . You probably think it's wrong to rob the dead, but what harm could it do them, answer me that."

"It could not harm them," said Nyctasia seriously, "but perhaps it could harm you."

"Ghosts, do you mean?" said Corson, frowning. Had she heard something in the tunnel, just ahead of them? Not listening to Nyctasia's answer, she peered into the dark corridor, trying to pierce the shadows, but there was nothing to be seen. She stopped and slowly drew her sword, motioning for Nyctasia to do the same. "I think there's someone ahead of us," she whispered, no louder than a sigh. "I hear breathing."

Nyctasia heard nothing at first, but as they both held their breath to listen, the sound of heavily drawn breathing came to her out of the darkness. "Shall we go back?" she asked softly.

"No. I think I know who's skulking down here, and I want to meet them face to face," Corson said, with an almost wolfish grin. "This is no crew of whispers and shadows. Ghosts don't breathe." She blew out her lantern. "There'll be light ahead, I wager. Stay behind me."

As she strode eagerly up the passageway, all her fears seemed to drop away from her. For an instant, Nyctasia lost sight of her in the gloom. As she hurried to catch up, she heard Corson's shout and the unmistakable clang of blade against blade. Someone screamed.

Corson was framed by the entrance to a large cavern lit by wall-torches. A body lay sprawled at her feet, and she was fighting with a squat, strongly built man. Nyctasia could only stop and watch in fascinated horror. She knew who would win this battle, and so did Corson's opponent. He had the face of one who sees his own death plainly before him and knows there is no escape. Corson's back was to Nyctasia, but she had no doubt that Corson was smiling.

There was a flicker of steel, and the man's sword struck sparks from the stone as it dropped to the floor. He seemed to Nyctasia to take an impossibly long time to fall.

Corson stooped over him. "Take the sword from the other one, Nyc," she said, without turning around. She was removing a ring of keys from the dead man's belt. "Here's the mystery of these ruins—it's a slavers' den. No wonder folk have disappeared here. Disappeared right into the slave markets of Celys, that's my guess." Swinging the keys jauntily at her side, she walked into the large cave.

Nyctasia followed, marveling at the mystery that was Corson herself. One moment she was trembling because she'd found a few graves, and the next moment she was putting other folk in their graves as carelessly as a cat killing mice. She was obviously reluctant to plunder the tombs, despite her bravado, but she stripped the bodies of her own prey without a qualm.

"See for yourself," she said to Nyctasia, sounding very pleased with herself.

The cavern was large and cold, and the roof was very high—

beyond the reach of the guttering torches. Another passageway entered it at the left. The chamber could easily have held fifty people, but there were only five, three men and two women, manacled to the wall. All of them were looking back at Corson and Nyctasia with frightened, apprehensive eyes.

Corson raised the keys and smiled. "Don't worry, those vermin are dead. We'll set you free."

The prisoners twisted their necks to look at each other. A woman said something to them in a language Nyctasia couldn't understand, but Corson's years in the Imperial Army had made her familiar with more than one eastern dialect. Much to Nyctasia's surprise, and rather to her annoyance, Corson answered the woman fluently, and the two began talking rapidly to each other. The others listened avidly, and one of the men started to cry. Nyctasia grabbed the keys and hastened to unlock their chains.

A slight, fair-haired man, shorter than the others, said to her, "I thank you, mistress Edonaris. How did you come to find us?" He rubbed his wrists slowly.

"By chance," said Nyctasia shortly, busy with the clumsy locks.

He followed her. "But what are they saying?"

"I haven't the slightest idea," she admitted.

Corson, looking more pleased than ever, told her, "They're from beyond the Spine. Can't you understand anything of what they say? With all your learning, I thought you'd surely be easy with their tongue."

"I have, of course, studied both Ancient and Modern Liruvathe from texts, but one learns only the literary forms that way," Nyctasia said, in obvious frustration. "If they wrote down their words, I believe I could read them, but it's not likely that they can write."

"That's not much use, then," said Corson smugly. "Now this lass tells me that all of this group except him"—she jerked her thumb at the man who'd spoken to Nyctasia—"are from Mount Eilas, in Liruvath. They were on their way to Amron Therain when they were ambushed and brought here. Probably they'd have been smuggled to Osela and sold."

One of the men broke in, gesturing wildly and shouting. The others seemed to agree with whatever it was he was saying.

Corson translated, "There's at least three more of the bastards about. He also says that they're dung-eaters, the spawn of scrofulous pigs, and that they rut with dogs in the gutter."

Nyctasia shook her head, smiling. "Even if he did write that down, I don't think I could follow it. Unquestionably the vernacular, and probably a corrupt dialect. Let's get these people out of here before the rest of the misbegotten offspring of unhealthy swine return."

Her words made no impression on Corson. "They want to kill them," she said simply, handing out the weapons that had belonged to the dead guards. "Let's wipe out this rat's nest now. Why not?" The four easterners took down the torches and gathered a few large rocks.

"I can think of any number of good reasons why not, but surely—"

"Nyc, these folk want vengeance, not reasons."

"I don't," said the fair-haired man tensely. "I want to leave, and if you've any sense you'll tell them to do the same."

"He's right, Corson. Why take the risk?"

"Because if we don't catch those scum now they might get away!"

"Yes, but so might we. We're probably outnumbered. They'll be better armed than we are, and they know these tunnels." She pointed at the knot of haggard, grim-faced prisoners. "They must be weak, they're in no shape to fight. Tell them to come away now, and we'll send others to hunt down the slavers."

Corson translated her advice to the Liruvathid, but she did not need to translate their answer. One woman spoke for all of them, and Nyctasia understood her well enough. They all clutched at their weapons and stood firm. Nyctasia sighed and drew her shortsword. The woman smiled.

"Fools!" exclaimed the other man. "You've no right—"

"Go, if you want, no one's keeping you here," Corson told him sharply, but a moment later they all knew it was too late for that. There were heavy footsteps approaching down the tunnel on the left.

Barking a few curt orders to the prisoners, Corson grouped them on either side of the opening. The fair-haired man caught Nyctasia's eye, and she shrugged. They joined the others and waited.

"We should have gone while we had the chance," he muttered.

"If you don't mean to fight, stay out of the way," Corson said softly, "or you may find a knife in your gut by mischance. Now keep still."

They listened, barely breathing, as the footsteps came closer.

Despite herself, Nyctasia began to feel the same eagerness to strike that inflamed the others. She recognized the thrill of waiting, with an arrow on the string, for the great eagle to swoop lower, waiting for the perfect moment to loose the arrow and bring down the bird that would harry her flocks no longer. . . .

But it was people they waited to slaughter here, she reminded herself. For, although she had urged caution, Nyctasia did not really doubt the outcome of this fight. Yet the bird of prey carried off a lamb only to feed its young, while the human raptors they were hunting preyed on their own kind, for gain. If it had been her duty to kill the one, why should these be spared? Were such people fit to live?

It had seemed to Nyctasia from the beginning that these caverns somehow called forth thoughts of death and destruction, nourished them, fostered them. . . . But, right or wrong, her choice had been made, and she was determined to see it through.

Then the first of the slavers entered the cave. Instantly, one of the foreigners clubbed him over the head, and the others fell on him. Nyctasia turned her head—clearly, they didn't need her help. It was soon over.

She looked up to see four more of the bandits at the tunnel's mouth, and for a moment her eyes met theirs. They were heavily armed, but to Nyctasia's surprise they suddenly turned and fled back up the passage. Corson and some of the others gave chase, but they soon returned. The one large tunnel had split up into a maze of smaller ones, Corson reported, and their quarry had scattered and quickly disappeared. "Rutting cowards!" she spat. She hated to let the slavers escape, but she knew better than to run blindly into those twisting tunnels.

"It was the sight of an Edonaris that chased them off," the fair-haired man explained. "They know their game's up if the Edonaris have found them out."

"*That's* why they turned tail so quickly the morning they attacked us, Nyc. They saw you. And I thought it was my mighty prowess that drove them away!"

Nyctasia nodded slowly. "The Edonaris would search the ruins stone by stone if one of their own disappeared. No wonder the ghosts have never troubled them." She began to laugh and could hardly stop, despite the puzzled looks the others turned upon her. The fight was over, and she'd not had to do a thing. Nothing at all!

22

A CURSORY SEARCH of the tunnels did not reveal the Cymvelan treasure, but gold and goods belonging to the slavers were discovered, including copies of the slave-brands used by all the major and minor municipalities of the Midlands. Diastor gave orders to have them taken at once to the smithy and destroyed. "It's not lawful for anyone but the City Magistrates to possess them."

"I repent that I doubted Aunt Mesthelde," said Raphe grimly. "Small wonder if screams have been heard at the temple."

For the time, the Liruvathid captives were quartered in an encampment of their own, provided with tents and clothing and food. Nyctasia was surprised at first to find that all of them were in sound health, suffering neither from starvation nor ill-treatment. But she soon realized that this was simple common sense on the part of the slave-traders; weakness or injury would only have lowered the value of their merchandise.

"I must take this opportunity to learn how Liruvathe is really spoken," she said to the others, after the new guests had been settled. "The rift between theory and practice has been the undoing of more than one scholar."

"If that means that you don't know anything useful, it's the truth," said Corson. "I've told you as much myself."

"That's what it means," Nyctasia admitted.

"It's well for us that you're here, Corson," said Diastor. "My wife and her brother know enough Liruvathe to deal with the eastern traders at Amron Therain, but they won't be back from Osela for a fortnight."

"Do you ever travel to the imperial markets yourselves?" asked Nyctasia.

He shook his head. "It would be quite an undertaking to transport the casks so far as that. We can't spare that many people for so long."

"It might be a saving, though, in the end," said Mesthelde thoughtfully. "We'd get a better price from purchasers than we do from other merchants. We should give some thought to it, perhaps."

"A splendid idea!" urged Jenisorn. "Now if you sent me to the Imperial University, I could find out all about the markets at the capital—"

"Or me!" said Tepicacia, who was a year or two older than Jenisorn.

"We should send you both back to the nursery," said Mesthelde. "Get along with you!"

Nyctasia smiled. "I wanted to go to the university too, when I was a girl, and my family wouldn't hear of it either. Perhaps it's not too late." In truth, the idea appealed to her a good deal, and she wondered why she hadn't thought of it before. She would be sorry to leave her new kin, but the pursuit of her studies would be work far more satisfying to her than grape-farming and winemaking.

"You won't learn anything useful there either," Corson scoffed. "Of all the feckless good-for-nothings born of woman, students are the worst of the lot."

"There's good sense speaking," said Diastor warmly, and even Mesthelde looked at Corson with approval. "Don't be stirring up the youngsters to long for Liruvath, Nyctasia," he cautioned. "It's only the tidings of Rhostshyl that's turned their thoughts from running off across the mountains to study a lot of nonsense—"

"And live like wild swine," put in Mesthelde. "Students! As if philosophy ever put bread on the table!"

Nyctasia winked at Jenisorn. "Admittedly, scholarship is a

luxury for the few," she said mildly, "but consider what valuable connections your young folk could make at the university. Children of wealthy and noble families—the very patrons for fine and costly wines."

This possibility had not occurred to Mesthelde, and for a moment she weighed the commercial advantages of a university education, but they were not sufficiently tempting to change her mind. "More likely they'd fall in with a lot of tosspots and troublemakers, and take to gambling and Hlann knows what mischief. Even if they did mix with scholars of good family, they'd only pick up extravagant ways and come home in debt—if they came home at all."

'Deisha resented her elders' remarks, on Nyctasia's behalf, far more than Nyctasia did herself. "Well then," she snapped, "why not send Jen and 'Cacia and 'Corin into the Imperial Army instead? They could have a practical education like Corson's, all at the crown's expense. Only think of the savings!"

Diastor began to remonstrate with her, but Mesthelde cut his words short. If she was perturbed by her niece's insolence, she nevertheless had the grace to laugh. "That's a very good idea, my dear—it would satisfy their restlessness and teach them some discipline into the bargain. And now that we've settled what's to be done with them, it's time we decided what to do about our unfortunate guests. What's to become of them?"

It did not occur to any of the Edonaris that they were not responsible for the welfare of the hapless foreigners. Their position clearly made it their duty to assist the victims of the slavers. "I don't see any great difficulty," said Diastor. "The money that was found probably belonged to them—the *vahn* knows they've a right to it. Divided among them, it will be enough to see them home."

Nesanye nodded. "They can travel with Leclairin and Aldrichas as far as Amron Therain, after Harvest Festival, and they're sure to find their own people there. There's always a party of merchants bound for the Spine."

"I'll be going to Amron Therain soon, to take a riverboat," Corson said. "I can see them safe that far."

"But you're not leaving yet," said Raphe, dismayed. "Not before harvest-fest, surely!"

The others laughed. "Well, not before I've had a chance to

explore those tunnels more carefully," Corson assured him. "We've not yet found a lock to fit that Cymvelan key, you know."

The fair-haired man among the prisoners was himself a Midlander, who introduced himself as Garast brenn Vale. "I've lived most of my life downriver, but I was born in these parts," he explained. "My people deal in silk and Iakosian tapestry. We were on the way back from Osela fair, and when we passed through Vale I left the others, to have a look at the ruins. I had some schooling among the Cymvelans as a child, and I—"

"You must understand Liruvathe well, then, if you trade in imperial goods," said Raphe, who'd been talking to Corson.

"Well, no, not really, but my wife . . ."

"It's strange your folk didn't make inquiry for you when you failed to return," Mesthelde interrupted.

"Didn't they? But they must have," said Garast uneasily.

"We'd have heard about any disappearances from hereabout."

"You don't understand," said Garast, but he made no attempt to explain.

"We understand well enough," said Raphe. "You're not the first treasure-seeker to come sneaking about here."

"The dogs catch them betimes," 'Deisha put in. "I wonder how many others have fallen into the hands of those slavers, though, and we none the wiser."

"They'd only themselves to blame if they did, for not seeking our leave in the first place," said Mesthelde. "If we'd known they were there, we'd have known they were missing."

Raphe frowned. "It must have been you stealing food from my harvesters, scaring folk away from the temple."

Garast protested his innocence with some indignation, but Diastor silenced him with a wave of his hand. "We don't much mind if every fool in the valley wants to waste time looking for that treasure—begging your pardon, my dear Corson—but we do object to prowlers who don't make themselves known, thief or no."

"I—I couldn't make myself known. I have enemies in these parts."

"I daresay," said Mesthelde, folding her arms.

"Garast, you really may as well speak the truth," suggested Nyctasia. "The Edonaris were always friends to the Circle. There's nothing to fear."

The others turned to her in surprise. "The Circle—?"

"It's not true, I'm no Cymvelan!"

"No, of course not. But you were as a child, no? You see, I think I have something that belongs to you," said Nyctasia, handing him the page of Cymvelan rhymes and riddles.

23

THE EDONARIS HAD no time to spare for treasure-hunting, but
Corson, Nyctasia and Garast undertook a thorough search of the
underground passageways without delay. A few led to empty
chambers of stone, others ended abruptly in a solid wall, but
there were those which opened into deep caves high in the foothills of the Spine, some of them leagues from Vale, and more
than one on Saetarrin land.

"Most convenient for smuggling people to foreign slave markets," Diastor observed, when the family was told of this discovery. "The first thing we'll do when the pressing's over is have
masons seal the entrances on this end. I daresay the Saetarrin will
do the same when they're told of it."

"They'll have to," said 'Cacia darkly, "but I wonder how
much Lady Avareth knows of it already. . . ." From the looks that
passed among them, it was clear that they all had been thinking
something of the sort.

"It's no use asking that," said the practical Raphe. "You know
we can't afford to make enemies of the Saetarrin. If they've been
in league with outlaw slavers, we could never prove it. We'll
have to be satisfied with putting a stop to it."

"Yes, you're all to keep your suspicions to yourselves," said

Diastor firmly, but he couldn't help smiling as he leaned back in his chair, regarding the vaulted ceiling thoughtfully. "Of course, if any of the malefactors are caught, it will be interesting to hear what they have to say of their dealings with our noble neighbors. But till that happens, there's to be no talk of the matter, is that understood?" He looked pointedly at 'Cacia.

"Yes, sir," she sighed.

"And you three, if you must keep up this treasure-chase of yours, be careful. Take care you don't lose yourselves in a tunnel that leads right to the dungeons of Castle Saetarrin."

"And 'ware another thing," said Raphe seriously. "If any of those tunnels lead beneath the temple, remember how unsound the flooring above you is. The treasure won't do you much good if you're buried in a stonefall."

It was Mesthelde, as usual, who put in the last word. "Treasure!" she said. "If there ever was a treasure, those slavers would have found it. It's trouble you're looking for, not treasure, you mark me."

* * *

"I hate to admit it, but Lady Mesthelde is probably right," said Corson, discouraged. The tunnel they were exploring had forked into two branches, and they had taken the left way, only to come up against another dead end. "This is fool's sport. We may as well fish for hake in a hayloft."

They slowly made their way back through the narrow stone corridor and started along the other branch of the tunnel. "Fool's sport is better than none at all," said Nyctasia. "I myself have always liked the chase better than the kill. I don't even believe in this treasure, but hunting for it does pass the time."

They were surprised when Garast, who spoke little, suddenly said, "I never believed in the treasure either—none of us did who'd lived here as children. Members of the Circle worked hard and lived simply. There were no riches to be seen."

"So Rowan told us," said Nyctasia. "And the Edonaris, who knew them well, say the same."

"Then what are you looking for here?" Corson demanded.

"I don't know, but there's something here they want—the ones who survived the attack. Something they were forced to leave behind when they ran away—saved themselves and left the rest to be slaughtered."

"I suppose they escaped by means of these tunnels, then."

"They must have," he agreed. "They probably hid down here until . . . until it was over, then sneaked away. My whole family was killed that night. I was the youngest—just a small child—but I remember. Now they mean to come back and claim their own. But it belongs to us—to Rowan and Jocelys and to me—not to those traitors. It's our birthright!"

Nyctasia forbore to mention that any treasure found on Edonaris land would in fact belong to the Edonaris. Time enough to deal with the rights of the matter if any treasure really did come to light. She said only, "Rowan wanted no part of it, though."

"Rowan's a coward. I know he thinks I'm crazed to come here, but he told me what he remembered of the riddles, and so did Jocelys, though she fears for her family. I don't think they'll refuse to share in the treasure when I find it."

"When *we* find it," Corson reminded him.

"*If* we find it," said Nyctasia.

"If we find it," Corson continued, "I'll not refuse to share in it either."

There was a long silence before Garast said, hesitantly, "I don't think it's anything you'll want, whatever it is, but you'll want to find it before the Cymvelans do. They mean to use it somehow to avenge themselves on the Valleylanders for destroying the Circle. I learned that much when they first sought me out, and they told Jocelys the same."

"With gold enough they could hire an army of mercenaries and lay waste the whole valley," said Corson. "The land's ill defended." She sighed, thinking of other uses she could find for such a sum.

For Nyctasia, the quest had ceased to be a game. She had lost one home, and was Vale now threatened as well? "Why didn't you tell us this before?" she asked sharply.

He stopped and turned to face her. "Ask rather why I tell you now! It's not from any love of the Valleylanders, I promise you! And the Edonaris—you call them friends of the Circle, but what did they do to help that night while their neighbors murdered the Cymvelans? I'd not raise my hand to save the whole of the valley from sure doom!"

Corson gripped the hilt of her dagger, ready to use it. There was no room in the tunnel to wield a sword. Rowan was right, she thought, he is mad.

"Very well, then, why do you warn us now?" Nyctasia asked calmly.

"Because I need your help to carry out the search. You have the favor of the Edonaris. And time is passing—the last of the Circle are to meet here at the temple on Yu Valeicu. I'll prevent them from claiming my heritage if I can, and you'll not abandon the search now either, if you care about the fate of the valley."

The Turning, the harvest holiday called Yu Valeicu—the Changes—in this part of the world, was less than a fortnight away. "I don't believe a word of it," said Corson, before Nyctasia could reply. "You needn't try to frighten us into keeping on with the hunt. If there's any treasure to be had here, we'll find it, and we'll deal with the Cymvelans when they appear—if they do. They could be kept out of the temple, you know, even if they know a dozen secret entrance-ways. The Edonaris can post guards."

"That's so," said Nyctasia, glad as ever of Corson's matter-of-fact view of the matter.

Even Garast seemed satisfied. "That would suit my purposes. I don't care why you help me search, so long as you do it. But for your own sake, I suggest we try to find it before Yu Valeicu, all the same."

"By all means," said Corson, "the sooner the better. And we won't find it by standing about here while our lamps burn low. We'd best go on or go back, before we run out of oil."

"I'm going on," said Garast promptly.

Nyctasia blew out her lamp to save the oil. "We might as well go on for a way, since we've come so far." They set out again, Nyctasia walking in the middle between the two burning lanterns.

"It can't be much farther to the end," Corson said. "We must be halfway to Osela by now. What's that—not another blind end—!"

She groped ahead of her uncertainly. The passageway narrowed to a sharp angle overhead, but the obstruction didn't seem to be solid stone. She pushed against it and felt it give way slightly. "This is wood!" Handing her lantern to Nyctasia, she set her back against the sloping planks and slowly forced them up and outward. A shaft of bright sunlight startled them all.

Nyctasia slipped through the narrow opening and pulled at the door from above. Garast followed her, and both held it open for Corson. They found themselves in the middle of a stand of pear trees. Garast went to investigate a nearby building.

When they let the door fall back into place, it seemed to become a part of the gently sloping ground. The boards had been covered with a deep layer of turf, its moss and grass rooted in the very wood.

"Clever," said Corson. "Hard to find, but not too hard. And those who find it don't come back to tell of it."

"And their disappearance feeds the rumors that the place is haunted, so most folk stay clear of it."

Corson spat. "A tidy profit for the slave-dealers all round. But they won't find it so easy to smuggle their wares through the valley in future. Blood of the Hlann, I hope they're caught! I want to see them hang."

"Perhaps you will," said Garast, rejoining them. "Come look at this—someone's been hiding in the ruins here. Maybe some of them are still lurking around these parts, hoping to recover their gold." He led them around the corner of a tall stone wall and climbed the white marble steps, now neglected and muddy, littered with leaves. "These were our living-quarters... we were sleeping here that night, when—" He shook his head. "There, you see, someone's camped here recently."

"Why, this is where *we* sheltered for the night, on our way to Vale," said Nyctasia. "It looks different by day."

Corson looked round with distaste. "I remember that filthy pool well enough. So that's how those bastards who attacked us got away from me—just vanished down a hole in the ground like the weasels they are. It was too dark for me to find the door." She examined the remains of the campfire, and frowned. "But you're right, someone has been here since we were, and not long ago." What interested her more than this discovery, however, was that she no longer sensed the disquieting presence of magic in the place. Could it really have been a dream, after all? She wanted to question Nyctasia, but would not do so before Garast, and said instead, "More likely it's our harvest-thief hiding here than—"

Then, as if to resolve the question, someone suddenly broke from the cover of the bushes nearby and darted behind them into the building.

They gave chase on the instant, but within the roofed entrance-way were corridors leading left and right, and just before them was an open room with another door in its far wall.

Corson cursed. "We'll never catch him. Nyc, stay here and guard this doorway." Corson ran down one corridor and Garast the other, looking into each empty room as they passed. Some still held simple wooden pallet-beds, or tables. But the roof and walls were so broken down in places that Corson saw that their quarry could easily have climbed out through a hole and escaped. Discouraged, she slowed to a walk and looked around her carefully, but saw no sign that someone was hiding in any room she passed.

The corridor finally widened to a hall, cluttered with the remains of long tables and benches. Garast was wandering through the room aimlessly, as if looking for something he'd lost. "We had our lessons here, and meals," he said.

"Are there cellars?"

He pointed to an inner room. "Beneath the kitchen. But I doubt there are any secret passages out of them—they were only used to store potatoes and preserves and such. In here, through the bakery, I'll show you."

Corson peered down the stairs to the dark cellars and considered whether to send Garast back for a lantern while she kept watch. But the very dust on the flagstone floor showed that no one besides themselves had been there for a good while. "It's no use," she said. "If he knows of a way out, he's gone already. There are probably dozens of hidden ways in and out of this warren."

Garast turned away and pushed wide the back door of the kitchen, which opened onto the large inner yard with the old well at its center. Corson now saw that there were cloistered walkways on three sides of the yard, their tapering arches supported by a colonnade of slender pillars. Where there had once been neatly laid out kitchen gardens and flowerbeds, there was now a wilderness of weeds and greenery run to seed. Nyctasia was kneeling in a tangle of overgrown foliage in the far corner of the yard, gathering sprigs of a few low-growing plants. "These were knot-gardens," she said delightedly, as they approached. "In all four corners—look, you can still see the designs."

The plants had been arranged in a symmetrical swirl of interlaced lines, Corson saw, though the pattern was now partly obscured by new outgrowths and uninvited wildweeds. "Trust the Cymvelans to make a puzzle of something simple," she said.

"Oh, this isn't a Cymvelan notion. It's traditional to grow certain herbs together in patterns. Some of the designs are hundreds of years old. This one's called Lace of Ease, because these three herbs all—"

"Why weren't you watching the entrance?" Corson demanded, dismissing the lecture in herb-lore.

"I was—you can see it from here, through the doorway. No one's gone by, I assure you."

Corson shrugged. "Never mind. He's far away by now, whoever he was. What have you got there, fresh cuttings of poisonous plants for that nasty herbal of yours?"

"Unfortunately, I left that in Hlasven. But I have an herb here that would be good for you—dumbcane. It causes muteness. A pity the effect is only temporary."

Corson grinned. "Have you got one that causes deafness? That's what I really need when I'm in your company."

"Those who will not hear are worse off than those who cannot hear," said Nyctasia sententiously, turning back to the tangled herb-bed, and pretending not to see the rude hand-sign with which Corson answered her. "It wouldn't be difficult to restore these gardens," she mused. "They must have been very well tended once."

"They were," said Garast, "and very pretty they looked, but we children didn't like them, because we were expected to help weed and water them. I used to carry pails of water from the rain-barrels for these herbs."

"Hornwort . . . ?" Nyctasia muttered to herself, frowning at a curled, yellow leaf.

"Why?" Corson asked Garast.

"Why—?" he echoed.

"Why did you fetch water from the rain-barrels instead of drawing it from the well there?"

Garast looked startled. "I don't know . . . I don't remember that we ever used that well . . ." he said slowly.

Nyctasia looked up, then got to her feet. The three of them all started to speak at once, and stopped. Then, without another word, they dashed to the well and stared down over the edge.

They could see nothing but the silhouettes of their own heads and shoulders darkly reflected below, and the well-rope hanging down the middle of the shaft. Corson grabbed it and pulled it up easily. There was no bucket at the end, but large knots had been tied in the heavy rope at regular intervals, to serve as footholds.

"This rope's new," she said.

"Why isn't it wet?" puzzled Nyctasia.

"We'll soon find out," said Garast, and started to climb over the side, but the others persuaded him to wait till they'd lowered a lantern into the well to judge its depth.

It struck bottom far sooner than they'd expected, and with an abrupt clatter instead of a splash. "It struck sparks!" exclaimed Nyctasia. "It must have hit stone." In the faint glow of the overturned lantern, they could see that it rested on a flat, unyielding surface that was dark and highly polished. "Black marble?" she suggested. "Do they mine marble this side of the Spine?"

No one answered her. Corson and Garast were both straining to see into a large, dark shadow on one side of the shaft. "That must be the opening," breathed Garast. "You two stay here and discuss it if you like—I'm going down there."

They watched him drop to his feet on the smooth, dark flooring, take up the lantern, and disappear into the arched opening in the wall. Corson climbed down at once, and Nyctasia lowered the other two lanterns to her before following. The knots of rope were too widely spaced for her to reach easily, and she had to inch her way down slowly and cautiously.

"Hurry up, can't you!" Corson said sharply. She felt buried alive in the narrow ring of stones that pressed in on her from all sides. Her heart pounded in panic, and her throat clenched like a fist at each breath, but she set Nyctasia on her feet before she hastened through the open archway into the stone corridor beyond.

Here, at least she could move forward, and she breathed more freely. "I am so rutting sick of holes and tunnels and scurrying around in burrows like a mole," she complained. "People belong on the earth, not under it—unless they're dead. And don't you tell me there's an old Eswraine legend that folk first sprouted from the ground like carrots!"

Nyctasia chuckled. "I don't know of such a legend, but really there ought to be one. Corson, I believe you have the makings of a genuine philosopher."

Corson was uncertain, as ever, whether Nyctasia was mocking her. "I believe you have the makings of genuine half-wit. Come along, we'll never catch up to Garast at this pace. I don't trust that one out of my sight." She stopped to wait for Nyctasia. The corridor had widened enough to allow them to stand side by side.

"I can't keep up with those long legs of yours, you know. If you're in such a hurry, you'd best go on without me." But despite this advice, Nyctasia took her hand, and they went on together.

Corson soon began to feel calmer. "The worst of it is," she said, smiling, "that Steifann won't believe a word of all this."

24

WHEN THEY CAME to the first bend in the tunnel, they made their way around the corner warily. "If it branches into two ways, I swear I'll turn back right now—" Corson began.

But the tunnel ended only a few feet ahead of them. They stood at the edge of a terrace of sorts, overlooking a vast round cavern that stretched far into the distance in every direction. A waterfall plunged down the wall on one side, filling a wide pool and flowing on in a stream that meandered through the great chamber to disappear beneath the facing wall. The water had cut deep winding channels into the bedrock, and even pierced the masses of stone to form natural bridges in a few places.

"The whole hill must be hollow," Corson said, and her voice echoed back to them from the empty air.

"Honeycombed, in fact."

A low parapet wall guarded the ledge from the sheer, steep drop to the stone floor below—probably to protect the children, Nyctasia thought. Corson took one look over the side and backed away hastily. "I hate heights," she muttered, "especially when they're depths."

They could not have seen so much by lanternlight, had the light not been given back a thousandfold by the facets of the

gleaming gemstones that studded the walls of the cavern on all
sides. Corson and Nyctasia seemed to be standing in the jeweled
heart of the earth.

Corson lost no time in prying loose one of the brilliant stones
with her dagger and testing it, but to her disappointment she
scratched it easily. "Well, the treasure's not a diamond-mine,"
she said sadly. "This is a lot of worthless crystal."

"Pity," said Nyctasia. "Listen—Garast's calling us." She
leaned over the stone balustrade to search the expanse of the great
cavern. Echoes chased the sound from place to place, but she
finally saw Garast standing on the far side of one of the bridges
and waving for them to join him.

"How did you get down there?" she shouted, but her words
were lost in meaningless noise, along with his answer.

They went on in the direction he pointed, following the terrace
along toward the cascading water. They came to the mouth of
another tunnel, but Garast waved them on, still pointing to the
waterfall. He seemed much excited by something he'd found.

"Does he expect us to *dive* down there?" Corson said, but the
ledge did lead behind the wall of falling water, and there they
found the opening to a deep spiral stairway.

Nyctasia cupped her hands to catch a drink of the rushing
water, and savored the clean, secret taste of ancient stone. "Perhaps the Cymvelans did have water for their gardens during the
drought, after all," she thought, as she followed Corson down the
winding stairs. The descent was an easy one, since Garast had lit
the wall-torches and left wide the heavy brass door at the foot of
the stairs. A flagstone path bordered the broad pool, and they
emerged from behind the waterfall a little dizzy, and dazed by the
noise, but quite dry. Garast was waiting for them, trying to shout
over the roaring of the water, beckoning them on.

The immense chamber was even more breathtaking from
within than from above. They followed the curving stream as it
wound across broad shallows and swirled into small, perfectly
round pools. It ran through deep, straight channels and fell into
purling cataracts over stairlike formations of stone. The water,
cutting through bare rock, was as clear and bright as the crystals
that glittered all around the chamber. Nyctasia suddenly remembered how she and her brother Emeryc had played as children,
lighting candle-ends stuck to bits of bark and floating them
downstream at night, to see whose would burn the longest. What
games children could have in a place like this!

Strangest of all was a spring of seething hot water that bubbled up from a cleft boulder to fill a deep, steaming pool. Corson tested the water in disbelief—the pool was as hot as soup, and the spring was actually boiling at the source. "I don't understand this," she said, frowning. "How did they do it? It doesn't seem like a spell, somehow, but how could it be natural?"

"No one knows," Nyctasia said quietly. "I've read of such springs, but I never thought to find one. This could be the true treasure, everlasting, precious beyond measure—the wellspring's weal. Waters like this may possess astonishing healing properties!"

"What about the danger and treachery?" asked Corson, who had begun to expect the worst of everything.

"I've no idea. It's said that all the world was water once, and that these are all that remains of the Mother of Waters. There's no telling what powers this spring may have."

"So you know no more about it than I do. You're just happy about all the baths you could take in it." Corson turned to Garast. "Is this what you wanted to show us?"

"No. It's over there." He started across the floor toward the far wall, and was soon lost to view among the strange stone structures that hung in graceful pillars. Some had been carved by wind and water into fantastic curving shapes, others sculpted by hand into beautiful or bizarre figures. A few of these natural columns had been hollowed, filled with oil, and fitted with wicks of waxed rope to create giants' candles which Garast had already lit. Their light flickered eerily, glinting on the crystals and casting monstrous shadows over the walls, and behind every stone form. Bats began to skitter and swoop about the cave, disturbed by the unaccustomed noise and light.

Corson and Nyctasia filled their lamps with oil and followed after Garast. Nyctasia would have liked to linger to study the detailed carvings, but he hurried them on to his new discovery, a large crack in the cave wall.

Irritated by his look of self-satisfaction, Corson shoved him aside to look through the rift herself. "There's something behind this wall. Look, Nyc, you can see all the way through to another cave."

But not even Nyctasia could fit through the fissure. "I knew I should have brought 'Lorin instead of you," Corson grumbled as they followed along the wall, looking for another way in. When they came to the end they turned back, this time climbing over

the high outcroppings of rock in the way, instead of skirting
them. From the top of one of these, and only from the top, they
could see the dark opening into the wall behind it. Corson clam-
bered down the other side in an instant, followed by Garast. He
pushed past her and went in while she was helping Nyctasia descend.

Inside, they found a stark stone chamber, a low-ceilinged cave
with none of the skillful embellishment of the crystal cavern. In
the center of the floor was a small enclosure made of heaped
stones, just large enough to hold one crouching person. Above it,
crudely painted on the rock, were more of the bestial figures they
had seen in the crypt, and they could just make out that something was stacked in small separate piles on the ground. They
huddled closer to look at them and saw that they were animal
skulls, dark brown with age, each lying atop a heap of bones.
Finally, level with the top of Nyctasia's head, was a large hole in
the wall that was clearly some sort of passage. Two slabs of stone
served as stairs leading up to it.

"Where are we?" asked Corson, after a silence.

"This," Nyctasia said softly, "is the way to life and knowledge."

Garast agreed. "I remember whispers about the last part of the
path—that it was narrow and arduous. That it led to the light
through darkness, and to the new knowledge through the old. I
was too young to understand all that, of course. We were supposed to learn the riddles first, and the dances. . . ."

"I'd guess that the Cymvelans used this place, made it part of
their pattern," said Nyctasia, "but it must have belonged to those
who worshiped here before they came. That sort of tunnel"—she
pointed to the hole—"is found in a number of very old, primitive
fanes dedicated to the Mother of the World. To pass through it is
to be reborn, you see."

"This is all most fascinating," Corson broke in sharply, "but
do you mean to say that we have to crawl through there?" The
well had been nearly unbearable, but this narrow space would
drive her mad. The thought of being trapped in the grip of stone,
unable to move, with only the tunnel stretching before her, sent
chills of unreasoning terror through her. She couldn't climb into
that hole. It was impossible.

"Certainly we don't have to," said Nyctasia. "But whatever
we're seeking is probably on the other side." Ever since she'd
seen the empty crawlspace, Nyctasia had felt a keen desire to

explore it. She saw that Corson was horrified at the prospect, and even Garast reluctant, and she wondered how they could resist the mystery of the tunnel, which drew her as strongly as it re-pelled Corson.

"You don't have to, perhaps, but I do," said Garast grimly. He held his lantern up to the opening and peered down the passage, but could not see to the end.

Nyctasia climbed the stone stairs to have a look. "It's dry as far as I can see," she said, pleased.

"Oh, *good,*" said Corson, "we wouldn't want to get *dirty*, would we? Nyc, you're not going in there?"

"I think I will . . . but perhaps you should wait here, Corson. The tunnel's cut to human proportions, not to yours."

"Yes, you might not be able to get through," Garast agreed—rather eagerly, Corson thought. "It looks as if it narrows farther on."

"We'll see," said Corson firmly. They were right, she told herself. They'd come too far to turn back now. And she'd die before she'd let the others think she was more frightened than they. "Nyc, you first. You're the smallest and least likely to get stuck before we know what's happening. You, go in after her. I'll bring up the rear." Her heart was hammering frantically, but she gave out her orders as sharply as an officer of the Imperial Army, and the others obeyed readily.

Nyctasia pushed her lamp into the tunnel then heaved herself up into the hole. "Corson, are you sure you—"

"Go," Corson snapped, "it's never going to be any easier."

It was just possible for them to move on their hands and knees, pushing their lamps ahead of them where the ground was smooth, or carrying them with their teeth. The oily taste of the leather strap made Nyctasia feel faintly ill, but she clenched her jaw tighter and crawled on as fast as she could. In places, the passage narrowed so drastically that they had to slide along on their bellies. We're in the stone throat of the earth, Corson thought. Any moment it will close and swallow us. A few times she thought she'd be stuck in a particularly tight place, and she only wriggled through with difficulty.

Once, panic-stricken, she called to the others to stop, sure that her shoulders were caught fast.

"Garast, pull at her arms," Nyctasia said calmly.

"I can't turn around," he said, "there's no room."

"No matter—Corson, dash some oil on the wall just above

where you're stuck. Once it seeps down between, you'll be able to slide through easily, or pull back, at the least." She sounded so completely confident that Corson took heart and tried to twist around to follow her advice, and her shoulders came loose of their own accord.

"Never mind," she said shakily, "I'm free, keep going." No one spoke again except when Garast's boot struck Corson in the face, and she cursed him roundly, which made her feel a little better.

Soon they were crawling through a tight tunnel of solid crystal, glorious to see in the lamplight, but brutally hard on their knees and their unprotected hands. When they had to pull themselves along flat to the ground, Corson could feel the sharp facets even through her leather vest. Nyctasia was already covered with bruises. There was nothing to do but move forward slowly and painfully, and hope for an end. Corson suspected that it would be impossible for them to back up and get out the way they'd come in, but she kept that thought to herself.

Nyctasia stopped abruptly. Garast tumbled into her and kicked Corson again. "What do you think you're doing, Nyc?" Corson demanded. "What's the trouble?"

"It slopes downward just ahead, be careful. And the air's getting colder. Can you feel it?"

"It must be another cave," Corson said. "It would be warmer if we'd reached the outside. Move!"

Nyctasia wriggled forward again, more slowly. Again, there was nothing but the sounds of their bodies scraping against rock, and their tired breathing. Then Nyctasia gasped, and the light of her lantern disappeared. "What's happened?" Corson shouted, and Garast, groping ahead, said, "I don't see her. Stop pushing me! There's a—" And he vanished as well. Corson was alone in the unbreakable hold of stone.

For a long moment she froze, unable to think or feel a thing. Then, panting like a cornered animal, she began to inch forward slowly, until her fingers found the edge. How steep was the drop? How far? "Nyc . . . ?" she called, in a strangled voice that did not carry far. She tried again.

"Get *off* me, you clumsy oaf! You'll set us both afire."

They were perhaps the most welcome words Corson had ever heard. "Nyc, where *are* you two?" she shouted.

"Wait, my lantern went out when I dropped it. There." Finally there was a light below, and Nyctasia's head and shoulders appeared, not as far away as Corson had feared. "Garast fell on me," she explained, "and knocked his head on the wall, too. He's all right now. Can you climb down here without falling, do you think? It's sloped, but quite sharply."

Unlike the others, Corson could reach to both sides of the passage to brace herself, and she managed to get nearly to the bottom before she lost hold and slid the rest of the way to the tunnel's mouth. She emerged head first into another cavern, smaller than the first, and divided by a tall wall of marble masonry. At first she only stared, without even rising to her feet. There before her, like a vision in a fable, was the end of their quest. She was lying at the threshold of a towering brazen door.

It was of a single bronze casting, molded to a masterpiece of sculptor's skill. A great tree filled the frame, its limbs laden with fruit, each leaf and petal perfect in detail. The strings of a wind-harp were stretched among the branches, and a spider's web delicately spanned two slender twigs. Golden bees clustered around the blossoms and ripe fruit, and Nyctasia saw with misgiving that the tree bore peaches.

Corson took more interest in the inscription carved in the marble arch above the door. She spelled it out triumphantly:

> "Here in the earthen embrace
> Of the last hiding-place
> Answered is every riddle,
> Run is the race,
> Done is the chase.

"I never want to hear another rhyme for the rest of my days," she said. "But this is the end, and no mistake—we've found it. Now, we've only to—" She stopped short with a wail of dismay. "The key! I didn't bring it with me—it's back at the house!"

"Fool!" exclaimed Garast. "We'll have the whole household swarming down here now. But there's nothing for it, we'll just have to go back and fetch the key. We'll not get in by standing here staring." He crouched down and crawled back into the tunnel without another word. They heard him scrabbling his way up the incline, sliding back then dragging himself up farther, cursing and kicking.

Corson got down on one knee at the mouth of the passage, to watch his progress. "Well, it can be done," she sighed. "You'd better go first so I can give you a push from below."

Nyctasia seemed not to hear. She still stood by the great brass portal, as if she were listening for something on the other side. At last she said in a low voice, "Corson, I'd not be in too great a hurry to open this door."

"Why not, in Asye's name? Look, it spells 'hoard'—what more do you want? This has to be the treasure."

"I fear you were nearer the mark when you said, 'This is the end, and no mistake.' Don't you see that the answer to this riddle is Death? The 'earthen embrace' is the grave, the 'last hiding-place' is the tomb. It is death that answers all questions and crowns every effort. It may be a charnel house we'll find behind this door, not a treasure-chamber."

A heavy silence hung between them for a few moments, till Corson said, "That would be just like my luck. 'Neither in the open air, neither in a dwelling,' eh? But we can't come this far and not look, Nyc. I'd go mad wondering."

Nyctasia laid her hand against the tall bronze door. "You don't feel it, then?"

"What do you mean?" Corson asked uneasily.

"The power—the spell—that we sensed at the ruins on the night we camped there." It seemed a lifetime ago, somehow. "The source is here, I'm sure of it."

"You feel it still? I thought it was gone—I meant to ask you. Why don't I . . . ?"

"I can't say for sure, but I think it's because it's daytime now, and the Valeice isn't in the sky—the star of change."

"The Reaper's Eye . . . Well, I'll make sure it's daytime when we unlock this door, but I have to know what's in there, spell or no spell. Let's get out of here now, before nightfall."

Nyctasia nodded. "We must open it, I suppose. But I thought you should be warned—there's no telling what the Cymvelans regarded as treasure." She took up her lamp and knelt before the tunnel-mouth. The urge she'd felt to plunge into it before was gone, but there was no other way back to the great cavern. With Corson's help she managed to climb the slope, gripping the knobby crystals and inching upward till she could pull herself over the edge again. Garast was already out of sight, but she rested and waited for Corson, nursing her scraped and bleeding hands. They were so painful she could hardly flex her fingers. She would have given half her fortune at that moment for a pair of thick leather gloves.

Corson followed, steadying her legs against the walls of the

tunnel, and clambering up without much difficulty. Even the passage itself seemed easier to bear, now that she knew how far there
was to go. Nyctasia was slower this time, but they made their
way steadily back to the bone-strewn chamber and had no serious
trouble until they reached the foot of the spiral staircase, hidden
by the waterfall. The door had been pulled tight, even with the
sheer stone wall. Garast had bolted it shut behind him.

25

"CORSON, I'M SORRY," said Nyctasia. "This is my fault. You knew enough to keep him in sight, but I—"

"Quiet, there he is," Corson whispered tensely. On the stone terrace high above them, near the tunnel leading to the well, Garast stood leaning over the balustrade, as if waiting for them to catch up with him. They walked slowly across the great hall, and Nyctasia waved up at him. "The door's stuck fast," she called quite calmly. "You'll have to come back down and push it open."

Garast did not move.

"Hurry up, man! We have to fetch that key."

"I'm sure I can find it for myself," he said. "I'll not be needing your help anymore."

"If you make me climb up there myself, I'll tear you into dogmeat!" Corson shouted, but the echoes threw her words back at her mockingly. She could no more scale that steep stone cliff than she could fly over it, and Garast knew it. She looked desperately around the vast, shadowy cavern, outraged at her helplessness. "There's sure to be another way out of here!"

Garast leaned farther over toward them, as if to confide a secret. "I think there is," he said, "and do you know where? I think the only way out is through the door of the last hiding-place. . . . And that door will never be opened by an outsider, nor reveal its secrets to the unworthy, while I can prevent it. You've seen more than is fitting already, but you'll pay with your lives for profaning the sacred places! And when you've starved for your meddling, I'll return to claim what is mine. No one but I has the right to use that key."

Nyctasia had a sickening feeling that he was right about the way out of the cavern. It suited altogether too well with the ways of the Cymvelans. But it would be a long while before she and Corson starved to death, she reflected. There was plenty of water. She herself was accustomed to fasting, and Corson was exceptionally strong. Could they eat bats? "It is only a few days to Yu Valeicu," she said to Garast. "Have you forgotten?"

"Let the Edonaris guard my inheritance for me. When I tell them you've gone astray in the tunnels, they'll comb the ruins for you, won't they, my lady? They'll keep watch day and night— but I don't think they'll seek you at the bottom of an old well. I'll help them search, though, just to be sure." He laughed, obviously pleased with himself. "I'll show them just where I lost you, and I'll direct the searchers tirelessly, I promise you—"

But his laughter suddenly swelled to a shrill cry, and then he was plummeting toward them, down the long fall from the ledge, to strike the stone floor at their feet with a hard, hideous sound.

"Watch out!" called a familiar voice from overhead. "He's the crazed bastard we stole the pouch from—that one's dangerous!"

Nyctasia had knelt beside the still form of Garast, but now she rose and turned away. "Not anymore," she said heavily. "His chase is done. In truth, he found the way without our help."

"Dead?" said Newt uneasily. "Hlann, do you mean I've killed someone? I thought he'd break a few bones."

"Never mind him—what are *you* doing here?" Corson demanded.

"What do you think? I knew you'd come after the treasure with my page of clues. I've been here for a good while waiting for you to find it, and it's taken you long enough! I watched the slavers, I watched you, I watched the slavers watching you, and the lot of you led me round in circles," he complained. "And the rutting watchdogs nearly had me a score of times, too."

"We really seem to give you no end of inconvenience," said Nyctasia, leaning wearily against the wall. "But might we just trouble you a little further, to come down here and open the door to the stairway? I want to get back to the house and have a bath."

Newt straddled the balustrade and grinned down at them. "Why should I? I could steal that key from your room and wait for you both to starve, like he said. Then I'd have the treasure for myself."

With a motion almost too fast to follow, Corson snatched the knife from her boot-sheath and straightened up again, arm poised to throw. "Try it, you sneaking flea," she yelled. "Make a move anywhere but toward those stairs, and I'll have a knife through your scrawny neck before you know it!"

Newt froze. "You daren't. No one else knows you're here. If you kill me, you'll never be found."

Nyctasia sighed, as if irritated at the quarreling of children. "Oh, she's mad enough to do it, I'm sure. Corson, do try, please, not to be so hasty." She pushed herself away from the wall, with an effort, and wheeled to face Newt, throwing out one arm to point at him threateningly. "As for *you,* thiefling, if you *dare* go off and leave us here, I'll cast a curse on you with my dying breath that will shrivel the flesh from your bones! Now come open that door before I lose my patience."

"All right, I'm coming!" He climbed off the balustrade and slid down to shelter behind it, glaring down at them between the stone palings. "But I don't believe you can cast a spell like that, lady. Why'd you run away from Rhostshyl if you can do such things?"

Nyctasia laughed. "You're no fool. Now why couldn't my accusers in the city take such a sensible view of the matter? The truth is that I don't know whether I can do it or not, because I've never tried. Perhaps I can't, but—"

"But we'll all find out soon enough, if you don't make haste," Corson told Newt grimly.

"Yes," Nyctasia agreed, "I don't like to be kept waiting. Stop pretending that you'll abandon us here, Newt. You're a thief, not a murderer."

"Well, I want a share of the treasure in return."

"Any treasure on this land belongs to the Edonaris of Vale," Nyctasia pointed out. "But I believe that I can answer for them. That seems fair enough to me." She disregarded Corson's muttered promise to see to it that Newt got everything he deserved.

"And there's another thing," he said suspiciously. "That one" —he pointed to Corson—"is quits with me for good and all if I help you. Your word on it!"

"Ho, I said you were no fool. But I'm afraid I can't answer for her. What say you, Corson?"

Corson spat, disgusted at the perverse, everlasting injustice of her lot. "Oh, very well. Agreed," she said.

* * *

Corson lifted Nyctasia over the lip of the well and then turned to look down at Newt as he struggled his way up the knotted rope. She chuckled. "After all, it consoles me to know that Raphistain ar'n Edonaris will have your head when I tell him it was you stealing from his harvesters."

A hollow-sounding exclamation of protest rose from the shaft, followed before long by Newt's head and arms as he climbed into view. "Thankless bitch!" he sputtered. "If not for me you'd have rotted down there forever!"

"Now, Corson," Nyctasia interceded, "Raphe's so enamored of you, I'm sure he'll forgive Newt when he hears that he saved your life."

Corson shook her head. "He loves those grapes of his better than me and the whole world beside," she said confidently, delighted with the effect of her words on the dismayed Newt. Then, with a laugh, she grabbed his arm and hauled him up over the rim of the well—not very gently, perhaps, but she did it without breaking his arm.

26

CORSON HESITATED BEFORE the bronze door, key in hand. Now that nothing prevented her from unearthing the hoard of the Cymvelans, she felt, despite herself, that it would be unwise to go further. Though Nyctasia stood by, waiting quite calmly, seemingly untroubled, Corson could sense her apprehension and could not help sharing it. But she knew that it was too late to turn back now, no matter what lay beyond. Ever before her mind's eye was the vision of a chamber heaped with gold and precious gems, hundreds of years in the hoarding, enough and more for a lifetime's spending. . . .

"What are you waiting for? Get on with it, woman, can't you?" said Newt, who harbored much the same hopes, and was impatient to commence his new life of opulence and luxury.

"Hold your tongue," Raphe said sharply. He was resigned to tolerating Newt's presence, but he did not pretend to be pleased about it. Certainly he would not allow him to speak disrespectfully to Corson. In truth, he too would have liked to tell Corson to hurry, but he was restrained by good manners, as well as a certain well-bred reluctance to reveal his own eagerness for the treasure. But he thought hungrily of the new land that could be bought and cultivated with such a fortune. . . .

"Yes, hush," Nyctasia said quietly. "Whatever we shall find has waited a very long time, I think. It can wait a little longer. We have time enough."

She had insisted that only the matriarch be told of their discoveries, and of Garast's death. Corson had willingly deferred to her judgment in such a matter, and Newt, indeed, had no desire to tell anybody. He refused even to accompany them to the house, arranging instead to meet them at the well next morning.

Lady Nocharis had summoned Diastor and Mesthelde to hear their tale, and they in turn had consulted with a few of the others. None of them was much inclined to join the search, when they heard how arduous it was to negotiate the passages to the locked door. Yet it was clearly impractical to entrust the affair to one of the youngsters, since all of them would insist on going along and getting in the way. In the end, only Raphe had been sent to look after the interests of the Edonaris in the matter, though he'd urged 'Deisha to go in his place. "You're smaller than I am," he teased. "You'd fit through all those ghoul-haunted holes, and dark tombs and such, better than I."

"But you're stronger, brother mine. You'll be more use for carrying out the heavy bags of gold and chests of jewels you'll find down there." She changed her mind when she realized that Nyctasia planned to return to the underground chamber with Corson, but Nyctasia discouraged her from coming along.

"There's really very little room for us all in those passages," she'd explained, more or less truthfully. "And you're right—the stronger the better for climbing about in there, and possibly for digging too." And 'Deisha had reluctantly agreed to wait for them at the well.

Nyctasia could not honestly have explained why she felt that the practical, realistic Raphe would be less at risk among these shadows than his fanciful, romantic sister, but as she watched Corson raise the key that would unlock the Cymvelans' secret, she was relieved to think of 'Deisha safe in the sunshine above.

The door swung out easily, as soon as Corson turned the key, and the others pressed forward anxiously to follow her into the dark room beyond. They stood in a knot in the middle of the floor, their lamps raised, and stared around them at the full-laden shelves that lined the walls of the inner chamber.

They had found the library of the Cymvelan Circle.

"Books!" shouted Corson. "Nothing but a lot of moldy, old,

rotting, rutting books! I might have known it would be something
not worth a heap of dried dog dung—" Words failed her. Even
curses failed her. Nothing could express her bitter disappointment
and rancor. Had she been alone, she'd have burst into tears.

Newt had taken a quick look around, then hastened to open a
pair of stout chests that stood on either side of the door. But
finding both filled with rolled vellum scrolls, he slammed shut
the second one, kicked it viciously and sat down on top of it,
head in hands, the picture of dejection.

"I don't suppose any of these are worth anything?" Raphe
asked Nyctasia, who was eagerly examining one volume after
another, exclaiming over them with delight.

"Worth anything? This collection is priceless," she cried.
"This *is* wealth beyond a lifetime's spending, because one could
spend many lifetimes studying it." Clearly, she intended to spend
her lifetime doing so.

"Oh, you could rot down here for all eternity, I've no doubt,"
Corson said. "You were right about that inscription—this is
nothing but a tomb for old, dead words. If they're so priceless,
why would the Cymvelans let children get at them?"

"The library wouldn't have been unattended in those days, I'm
sure. There would always have been people here studying or
writing. I imagine that once the children were clever enough to
find their way here, they were deemed ready to begin their studies—"

"Poor little mites," Corson put in sympathetically.

"It was probably part of their initiation, the approach to wisdom. We were a sad lot of fools to think that the riddles might
lead to anything else. What treasure but knowledge does one put
into the hands of children? What other power can be shared with
all, but never lost? Who can measure the worth of such riches?"
She gazed at the precious books as if they might turn to dust and
smoke if she turned her eyes from them. "Look, this is Threnn's
translation of Iostyn Vahr's *Treatise on the Manifold Ills of the
Flesh,* all seven volumes! The man knew more about diseases of
the inner organs than anyone who's ever lived. For years I've
been seeking just for scraps of the Fourth Book—I didn't think
the last three still existed! There are books here that I've only
read of in ancient commentaries. And there are recent works too
—here's Raine of Tièrelon's *Account of His Sojourn Among the
Wolf-Folk,* and the *First Precepts* of Isper the Mad ...! The
Cymvelans must have been devoted to learning absolutely, both

in body and spirit, to create such a complete collection of scholarship."

Newt, grieving over his lost treasure, listened to her transports of rapture with heartfelt loathing. "How can you *stand* her?" he asked Corson, between clenched teeth.

"I can't," said Corson promptly, feeling some goodwill toward Newt for the first time. "It's enough to wear away the patience of a stone. One day I'll tie her neck in a knot, I promise you."

Nyctasia paid no heed to either of them. "These must be taken out of here as soon as possible, to a dry, aired room—at least until I've had copies made. *Vahn*, it will take me years just to record what's been assembled here. I can't think where to begin."

Raphe shrugged. "We'll have to begin by opening out the passageway, if you want to move all these aboveground. That will take some time."

"But there must be an easier way in and out of here. They'd not have taken all that trouble every time they wanted to consult a book."

Once they'd lit the torches along the walls, and the great lamp that hung from the center of the domed ceiling, they soon found the door they were seeking. It was half-hidden by the shadows, but had not been deliberately concealed. It was locked, however, and built of stout, unyielding oak.

"We'll have to come back with axes," said Raphe, when they'd tried Corson's key without success.

Newt looked at him scornfully. "Any fledgling picklock could open this door," he said, and turned to Corson. "Let me have the use of that clasp you've got in your hair." He took it from her and knelt before the lock, peering into it and muttering. "The trick," he said, turning to the others, "is to get all the tumblers lined up at once. This lock's more for show than protection. I don't think they expected thieves down here." He inserted the long pin of the clasp and gave it a practiced twist. There was a distinct click, and the door opened a bit. Newt rose, dusted his knees elaborately, and returned the clasp to Corson, with a bow.

But instead of a way to the outside, they found another, larger chamber, surrounding a strange round enclosure with windowless stone walls that reached to the ceiling. The entrance to the inner enclosure was a gate, wrought of iron and embellished with the mark of the Cymvelan Circle. Nyctasia thrust her lamp between the bars and saw a series of walled pathways that twisted and intertwined. "It's the maze," she said. "I wondered why we'd never found it." She tried the gate, but it was locked fast. "Newt, come here and—"

"No need for that," Raphe called from the other side of the enclosure. "There's an opening on this side, and more doors."

They circled the maze to the point opposite the gate, and found an open archway to the enclosure, and two closed wooden doors equidistant from it, in the facing wall.

Newt had gone into the maze a little way, but quickly returned, fearful of losing the way. "This must be the way in, but then why—"

"The way out, more likely," Nyctasia said. "I think the initiates were brought in at the other side and locked in. They were meant to find their way through the maze to this opening, and then to one of those doors, I suppose. What's in there?" She thought she knew the answer, but she was reluctant to look.

Much to Newt's disappointment, the first door they tried was unlocked. It opened into a long, bare room, hewn by hand from solid stone. No attempt had been made to smooth the walls or ceiling, but the floor had been worn level in places from the tread of many feet over the years. One such path led to a large altar, made of one rough, flat stone balanced on four short stone columns. The whole was set on a natural shelf of rock, so that it was elevated above the ground. There was none of the elaborate decoration or painting that adorned the building above, but no one doubted that this too was a temple of sorts.

Nyctasia shuddered. "Let's try the other door."

Newt had already done so, since the first door had yielded nothing he could spend or sell. But the second revealed only a set of broad, easily climbed stairs, leading upward. A few faint streaks of light pierced the gloom at the top.

The flight of stairs soon ended in a strange, curved corridor no wider than the stairs, not carved from solid rock, but built of stone and mortar. "We're above ground," said Nyctasia, "but where?"

"Probably in a keep of Castle Saetarrin," said Raphe gloomily.

A few feet before and behind them was a stone wall, but on either side of the top step was a doorway covered with wood, and sunlight was seeping between the planks on one side. Corson lost no time in setting her back against the opposite side and kicking out the slats.

* * *

"It's been boarded up for years," said Raphe. "Of course the whole place was searched, but they only needed to uncover the main door to do that. I daresay no one thought to look *inside* the wall."

The four of them were sitting on the low wall outside the bell-tower, regarding the doubly boarded doorway. It did not seem to conceal a thing, either from inside or outside the tower. The stairway could only be seen from the very threshold.

"Neither out of doors nor in," sighed Nyctasia. "Perhaps the Cymvelans hid the way themselves. If they feared an attack they'd have wanted to protect the library."

"The Cymvelans or the Saetarrin . . ." said Raphe.

"Or the slavers," Corson suggested. "And if people did discover it, the slavers soon discovered them." She shook her head. "When I think of all the trouble we went through—that awful crawl through the tunnel . . ." Her voice trailed off in disgust.

"And all for nothing!" Newt agreed in an aggrieved tone.

"This will make it much easier to reach the library," Nyctasia said with satisfaction. "We've only to break open that inner doorway, and I can start removing the books at once."

"Hurrah," muttered Corson, seconded by Newt, who wished Nyctasia joy of them. Their differences forgotten in their mutual dissatisfaction at the outcome of the adventure, the two went off to get drunk together.

Raphe stood and offered his hand to Nyctasia. "I'll find you people to. carry the books," he promised. "The sooner it's done the better, I think. It's no wonder the structure's unsteady if the ground's not solid below, and half the wall's hollow. The shoring underneath looked none too healthy either. You'll have to take great care. I wouldn't like to lose my new kinswoman almost as soon as I've found her. When you're finished we'll have to seal the whole place off—especially from the little ones. The chances that someone will come to grief are too great."

Nyctasia agreed with him wholeheartedly, though she did not voice all of her reasons.

27

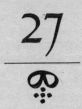

"WHY ARE YOU so set on finding this Jocelys, anyway?" Corson asked. "What's the use? The riddles are answered, you've got your precious books—what do you want with Jocelys, whoever she may be?"

Corson, Nyctasia and Newt were on the road to Amron Therain, all three traveling for different reasons. Nyctasia hoped to find Jocelys, the last of the Cymvelan foundlings on Garast's list. "She ought to be told about the library," she explained. "It is her birthright—Garast was right about that. And she should be told about his death, too. She and Rowan are as close to kin as he had."

Corson shrugged. "If she's at all like Rowan, she'll not thank you for the information. Probably she doesn't want to know anything about it."

"Likely enough," Nyctasia agreed. "But there's another reason I want to find her. Garast said that the Circle meant to use the treasure for vengeance somehow. If they went to Jocelys too, she may know something about their plans."

"Garast made it all up, I daresay. That one was almost as much of a liar as you are. We didn't find anything in the library that would serve as a weapon for vengeance."

"That's just what worries me. Yesterday I had the last of the books removed. . . . There's a volume missing, and it was taken recently, to judge by the dust."

"It wasn't me!" Newt said hastily, looking guilty nevertheless.

Corson gave him a sidelong glance. "No one's accused you. Yet. Do you know what book it was, Nyc? Was it valuable?"

"It's rare, yes, and for good reason. For generations it's been forbidden to make copies of it, all through the Empire, and it's proscribed in most municipalities as well. Naturally there are those who'd pay anything for it."

At this, Newt took an interest. "What's in the thing?"

"It's a treatise called *On the Nature of Demonic Spirits*. No one knows who wrote it, or exactly when it was written, but it's old. The work's divided into two parts—the first is harmless enough, and not very hard to come by. I've read it many times. But the *Second Book,* you see, contains spells—spells only a mad fool would tamper with—for summoning and commanding certain elemental powers. . . .

"Perhaps the Cymvelans never had the entire work," she continued, after a long silence, "but there are other books just as rare in that collection. And the missing volume, whatever it was, was on the shelf next to the *First Book on the Nature of Demonic Spirits*. I think they had the *Second Book,* and knew very well the potency of its spells. That riddle about the peach tree is ambiguous—it doesn't spell out the answer. It could refer to the library, to the sweet fruit of study that nourishes the spirit, but holds a deadly secret. One spell from the *Second Book* could free the demonic Presence of the Cymvelan land, and give the power and riches that the riddles promise, but the danger is unthinkable. Corson, tomorrow is Yu Yaleicu."

Newt gave a low whistle. He felt that he'd chosen a good time to get out of Vale. He was bound for Amron Therain simply because it was the nearest town of any size where there would be a Harvest celebration, no doubt teeming with drunken folk with pockets to be picked. As he'd explained at dinner the night before, he'd had his fill of treasure and adventure, and meant to return to the safer occupations of thievery and swindling. After a few glasses of Edonaris wine, he had entertained some muddled but interesting ideas of selling worthless pieces of parchment covered with clues to the Cymvelan fortune. With his detailed knowledge of the site, he should be able to make them very convincing indeed. . . . But foremost in his mind was the desire to put some distance between himself and Corson and Nyctasia, whose company he considered unlucky.

As they reached the outskirts of Amron Therain, he reined in his horse and waited for them to pass. "I'll not enter the city with you, if you don't mind," he said, with a curt bow. "I'll wait here till you're out of sight."

"Good," said Corson. "If you're caught for a cutpurse, I don't care to have been seen with you."

Nyctasia gave him a present of money. "Farewell, Newt, and be careful. If you take up brigandry again, I'd advise you to go masked in future. You might rob another soldier with a memory as long as Corson's."

Newt grinned. "Many thanks, Your Ladyship. The generosity of the Edonaris is renowned. Your kinfolk won't object, I'm sure, if I keep this handsome horse, in place of the one you cheated me of, back in Rhostshyl Wood." Then he turned to Corson, shaking his head reprovingly. "And you, you're too careless by half. When you drink with a thief, guard your valuables well." To Corson's astonishment, he tossed her a large diamond she'd received from Nyctasia some time ago, in fee for her services as bodyguard. "I hate to give it back, but I fear our paths might cross again one day."

"Asye forbid!" said Corson. "Nyc, let's go before I forget my promise and break his neck." Newt drew aside and waved them on their way with a jaunty salute. Corson dug her heels into her horse's sides. "A strange little scoundrel, and no mistake," she laughed. "Good riddance to him, for all that he saved our lives."

Her object in Amron Therain was to arrange passage on the first riverboat sailing south to Stocharnos. From there it would be only a few days' ride overland to Chiastelm and Steifann. He had been on his own quite long enough, she felt. If there was no boat leaving soon, she'd return to Vale with Nyctasia for the three days of Harvest Festival, but if she could set sail on the morrow, so much the better.

She'd already taken her leave of the Edonaris. As was usual with her, her farewells had been brief—except with Raphe. Their leavetaking had occupied the greater part of the night. She'd tried to return the fine gold silk, since the material could easily be used again, but he had insisted that she keep it, declaring that it could not possibly look so charming on anyone else. Uncertain, she'd consulted Nyctasia, who'd assured her that it would be impolite to refuse. "Always accept a gift from one who can afford to give it," Nyctasia had counseled, and Corson accepted her advice readily. She was not likely to have occasion to wear the gown again, but she looked forward to showing it to Steifann, and she could have a shirt made from it afterward. A silk shirt would be an extravagance, but more practical than a fancy gown. There'd be enough left over to make a kerchief for Annin and some ribbons for that little peacock Trask to wear on his sleeves. It would be her finest homecoming yet—the stories she'd have to tell them, this time! And as for Steifann, she'd make him wish he'd never met that mangy cur Destiver. And after that, she'd make him forget that there were other women in the world. . . .

As she planned her reunion with Steifann, in vivid detail, they rode into Amron Therain, and Nyctasia halted her horse. "I can't go to the waterfront with you—I must find Jocelys. There's no time to be lost. I'll ask at the marketplace first. Shall I meet you somewhere later, in case you decide to go back to Vale with me tonight?"

Corson started guiltily. Nyctasia looked tormented with worry, and her voice was strained and anxious. "No, I'll help you look for her first. I can do that much. But I can't help you fight spells, Nyc. My sword's no use against ghosts and demons. I won't hide from you that I think I'm well out of all this. But if the danger's as great as you say, why not post guards and keep the Cymvelans out of the temple, like I told you before?"

"I'll see to that, of course. But I'm not sure that will prevent them from invoking the spell. I'm afraid that the time when it's done may be more important than the place where it's done. The Valeice is at its height now, at the turning point from summer to autumn. The celebration marks the weakening of the boundaries, not just between the seasons, but between all things. Nothing is certain at such a time, and the Balance is weighted toward death —not toward life, as it is in the spring. Something must be done, but I don't know what to do."

Corson sighed. "I surely don't know if you don't, Nyc. But I think we'd better stop talking and get on with searching for this Jocelys."

* * *

"Would it be Jocelys the tax-collector you want, milady, or Jocelys who keeps the dramshop?"

"The dramshop-keeper," said Corson hopefully.

"I don't know," said Nyctasia. "Was either of them a foundling from Vale?"

The man shrugged. "I don't know their histories. The one's a man, rather loud, rather fat, and the other a woman, rather quiet, rather thin."

"Ah, we're in luck," said Corson. "Where will we find her?"

"You've not far to go. If you turn down this lane and take the second alleyway to the thoroughfare, then cross the square, on the right side, you'll be nearly there, but it's a small place and easy to miss—"

"Show us the way," ordered Nyctasia, holding out some silver.

The dramshop was indeed a small one, and empty at this hour of the morning except for a woman who was mulling ale over an open hearth. The rich, savory scent filled the room.

"Two cups of that brew," said Corson, "and plenty of ground emberseed in mine, if you've got it."

The woman nodded to them. "Surely, mistress, but bide a breath, if you will. I've not quite finished with it." She tasted the simmering liquor with a long wooden spoon, then tossed in a handful of nutmeg from a row of jars on the mantel and stirred it in.

They sat down on a bench near the hearth. "If it's as good as it smells, it will be worth the waiting," said Nyctasia. "Would you be Jocelys brenn Vale, I wonder?"

The woman's eyes widened. "I am, and no reason to hide it. All in this town know me."

"We bring you news from Vale . . . about Garast," Nyctasia said gently. "He's dead, I'm afraid. We were all three exploring the caverns beneath the Cymvelan ruins, and he fell from a ledge. I'm sorry to bring such tidings across your threshold."

Jocelys bent over the kettle of ale, her face hidden. "What is that to me? I've nothing to do with that fool Garast and his schemes. I told him he'd find no treasure there, and I tell you the same. Let me be!"

"But we did find the treasure. It was knowledge the Cymvelans hoarded. We found their library, underneath the temple. Garast wanted you to know that, you and Rowan. You've a claim to it, after all."

"So, now I know, and you can take yourselves off. I trouble

no one, and I want no trouble from others. I've my family to think of. Get out of this house, both of you!"

"In good time," said Corson evenly. "We'll have that drink first, if it's ready."

"Jocelys, please hear me out," Nyctasia pleaded. "We've not come to make trouble for you. We need your help—it's a desperate matter. Garast warned us that the Cymvelans mean to visit some dire vengeance on the folk of the valley, and the time is near. Surely they sought you out as well. If you know aught of their plans, I beg you to tell us before it's too late to stop them."

Scowling, Jocelys turned back to her brewing. "So you believed that mad tale of Garast's?" she said scornfully. "There are no Cymvelans. How could they have escaped the fire, tell me that? Oh, Garast may have seen them, but who else ever did? Not I. Not Rowan, that I ever heard of." She paused to taste the ale again, and stirred in more spices. "If you're worrying over some nonsense that one told you, you can rest easy, by my word. And you're welcome to the library, and the root-cellar too, for all of me." She ladled out two mugs full of the fragrant drink and set it before them, clearly impatient to be rid of them. Though she spoke firmly enough, Nyctasia saw that her hand trembled as she poured their ale.

It *was* as good as it smelled, Corson decided. "Nyc, what she says makes sense. Maybe Garast did imagine that little visit from the Cymvelans. He was crazy enough for that."

Nyctasia sipped her drink thoughtfully. "I'd be glad to believe that. But there's still the book to be accounted for, and the uncanny power we sensed at the ruins. . . ." She turned to Jocelys. "You see, there are tunnels underneath the temple that they might have used to flee the fire. The *vahn* knows I hope you're right about Garast's story, but if you're not, many lives may be in danger—the innocent and the guilty alike. It might be of help if you told us what he said to you about their plans. He might have revealed more to you than to us. Please try, that's all I ask."

"If I do, will you go away and leave me in peace? I don't like to speak of it."

Nyctasia gave her promise.

"Very well," sighed Jocelys, "but I warn you, you'll be here for a good while, if you want the whole story." She refilled their mugs, then went to the door, pulled it shut and bolted it. "I'll have to turn away customers," she complained. "I won't have others hear me speak of this."

"Your neighbors won't hear of it from us," said Corson.

"And you'll not lose by it," Nyctasia assured her. "I can pay for your—" She stopped, puzzled. Her own words sounded strangely slow to her, and seemed to echo in her ears. I've taken too much ale, she thought, and at such a time! I should have known better. It had not tasted very strong, but she was not used to drink at all. Angry at herself, she shook her head hard, trying to clear her thoughts, but only felt dizzier for it. Jocelys was speaking now, but Nyctasia couldn't understand her. She turned to look at Corson, and even this simple act was almost too difficult for her. "Corson," she managed to gasp as she slid from the bench, "the ale—don't—drugged—"

Corson leaped to her feet with a shout and started toward Jocelys, but the floor suddenly shifted beneath her feet, and she staggered against the wall. Jocelys seemed to float away from her, white, terrified, whispering, "I'm sorry, I didn't want to do it, I had to. Garast told you about them, and he's dead. They threatened me. . . . My husband," she sobbed, "my child."

28

CORSON STIRRED AND groaned. She felt as if her head were in an ever-tightening vise, and her mouth tasted of swamp water. She sat up slowly. She could hear Nyctasia beside her, breathing harshly in her sleep, as if in pain. Corson shook her roughly.

"Wake up, curse you. Do you know where we are?"

"Leave me alone," Nyctasia moaned. "I want to sleep."

Corson seized her by the shoulders. "Come to what little sense you've got, fool. Hlann help us, but we're going to need every bit of sense we can muster, and between the two of us I don't think we make a half-wit. How could I be taken in by a colt's trick like that?" She pressed her fists against her aching head. "That bloody bitch," she added, with feeling.

"Well, where are we?" Nyctasia asked sullenly. "I don't like it, wherever it is. I knew it was a mistake to wake up."

"We're somewhere in the ruins, that's my guess—and it's night. The stink of magic's so thick I can hardly breathe."

Nyctasia sobered suddenly. "Carelessness," she said. "Always and ever carelessness. It's not only night, it's the night of Yu Valeicu. Sweet *vahn,* we've got to find them before—"

"Find *them!* We don't know where *we* are."

They rose unsteadily and groped around them in a darkness so dense that they could not even see one another, and all directions were alike. The floor beneath them was smooth stone, but Corson discovered that she could not reach the ceiling or walls from where she stood. "We're not in a tunnel, anyway," she said thankfully.

But her relief was short-lived. As they shuffled forward together, her outstretched hand soon met with an intricate web of metal that she took for part of the fountain until she remembered that the courtyard was not paved. "Oh no," she said softly, "they would do that, the rotten bastards. They wouldn't just kill us, not them. They wouldn't soil their pure spirits and clean hands with our blood—perish the thought!"

Nyctasia touched the bars, and understood. It was the gate to the maze, and this time they were on the wrong side of it.

Corson pulled furiously at the gate, but the ironwork held fast, for all that it had looked delicate from the other side. "I never thought to say it, but I wish we had Newt here now. He could pick this lock in the dark as easy as picking his teeth. But we'll just have to get through the maze. For Hlann's sake, if children can do it, I can."

Nyctasia's voice was flat and hopeless. "They didn't do it in the dark. There are torches on the walls which our hosts have neglected to light. And even if we should find the way through in time, what do you suppose they have waiting for us at the other end? Not, I think, a welcome to the ranks of the initiated."

"It's no use asking that now. We might as well take our chances as wait here for them to come fetch us. You know, we've been round the maze—it's not much bigger than a barn—it won't take long to cross it."

"Don't you see, it may be too late already. And the size of the space doesn't matter when all you do is go around in circles and wander in and out of the same blind alley over and over—"

Corson heard the edge of panic in her voice, and became immediately the stern commander. "No—hold your noise and listen," she said firmly, dragging Nyctasia into the maze. "We won't get lost if we're careful. I'll keep my left hand on this wall; you keep your right hand on the other side, and take a good hold of me with your left. We don't want to get separated."

They moved forward slowly until they reached the first junction of the path. "We'll go left," Corson decided. "As long as we keep going in one direction, it makes no difference which. We know there's an opening somewhere. If I always have my hand on the wall, it has to lead us there sooner or later, doesn't it? If we strike a dead end, we'll just retrace our steps and go the other way. Come on."

"One, left," said Nyctasia.

"Left, straight, right, not counting the blind ends. Remember that, it may repeat. There's sure to be a pattern of some sort. The Cymvelans did everything by design."

"Left, straight, right," Corson repeated. "No—it's straight, left, straight, right! The first bit was straight, remember?"

"Yes, I didn't see that it mattered before. Corson, I apologize for calling you a simple-minded barbarian."

"Spoken like a lady. There's a straight part coming now. How much will you wager that the next turn should be left?"

"I'll wager my life on it."

But they had followed the left turning for only a few paces when Nyctasia stopped. "Corson, I can't feel a wall on this side. I think we're out!"

Corson kept her hand on the other wall. "Are you sure? This side's still curving in. It should go the other way on the outside."

Nyctasia stretched to reach as far as she could without losing touch with Corson. "It's open over here," she insisted.

"Maybe it's just another opening in that wall, like the ones we've come through. We'd better keep to this wall for a while, and you go on feeling for the other."

"All right . . . but there's nothing yet . . . it's still open. . . ."

"This side's still curving around. Wait, here's another turning. We're still in the maze, then. There was only one opening on the outside."

"Yes . . . unless we've come full circle, and that's the same opening we came through just now."

Corson cursed. "It can't be! We've not come far enough. Have we?"

"I don't think so. But I can't judge in this darkness. I'm going to try to cross this space—if we're outside the maze, we should be almost opposite the door to the stairway."

"And the door to that other room," Corson reminded her. "Don't go far. The door's only a few feet away, if it's there. Make some noise so I know where you are." She released Nyctasia's hand with misgiving.

Nyctasia stepped away hesitantly, her arms outstretched, reaching into emptiness. "Stars are wheeling in the night," she sang, without thinking, "birds are circling in their flight, winter turning into spring, children dancing in a—" There was a long pause.

"Nyc? Are you still there?" Corson called anxiously.

"Oh, yes, we're still here, both of us. I've come across farther than the width of that corridor outside the maze, and I haven't found the wall. This must be an inner chamber, probably the heart of the maze. I can hear them from here, Corson. They've begun."

"The chanting? I wondered when you'd notice. Come back here—follow my voice. We have to keep following this wall, it's the only way. We must be halfway through, that's something."

"There's no time for that. Suppose the maze doubles back on itself? I'm going to try to create a spell-flame to light the way. There's power enough here to draw upon."

"If you can conjure up a light, why didn't you do it before, in the Hlann's name?"

"Because it's dangerous to tamper with an unknown Influence! But we've nothing to lose now. If we don't get out in time to stop them, it won't matter if we get out at all. Now be still."

Corson heard her scratching at the floor, and thought she heard her spit. Beyond the maze, the chanting had risen to a wailing song. Corson could not understand the words, but she knew well enough what they meant.

"Air is the element nearest to fire," said Nyctasia, after a long pause, and she breathed warmly into her cupped hands.

Slowly, the glow crept to the edges of the high, round room, and Corson could see that there were several entrance-ways to the place, evenly spaced around the circle. She pulled the ornament from her hair and left it to mark the place where she stood, then took a torch from the wall and hurried to Nyctasia.

She was kneeling in the center of the room, gazing into her burning hands. Corson soon found that those pale, flickering flames gave off no heat, but when she touched the torch to them, the pitch flared up at once in a reassuring blue and gold blaze. By its light, Corson saw that Nyctasia knelt on a wide circle of mosaic-work, surrounding the image of a huge, hideous spider made up of thousands of tiny chips of black tile. Nyctasia seemed almost to be riding on the back of the loathsome creature. Her face, lit from below by that eerie bowl of flames, looked unfamiliar and inhuman. Corson remembered how Nyctasia had seemed a different person when they'd traveled through the haunted Yth

Forest—a dangerously different person, and perhaps not a person at all. . . . Corson wanted to seize her and shake her from her spell, but she dared not touch that still, rapt figure, illumined by witch-fire.

"Nyc, get up from there! We've no time to waste, hurry!"

Nyctasia looked down at the decorated floor, then slowly raised her head. "The poisonous stone at the core of the sweet peach," she said. "The murderous spider at the center of the gossamer web. The forbidden spell hidden among the volumes of precious wisdom. And the bloodlust buried in the hearts of the peaceful. We are meant to remember it, but not to surrender to it. The Cymvelans have forgotten their own lessons."

"If you've quite finished your recitation, we could go stop the Cymvelans and their rutting spell. Do you want to get out of here or don't you? Make up your mind fast, because I'm leaving."

Nyctasia shook herself, and stood. "And douse that cursed spell-fire," Corson snapped, lighting another torch and thrusting it at her.

Reluctantly, Nyctasia pressed her hands together, quenching the livid flames. She took the torch and looked around in confusion. "But you've left the wall! Which door did we come through?"

Corson located her hair clasp. "This one. No, wait, we came through that one and walked to this one. Let's go on. Now that we've light, we can find which of these lead to blind ends in half the time."

Nyctasia ran to the door opposite the one Corson had pointed out. "This way. The maze must be symmetrical—the rest should be a mirror image of the first half, the same pattern in reverse."

"That sounds like the Cymvelans' tidy way," Corson agreed. "And this is as good a starting place as any. It will save us a lot of trouble if you're right."

"Nothing will save us if I'm wrong," said Nyctasia. "Don't you hear? They've stopped. They've completed the invocation." She disappeared into the waiting tunnel, with Corson close behind her.

* * *

The door to the underground temple stood open, and the ceremony within was well-lit by flaming brands and candles. Corson and Nyctasia abandoned their torches and grasped their weapons instead.

No one seemed aware of their presence. The celebrants, draped in skins and masked in the heads of animals, stood facing the altar, where one old man, who wore no mask, was speaking. He alone might have heeded their approach, but his eyes were fixed on some point in the air beyond them, where nothing was to be seen. His manner was commanding, and he intoned his words in a language like none Corson had ever heard in all her travels.

But Nyctasia, hearing him, gasped and suddenly screamed out, "Now, *now!*" and Corson let fly her knife.

"Run for help—I'll hold them off," she ordered.

"You can't—"

"Go!" Corson pushed her toward the other door and turned to meet the first of the horned, furred creatures that rushed from the temple, howling in fury and brandishing clubs of oak.

Nyctasia raced up the stairs to the bell-tower, leaving Corson to certain death below. The Cymvelans were not many, but they were surely more than one fighter could hope to overcome. Yet she knew that Corson had been right to sacrifice her life to give her this chance to flee. If neither of them escaped to give warning, many more lives would be lost. Even now, Nyctasia was not sure she could summon help in time to prevent the Cymvelans from finishing what they'd started.

Then at the top of the stairs, she saw at once what had to be done. Instead of running away from the tower, she dashed through the inner door and threw herself upon the bell-rope, pulling it down with the full weight of her body.

The rope held, but the great bell barely moved at first. Somewhere, she sensed, something was taking shape, drawing power into itself, becoming more potent with each instant that passed. Desperately, she dragged down the rope, again and again, with a strength she had not dreamed she possessed.

When the bell spoke at last, it seemed to take on a life of its own, and its powerful voice sounded out over the countryside, so loudly that Nyctasia thought she would be deafened. Its motion grew wild and violent, like the thrashing of a caged bird, frantic to break free, and Nyctasia was pitched to and fro in its wake as she clung to the rope, fighting to control the bell's great weight. She could not steady her feet against the floor, which seemed to shudder beneath her while the walls tilted drunkenly overhead. Not till Corson had seized her around the waist and dragged her from the toppling building did she see that the ground was really buckling underfoot, and the walls shaking. The whole earth seemed caught up in some terrible convulsion.

They flung themselves down the hillside in the darkness, falling, rolling, scrambling to their feet and plunging on, till they landed in a heap among the vines of the lower slope. "Idiot!" shouted Corson. "Didn't you see the rutting place coming down around you?"

Nyctasia struggled for breath. "But—but—what about you—how—?"

Corson pulled her to her feet. "They were . . . old, Nyc. Weak. They looked fierce in those masks, but some of them could barely stand. It was easy to scatter them. I felt sick, to tell the truth, cutting down such people. Are you hurt?"

"I don't know. Probably. I wonder if Jocelys was among them." She looked back at the fallen tower, where nothing stirred except the settling stones.

But there was much noise and commotion at the foot of the hill, as people came running to answer the call of the bell. As Corson and Nyctasia walked down to meet them, they saw that great bonfires burned in the fields, and that the crowd was dressed in gay finery and vine-leaf wreaths. Singing and shouting, they swarmed up the slopes, waving ribboned torches and leafy branches, carrying flutes and drums and tambourines. It was the first night of the Harvest Festival.

"And I left my new hair-clasp down there, too," Corson said glumly.

29

IT WAS ON the last night of the Harvest Festival that Nyctasia slipped away from the festivities alone, and toiled up the slope of Honeycomb Hill by moonlight. Overhead, the Reaper's Eye burned steadily, like a beacon warning ships of treacherous waters. Danger, turn back. Turn back, fool, she thought, but she continued to climb, passing the cave and the rows of sweet, overripe golden grapes left drying on the vines. She did not stop to rest until she saw the ragged pile of stones where the bell-tower had stood. The great iron bell had crashed through the flooring easily, to disappear into the caverns below. The temple seemed to have sunk beneath the earth, and now its painted dancers, the fair and the wild, lay together in the tomb with nothing to choose between them. Half the hilltop had caved in on itself, crushing the last of the life from the Cymvelan Circle for good and all. There was only a great pit now, like an open wound, to mark the place.

The Edonaris had argued hotly over the possibility of digging into the hillside to search for survivors of the cave-in, some arguing that it was their duty to try, others that the ground was still too unsettled to be safely disturbed.

But Nyctasia had assured them that no survivors were buried

under the rubble. She knew that all were dead, as surely as she knew that she had killed them—that the sound of the bell had finally shivered the weakened supports that upheld the whole hollow structure.

"But how can you be sure?" 'Corin had asked uneasily.

And Nyctasia, more composed and withdrawn than ever, had answered, "I know . . . that the One they summoned has been satisfied. The sacrifice has been accepted. I know because it was I who carried out the sacrifice. Let no one set foot on the hill for any reason. Even if the earth has settled, the land is more dangerous now than before, more dangerous than you imagine." But she had refused to explain further.

The superstitions of the countryside were well founded, Nyctasia thought, as they so often are. The land was unlucky indeed, the place was well and truly cursed, now, and it was for her to cast out the demonic presence that haunted it. The dragon had been wakened, and only she could bridle it.

But that would be a simple matter compared to the task that must be undertaken first. Before she could rid this place of its curse, she would have to cast out the demons of ambition and desire that haunted her own spirit. It was for that struggle that she doubted her own strength.

She had held vigil for days, fasting, solitary, silent, as she searched within herself for the guidance of the Indwelling Spirit. She had examined with uncompromising clarity the choice that lay before her, and sought the strength to choose aright, though each way she turned seemed to lead to a grave mistake.

But she could not delay any longer. The power that had been bound by the ancient spell, and guarded by the Cymvelan Circle, had now been invoked, and it had been waiting a very long time to be free. Corson is right, Nyctasia reflected with a rueful smile, I think too much. There's no time for that. Sometimes it's action that's wanted.

She could sense the newly roused, restless power of the place all about her, like an unseen radiance, in the earth, in the air, in the very stones at her feet—and within herself. It was easy, all too easy for safety's sake, to draw upon that power and use it to work her will. She felt as if she were again in the enchanted Yth Forest, whose untamed, predatory power had all but ensnared her once. The feeling was not in the least frightening. It was inviting, enticing, elating. It offered everything and demanded nothing, and though Nyctasia knew that it lied, she listened.

Without further thought, she reached out in spirit to summon the enemy, using its own power to compel it to come forth.

There was only a subtle shifting of shadows to show that it had obeyed, and a heightened sense that something was demanded of her. But Nyctasia had expected nothing more. This was a being that could not be imaged by the eyes of the spirit, and far less could it be seen by the eyes of the body. But its claim upon her was strong and undeniable. A bargain had been struck. A price had been paid, and paid in blood. But not until the service thus won had been received would that bargain be fulfilled, and the spell broken that had held this Power captive for so long.

It is an exile, as I am, thought Nyctasia, and probably less to blame for its plight than I for mine. It is fitting that I set it free. For she knew that this was not truly an entity of evil. It wanted, as she did, to return to where it belonged, and only the service it owed to her stood between it and its desire.

Had the Cymvelans succeeded in using its power to avenge themselves upon the Valleylanders, it would have carried out their commands as surely as it would carry out hers now. It had no ties to humanity, and made no distinctions among mortal beings. Certainly it did not care whether they lived or died.

Nyctasia could not blame it. She blamed only herself, for her reluctance to release the One that awaited her command, the temptation to turn its power to her own purposes. For the demon, believing that it could win its freedom in no other way, ceaselessly demanded that she yield to that temptation.

Among the rescued volumes of the Cymvelan library, Nyctasia had found certain works that she knew would be there, and she studied them carefully—not for the first time—before she set out to confront that which awaited her at the temple. But most especially she devoted herself to the *First Book on the Nature of Demonic Spirits*.

"There are other worlds than our own," she'd read. "And that which we call a demonic spirit is no more nor less than a denizen of another world who has become ensnared in this world of ours, through magic or mischance. And if beings such as ourselves were to be drawn into the world whence such Ones come, we should ourselves be as demons to those who dwell there, and it may be that this has come about, betimes, and none returned thence to tell of it. Or mayhap some have returned but been

accounted mad by their fellows when they spoke of the strange
regions they had visited. And some of those whom we deem mad
were perhaps made so by sights incomprehensible to humankind,
witnessed in worlds beyond our own.

"Then it is little wonder if those beings known to us as
Demons should be desperate and dangerous in nature, and unpre-
dictable to deal with, as mad folk are. And this is seen in those
who are possessed by them, such that the most skilled physicians
are oft hard pressed to decide whether some certain unfortunates
are in truth possessed by demonic spirits or have indeed simply
lost their wits.

"Now such a One, being out of Its own rightful place, does in
consequence forfeit its proper form and nature, and appear to
mortal eyes insubstantial, as an Absence rather than a Presence.
But by virtue of Its displacement and discorporate essence does
such a Being acquire sundry Powers which in no wise answer to
the Laws governing substance and matter, even as the Indwelling
Spirit submits not to be thus constrained. And thereby It may
assume what guise soever should serve Its ends, albeit in illusory
wise.

"Only by the Laws governing Immaterial Influences may such
a One be compelled, and Its powers made to serve the Will of
another. But this ought in no wise nor manner to be attempted,
for the Power thus won may well be beyond price, but will prove
well beyond the price that any one alone can pay. For even as the
Invited Power is drawn from Without, so must the recompense be
made from without, if Balance is to be restored, and such a Sacrifice the Spirit of Harmony forbids. . . ."

Excellent advice, thought Nyctasia, if it did not come too late.
For the recompense had been paid already, and now it remained
for her to assign a service, as It demanded. But if she consented
to take advantage of that sacrifice, then the blood of the Cymvelans would truly be on her hands.

"Balance must be restored." It spoke to her, silently, word-
lessly, but its meaning was unmistakably clear to Nyctasia. "Take
what is yours! Ask! Command!"

What's done is done, Nyctasia told herself. It will not be un-
done if I refuse, they will still be dead. If I accept, they cannot be
more dead than they are. And though this seemed like reason, yet
even as she voiced her command to the demon of the hill, she
knew that the *vahn* within her replied, "Not they, but you can be
more dead than you are. . . ."

But Nyctasia gave the one command she had known she must give, whatever the cost to her own spirit. "Tell me of my city. Will there be war?"

And before she had finished speaking, she saw the answer, inwardly, as one sees memories, not before her eyes but behind them. She could envision, as if she had been a witness, the burning buildings, the barricaded streets, already littered with the dead and wounded. Fire raged unchecked from house to house, and the gates of the palaces were broken and undefended. Rhostshyl, the proud city, the city of marble and silver...

"No more!" Nyctasia ordered, but she could not forget what she had seen.

She was offered other visions, then, which said as clearly as words, "By my power you could prevent this. Use it. Use it. You could have the power to impose peace on the city. Take it. Take it. Your enemies will do your will. You will be hailed as peacemaker and savior of the city. Rhostshyl need not perish. Do it. Do it. You must. It is your duty."

Was it not, in truth, her duty? If she could prevent the death and destruction she had seen, had she the *right* to refuse?

But these thoughts were not her own. They were the work of One who sought to serve her for Its own sake. "You lie," she said. Power won at such a price could not bring peace, could not give life, could not—whatever her intentions—be used innocently. This Nameless Being knew her every weakness, she realized, knew her deepest desires and her very thoughts. Such a servant is too dangerous, she decided, and ordered, "Show yourself! Take a form that I can see. Speak in words that I can hear."

Again it obeyed. In man's shape it walked out of the shadows and approached her, stepping into the moonlight to reveal the form and features of Erystalben ar'n Shiastred.

"I can bring him back to you," it said, in his voice.

30

"WHAT MAKES YOU think she's gone up there?" Corson asked, as she and 'Deisha climbed the cart-track up Honeycomb Hill, stopping occasionally to shout for Nyctasia.

"I don't know.... Nobody'd seen her at dinner, and she wasn't in her room, or at the dancing or the bonfire. I just suddenly felt quite certain that she'd gone back to the temple, I can't think why. Perhaps I'm wrong. I hope I am."

"Oh, you're probably right—it's just the sort of mad thing she'd do, the rutting half-wit. Every time I plan to set off for the coast, that one gets herself in some kind of trouble! I swear, if she's vanished into the earth now, I'll leave her there to talk philosophy to the moles. I mean to be back in Amron Therain in two days, without fail, even if the ground opens up and swallows all of Vale." She called again for Nyctasia, but there was still no answer. "Curse her, if she's hurt herself, I'll throttle her!"

'Deisha reached for Corson's hand and squeezed it. "No wonder Nyc's so fond of you. And Raphe will break his heart when you go."

"Did she tell you she's fond of me?"

"Oh, anyone could see that, but in fact she did tell me so."

"Ah . . . well, you can't believe everything that little liar says.

197

The Imperial Head Questioner couldn't get the truth from her on the rack if his life depended on it. Sometimes I've come within a hair of—"

'Deisha laughed. "Corson, how do you deal with people you *don't* like?"

"Ask Newt," said Nyctasia out of the darkness ahead of them. "He can tell you all about that, but it's not a pretty tale, I warn you."

"He deserved it," said Corson promptly. "Nyc, you fool, what were you doing up there?"

"Have you been looking for me? I'm sorry you had the trouble of coming out here—I was on my way back."

Corson turned to 'Deisha in exasperation. "There, that's what I mean. She can't answer a plain question. It's not in her nature. Oh, no, we weren't looking for you, of course not. We climbed all this way in the dark because we wanted to fall in a pit and break our necks. Come along, scatterwit, let's get back to the feast."

"I really shall miss you, Corson. It will be rather a bore being among civilized people again, but I daresay I'll get used to it in time." She took Corson's hand, then 'Deisha's, and they started back down the path together.

'Deisha leaned across Nyctasia to say to Corson, "You're right, she never did answer. And just now she tried to provoke you, to turn the subject. It's remarkable."

"Now you're catching on to her tricks. She can talk you into swearing your hat's a hen, and believing it too, if you don't take care. But maybe you'll prove a match for her—you're of the same blood."

"Yes," said 'Deisha, "we're of the same blood. Nyc, why were you at the temple? It's dangerous there, you said so yourself."

"It's not as dangerous now."

"Hmmm, I thought as much," said Corson. "It's changed, I can feel that. What did you do?"

Nyctasia was silent for a time, but then said quietly, "I didn't do it, but it's done. That's all that matters."

For it was not she who had spoken, in truth, but the Indwelling Spirit which had spoken through her. Faced with a temptation which she could neither refuse nor receive, she had desperately thrust from her the very will and power to choose. Guided only by the thought, "Don't hesitate, act!" she had cried inwardly, "Let it be as it will, whatever may befall. Let it be as it will." When she drew breath to speak she did not know what she was about to say, and then she heard her own voice commanding, "Begone. Return in peace to thine own place, and there remain. This and this alone I require of thee. Obey!"

She had no sooner ceased speaking than she was alone on the dark hillside, and only a fleeting sense of wild, inexpressible thanksgiving remained to mark the passage of the Cymvelans' curse.

Nyctasia was past doubt or disappointment. If she had lost her only chance to save her city, to be reunited with her lover, yet she knew a great relief that the choice had been taken from her. She might so easily have made a mistake, but now she had only to trust in the *vahn* and believe that the right decision had been made. She had—thank the stars!—no choice.

She did not know how long she'd been away from the harvest celebration till she heard Corson and 'Deisha calling for her. Then she hurried downhill to join them, suddenly eager to be with the others, and to forget about what might have been.

"It's done," she said. "Done is the chase, and you'll not have to come hunting for me there a third time, I promise you. I don't mean to climb this hill again till next crush. And perhaps I won't be needed then—I don't think the workers will shun the place anymore, by then. But *I* will. Now I only want to have some of Raphe's new wine. In fact, I want to have a great deal of it." The first barrels of the golden wine had been opened on the first day of the Harvest Festival. The new vintage had been a great success, a striking blend of sharp and sweet that even Nyctasia had appreciated. Raphe had named it, in Corson's honor, "Corisonde."

"*And* some food," Nyctasia added. "I've not eaten all day, I'm famishing."

"What, not eaten a thing at the harvest feast?" cried 'Deisha. "That's bad luck for the whole year to come! You must come eat plenty at once, or Aunt Mesthelde will never forgive you."

"That's right," said Corson gleefully, "and she'll surely be offended if you don't have some of her own special traditional zhetaris, Nyc."

31

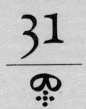

THE RIVERBOAT *HARBOR LASS* tugged against the moorings as it rode at anchor between the wharves. It seemed to Corson that the boat was as eager as she to be free and on its way to the next port. She watched the crew loading the last casks of wine, under the direction of Leclairin ar'n Edonaris. It would not be long now before they cast off.

"If you ask me, the Cymvelans brought it on themselves," she said suddenly to Nyctasia. "Maybe they did cause the drought, in a way, because they defied Nature. Everything they did was so controlled—making herbs grow in fancy patterns, making water flow in fancy patterns. Maybe the drought and . . . the rest . . . was Nature's way of rebelling and showing them her power."

Nyctasia smiled. Corson's nature had chafed at military discipline all during her years in the army, and left her with an incurable distrust for any form of restraint or confinement. "I doubt it," she answered, "but really you have a remarkable grasp of Elemental Balance." Still, it might be as well not to restore the knot-gardens after all, Nyctasia reflected. "Well," she continued, "since you disapprove of interfering with Nature, perhaps you won't want this little keepsake I made for you." She knelt and looked through her satchel for her parting gift to Corson, a small parcel wrapped in a scrap of leather. She moved stiffly and pain-fully—the result of a final lesson in swordplay from Corson.

At first Corson was puzzled when she unfolded the covering and found only a simple wooden comb. But then she remembered that Nyctasia had once told her about a certain perfume of ancient Kehs-Edre—a perfume for the hair. She sniffed at the comb ea-gerly. "I don't smell anything."

"I told you, only men can smell it, and only when it's combed through a woman's hair. Don't try it now, for *vahn*'s sake! Put it away—you must only use it when you're alone with the man of your choice, and then only in a place where you can wash your hair afterward. I'm serious, Corson, I warn you. In *your* hair, the scent might even be dangerous."

Corson believed her. When Nyctasia was lying she never seemed at all anxious to be believed. "I'll be careful," she prom-ised, putting the precious comb safely at the bottom of her pack. "Thanks! I'll write and let you know how I fare with it."

"Yes, do. You've almost learned to write legibly. You should keep in practice."

"And you, remember to use your shield arm. Always think of your shield as a weapon, not just a protection, even if it's only a cloak wrapped around your arm. Never let your shield arm hang idle—if there's nothing else to hand, grab some dirt and throw it."

"I'll remember," said Nyctasia with a grimace, touching her left forearm, which was bandaged. But then she started to laugh. "You're lucky 'Deisha didn't take up arms against you for the way you misused me. She'd have minced you to bits and fed you to her dogs, she was that furious. Now she thinks you're a brute."

"Well, I think she's a darling," Corson said generously.

"And that puts me in mind of something else—when Raphe wished you a good journey, why did you say, 'The same to you, and many of them'? What did you mean by that? He's not going anywhere."

Now it was Corson who laughed. "Why don't you ask him to explain it? You Edonaris are great ones for explaining."

"Never mind. I think I can guess. . . . It looks as if they mean to weigh anchor soon. Perhaps you should get on board. Do you have the letters I gave you? Remember, don't take them to Chiastelm with you. Give them to a courier in Meholmne or Lhestreq, except the one for—"

Corson picked her up and hugged her roughly. "I won't forget, don't worry."

"Put me down, fool!" said Nyctasia, and kissed her on the nose.

Corson obeyed, and took up her pack instead, slinging it over her shoulder. They started down the wharf to the gangplank of the *Harbor Lass*.

"Take care of yourself, Corson. And send me word if there's ... news ... of Rhostshyl."

"I will. Maybe I'll bring you word someday. I'm bound to be in these parts again, sooner or later. I'll come for a visit."

"You'll be most welcome—especially to our Raphe. But if you had any sense, you'd stop your vagabonding and settle down in Chiastelm, you know."

"Sense! If I had any sense, I'd not have taken up with you in the first place."

"True. But I didn't hire you for your sense."

"No, you hired me because you were so *fond* of me," said Corson triumphantly. Before her startled companion could reply, she raced up the gangplank to the deck of the *Harbor Lass*, well satisfied that she'd finally managed to have the last word in a conversation with Nyctasia.

When she looked back, Nyctasia had gone to join the other Edonaris. Leclairin was concluding their dealings with the trader who'd purchased their wine for shipment to distant markets, while her brother Aldrichas paid the hired wagoners. Nyctasia looked on patiently, without comment.

Soon the call was given to weigh anchor, and the lines were cast off, the plank drawn in. Corson watched the sails unfurl and swell as the *Harbor Lass* moved slowly away from the wharves. The sight reminded her of something, and she chuckled at the idea. The sails, the rigging—what were they but a web to catch the wind? "I'll have to remember to write that to Nyc," she thought. "She likes that sort of nonsense."

Nyctasia waved to her from the dock. For a while she watched the graceful vessel sail out of the harbor and head downriver, then she turned back to her waiting kinfolk, ready to start for home.

Stories

✠ of ✠

Swords and Sorcery